# Cowboy Country Christmas

## by

## Gail MacMillan

*Cowboy Country Connections Series,*
*Book Three*

**Cowboy Country Christmas**

Cover Art by *RJ Morris*

The Wild Rose Press, Inc.
PO Box 708
Adams Basin, NY 14410-0708
Visit us at www.thewildrosepress.com

Publishing History
First Yellow Rose Edition, 2017
Print ISBN 978-1-5092-1678-9
Digital ISBN 978-1-5092-1679-6

*Cowboy Country Connections Series, Book Three*
Published in the United States of America

**"Hello." He paused in front of her, wet bottle in** hand. "Cinderella?"

"What?" The word came out in what sounded to her a ridiculous squeak.

"Cinderella. The girl from the round pen. The girl whose name I was too dumb to find out. I didn't get a glass slipper…or even a running shoe, to help me find her again. You are her, right?"

"I guess…yes." His left hand holding the bottle had the jagged scar down its back that she remembered from the cowboy who'd given her a riding lesson.

"Nice to see you again." He extended his right hand. "I'm Travis Masters."

"I know." She was only vaguely aware of accepting his offer, too astonished to feel any of the famous tingle she'd so often written about that occurred when her hero and heroine made their first physical contact.

"And you're…?" He was looking into her eyes, strangling speech in her throat.

"Et…Etta Prescott. My name is actually Henrietta, but everyone calls me Etta." *Oh, damn, I'm stuttering…and rambling. Get a grip, Etta, get a grip. Tell yourself he's only another good-looking guy.*

*Not exactly.* The disconcerting thought rattled around in her head. *He's Travis Masters, number one country singer, and you're quite possibly his biggest fan.*

"You met everyone?" He waved his bottle around to indicate the crowd.

"More than whose names I can keep straight." This time she managed to speak coherently.

*Calm down, calm down. Ignore the fact of who he is.*

## Dedication

To my friend Sue Owens Wright
and the memory of her beloved basset hound, Beau

**Gail MacMillan's books from The Wild Rose Press**

Non-Fiction:
*How My Heart Finds Christmas*
*To All the Dogs I've Loved Before*

~

Historical Romance:
*Shadows of Love*
*Caledonian Privateer*
*Lady and the Beast*

~

The Riverhaven Rogues Series:
*Privateer's Princess*
*Heather for a Highlander Harry* (winner of "Best Heroine" in the 2014 Canadian Romance Writers Maple Leaf Contest, with the hero taking second best and the ending awarded an honorable mention)
*Highland Harry* (winner of "Best Opening" in the 2015 Canadian Romance Writers Maple Leaf Contest)
*Bandit's Bride*

~

Contemporary Romance:
*Phantom and the Fugitive*
*Rogue's Revenge*
*Ghost of Winters Past*

~

Cowboy Country Connections Series:
*Holding Off for a Hero*
*Counterfeit Cowboy*
*Cowboy and the Crusader*
*Cowboy Confessions*
*Cowboy Country Christmas*

Chapter One

"Emma, this has to be the wildest birthday gift ever!" Grasping the collection of tickets, Etta Prescott stared at her twin sister. "I can't believe you got these, never mind afforded them!"

"Hey, I work." Emma MacKenzie picked up the bottle to replenish their wine glasses. "We deserve a treat. If you have to put a practical spin on it, you can consider it research for your books. It's always amazed me that you've become the successful author of a dozen or more cowboy romance novels and yet you've never been west of Ottawa or ridden a horse."

"But plane tickets across the country from New Brunswick? And to events at the Calgary Stampede, including for the Travis Masters show? Wow!"

"It's too bad you weren't living here at Loon Lake last Christmas. He always comes home for the holidays, I've been told. I could have arranged for you to meet. Did you know he grew up on a farm fifteen miles down shore from Carleton, no more than an hour's drive from these cabins? I'm told he still regards it as his home. His sister, a veterinarian who runs the place, is married to Jordan Brooks, Jake Brooks, as he now calls himself, retired number-one country singer. That's how Travis got his start…when Jake quit the business and needed someone to take over his band."

"Really? I didn't know."

"Well, you are his biggest fan, aren't you?"

"Probably, maybe, I guess. But, Emma..." Etta looked over at her, eyes narrowing with suspicion. "This hasn't got anything to do with the fact that you think Frasier may be working undercover in the Calgary area, does it? He's warned you never again to insert yourself into any of his cases after that near-death experience here at the lake last winter."

"Back then I didn't know I'd be celebrating our birthday nearly a year later at one of the rustic, romantic cabins where he and I met, alone except for my romance-novel-writing sister, who prefers seclusion to a walk on the wild side with the man of her dreams. At this moment, being married to Sergeant Frasier MacKenzie of RCMP doesn't seem all that great."

"It's his job that's keeping him away, Emma. You knew that would be the situation when you married him."

"Frasier is a great undercover agent, but sometimes he fails to realize what he needs." Emma stood and sashayed across the room to add a log to the dwindling fire on the hearth. "After three months of celibacy, he needs me, his loving, audacious wife." She tossed an impudent smirk at Etta as she knelt by the fieldstone fireplace.

"If you say so." Etta took a sip of wine before continuing. "Still, I don't plan to be around if you meet up with him out there. The man may be head over heels in love with you, but he's also determined never again to involve you in a sting operation."

"Oh, Etta, Etta, I love you, but you do have to get your game on if you ever want to catch a man as handsome and exhilarating as my Frasier." Emma heaved an exasperated sigh as she resumed her seat on the couch. "At times like this it's so blatantly obvious we're fraternal, not identical, twins. You're a shy honey blonde, and I'm an outgoing chestnut-haired rogue. You're the introverted author of western romance novels, while I'm an out-there, frequently personally involved guidance counselor to Carleton High School kids with all kinds of problems."

"Okay, okay, we're different. Not entirely a bad thing." Etta quirked her mouth at one corner. "Remember, there have been a number of times my good old-fashioned common sense has gotten you out of scrapes that your exuberance has gotten you into."

"I suppose." Emma paused, swirling the wine in her glass. "But in affairs of the heart, you'd do well to take my advice. Keep in mind I'm the gal who snared the dashing RCMP Sergeant Frasier MacKenzie. And that's not the only fascinating fact about the man. You'll recall Frasier was the star of the rock band The Sound before he joined the Force. I loved Frasier's music probably as much as you enjoy the tunes this Masters guy plays. But was I content to sit around and have fantasies about him? No way."

"Yes, well, as you've said, we're fraternal and not identical twins. I don't plan to make any wild, crazy moves to attract Travis Masters' attention. I'm not foolish enough to think a man who has thousands, probably millions of female fans chasing after him would give me a second glance." She threw her sister a disdainful glance. "I've got too much common sense to try. I'm not about to make a fool of myself over a country music superstar."

"Maybe it's time you threw some of that common

sense out the window, stopped living in those fantasies you write, and got out there. This trip is my best effort to bring you into the real world, maybe long enough for you to capture the heart of that country singer with the shy grin. I think you two might make the perfect pair." She picked up a copy of Etta's latest book and turned the back cover with her sister's publicity photo toward her. "Here's how you can look. Don't tell me Travis Masters wouldn't give you more than a glance if you got yourself all glammed up like this."

"That's an absolutely ridiculous image." Etta snatched the book from her hand. "A hairdresser and a makeup artist worked nearly two hours to give me that cover-girl look. No one who actually knows me would even recognize me. That's Vanessa Dean, not Etta Prescott."

"So you're telling me your pen name and this photo are an entirely different identity?"

"That image certainly is. But Vanessa Dean, that's me, a rose under a different name."

"Now you're splitting hairs. If Travis Masters saw you all gussied up like you are in that picture, you can bet he wouldn't take his eyes off you no matter what name you were calling yourself."

"Don't be ridiculous."

"You mean seeing him once in the flesh will be enough to satisfy all your romantic fantasies about the guy, that he's not worth giving it your best shot to attract his attention? Come on, Etta. Get real. Don't worry. I'll figure out a way for you to meet the man. After that, you're on your own. If you don't seize this golden opportunity, you could end up a nasty old maid like Mildred Carter."

"Mildred Carter, the math teacher at Carleton High? I thought you'd forgiven her for all the ugly innuendoes she threw around about you and Frasier living together up here at Loon Lake last fall. You have managed to work in the same building with her ever since."

"I tried to forgive her. Believe me, Etta, I tried, but after Frasier left, she started up again. She implied we never actually got married, that the oh-so-pure Emma Prescott simply had an affair with a man who then deserted her."

"Emma, that's just downright mean! Maybe even libelous, given your position at the school."

"Maybe, but aside from getting into an all-out cat fight about it, the best I can do is avoid her as much as possible. I can only hope she either gives up on me or finds romance with Brandon Worth, the English literature teacher she all but accused me of seducing away from her. Forget I mentioned her. Let's get back to Calgary planning."

She looked down at her Pug, Bruiser, and Etta's basset hound, Beau, lying at their feet. "Can you believe this woman, guys? She's willing to let the opportunity of a lifetime pass her by, all because she's too timid to take the bull by the horns, the bit in her teeth, or whatever parallel applies."

In answer, Bruiser threw back his head and issued his Pug howl. Beau responded with a deep woof.

"See, our boys agree with me."

"You've trained Bruiser to give that yodeling howl at the tone of your voice whenever you want backup. Beau is just a good-natured guy who goes along. By the way, what is going to happen to these two while we're away?"

"Got it covered. They're booked in at the Pampered Puppy Pavilion just outside of town. They'll be enjoying an all-expense-paid luxury vacation. I've checked it out. It's terrific."

"Seems you've covered all bases."

"Except for your wardrobe. Tomorrow we're shopping. I want you out of that baggy sweatsuit and into a pair of hot jeans and a smokin' top, something red, with sequins. It'll give this Travis character a decent chance to spot you in the audience."

"Emma, what will be smokin' hot will be Frasier if he finds you've tracked him to Calgary."

"Maybe for a minute or two…until his hormones kick in. After that happens, he'll be ever so glad to see me. What time is it? I'm bushed."

"Pushing eleven thirty." Etta glanced at her watch.

"Etta, I can't believe it. You're still wearing that relic? It's ancient and more than a bit tacky, with that frayed leather bracelet. Why don't you get a new one?"

"It has a lot of sentimental value, sister dear. Remember, it was the prize in the first fiction-writing contest I ever won."

"Ah, yes. *Bushes in the Breeze*. You were all of sixteen when you got that award."

"Actually it was *Willows in the Wind*. I reread it this past winter and thought it wasn't all that bad…given my age and lack of experience." She stuck up her nose and pretended to take offense.

"Teasing, sweetie, teasing. Actually, if I recall the story correctly, you're absolutely right. It was pretty darned good." Emma gave her a hug. "You were destined to be a writer from the time you learned to print. Now I'm heading off to bed. Fortunately this place has two bedrooms. I'm not about to drive after drinking half a bottle of wine. See you in the morning. Come on, Bruise."

"I'll be going, too, shortly," Etta called after her sister as Emma headed into the cabin's second bedroom. "I'll finish my drink first."

When the sound of running water announced her sister's presence in the bathroom, Etta picked up her glass and headed for the veranda. Beau heaved himself to his paws and followed her.

Outside, she closed the door and took a deep breath of the warm summer evening air. Frogs and crickets sang from down by the lake. An owl hooted, and a coyote howled. Across the water, the mountains rose into a star-studded silver-gray sky. The soft sensuousness of the night enveloped her.

Gazing out over the still surface of the water where the moon cast its reflection, she sighed. She loved the beauty and privacy Loon Lake offered. Memories of her first years after she'd left her job on the magazine, writing in her parents' basement in Ottawa, flooded back.

While she'd appreciated her mother and father's support in granting free room and board until she got established as a romance writer, the tiny below-ground apartment had been such a dull, uninspiring place she'd all but given up. Finally, her savings and a decent level of success had allowed her to accept Emma's suggestion to rent one of the two cabins at Loon Lake. Last spring it had been a breath of fresh air to move to this lovely place, to have the peace, quiet, and setting she needed to write.

She knew it couldn't last. In winter the cabins would be isolated, the access road blocked by deep snow that the owner wouldn't be obliged to plow. While she loved the beauty of the surroundings, she didn't fancy being absolutely alone for possibly months at a time. She needed a bucolic location to live and work, secluded but not entirely cut off from the world...where she might meet someone special.

She glanced across at the cabin next door. Dark and deserted, it appeared cold and lonely in the moonlight. If only some strong, quiet handsome man would move in. Someone tall and dark, someone who loved the country and horses and dogs, someone who would understand her need for this lovely setting in which to work, someone who could appreciate the beauty of a night such as this one. Someone, she thought boldly, who could inspire her emotionally and physically the way her heroes affected the heroines in her books. The last condition brought warmth flushing up through her body.

*Dreamer! Come winter and snow, you'll have to move into Carleton and, hopefully, get an apartment in Emma's building. At least that place allows dogs and is on the edge of town. I'll reserve this cabin for the spring and look forward to the time when Beau and I can come back up here.*

After one last look at the midnight beauty that was Loon Lake, she turned and headed into the cabin, the basset shuffling behind her. Inside, she placed her wine glass on the mantel and picked up a CD from a rack beside it. Travis Masters' likeness grinned up at her, the members of his band looking equally happy behind him.

*He's handsome and incredibly sexy, yet there's something so down to earth, so unassuming about him. I guess that's what appeals to me most...the idea that he's a really nice guy, no star-studded entitlement about him.*

She replaced the CD and bent to add a log to the fire.

*Fool! Emma's got me entertaining her crazy fantasies. Definitely time for bed. How can I tell what the man is really like from a publicity photo probably as phony as my own? He might be the biggest jerk in the world. So what. I'll see him in that concert in Calgary, and that will be the end of it. And I'll get to see horses, horses, and more horses.*

\*\*\*\*

"Travis, Travis!" Lili Farrah stopped him as he was about to stuff a pair of jeans into a duffle bag. "Those have to be folded and put in a suitcase. Do you think I spent all day yesterday doing laundry and ironing for you and your band to have you mutilate my work? I won't have any of you going on stage in Calgary looking like you slept in your clothes."

"Sorry, Lil." Grinning, Travis Masters backed off as the woman snatched the pants from his hands and laid them out on the bed to fold them neatly. He loved Lili, a fifty-something-year-old woman, wife of the band's bus driver Joe Farrah. After his brother-in-law Jordan Brooks had quit the music business to marry Travis's sister, leaving the band to Travis, Lili and her husband Joe had taken over responsibility for the group of reformed delinquents: Matt, a former wizard at car theft; Jessie, previously a drug dealer; James, accused of a violent crime he hadn't committed; and finally,

Paul—Paulie to his friends—a talented composer once a serious drug user. Travis was the only one without a checkered past.

All four had been doing well under first Jordan's and now Joe and Lili's supervision, but lately Travis had noticed Paulie had been getting edgy, easily annoyed, and avoiding Lili as much as he could. He'd have to talk to Lili about the keyboard player when he had an opportunity to get her alone. Before marrying Joe at age fifty, Lili had been an addiction rehab nurse. She'd be able to recognize signs of trouble.

"Jessie, you need new underwear." The woman turned to the young man dozing on the couch of the luxury Toronto penthouse suite in which they were staying. "I'm ashamed to remove such things from a dryer in a public place. Take a walk to the nearest mall and do some shopping."

"Good advice." Matt slouched in a chair in front of the television set, the sound low as he watched the beautiful woman in the soap opera. "Who knows, Jess, you might get lucky some day, and you wouldn't want to strip down to rags. Wow!"—he sat up straight, suddenly focusing on the show—"that Michelle Latton is one sexy babe. Just look at the way she moves across that screen."

"Sure is." Jessie pulled himself to his feet and stretched. "She turned me on when we met her last spring at that recording studio in Nashville. Looks, acting talent, and now she's out to cut a country music CD. Even if she never sings a note, the cover will make the thing sell a million. I saw the proofs…Michelle wearing a Stetson and cowboy boots, and not much in between."

"Hot stuff." Matt leaned toward the television. "Paulie was ready to jump through hoops for her. I think she was trying to lure him away to write songs for her. Lucky you reminded him what he owed to our band, Travis, or he might have gone."

"Yeah, well, Paulie better watch himself around that one," Travis replied. "She cost my sister a fiancé a few years back. She might be eye candy, but she's got a nasty center."

"It all worked out for the best, didn't it?" Matt slanted him a glance. "Shelby went on to marry a far, far better guy. It would take a lot of man to outdo Jordan Brooks a.k.a. Jake Brooks. So maybe Michelle did your sister a favor. Kept her from marrying a cheat."

"Maybe I've never told you." Travis wasn't about to let the subject so easily rest. "She also ruined Shelby's shot at becoming a member of the Canadian Olympic Equestrian Team. Shel was by far the better rider, but Michelle's rich father bought her a state-of-the-art horse. There was no way Shel had a chance against it at the trials. To add insult to injury, after Michelle and her fancy horse were offered the opportunity to train with some of Canada's top riders, she turned it down flat in favor of her so-called acting career. I'm not sure her old man's money didn't play a part in getting her a role in that stupid soap, as well."

"Come on, Matt." Jessie had snatched up his baseball hat and sunglasses. "Travis is in a bad mood. Let's go hustle up new underwear. You can use some, too. Who knows, even you might get lucky."

Lili put her hands on her hips as she turned on the pair. "Well, any of you who plan to get lucky, as you put it, will have to do it between twelve p.m. and four p.m. You boys sleep until noon, either in a hotel room or on the bus, and you have to eat around four and be backstage no later than six. Of course, I'm not taking into consideration rehearsals, setting up…"

"Okay, okay, Lil, we get the picture." Matt planted a kiss on her cheek. "In other words, Mommy Lil doesn't approve of us getting it on with the ladies. Let's go shopping, Jessie." He slapped on a pair of sunglasses and a baseball cap. "Don't want to be recognized by adoring fans."

Travis knew he was joking, but the possibility existed. Easier to wear glasses and a cap than to suddenly find yourself surrounded by a bunch of screaming female admirers, some of whom, he knew from experience, could decide to take a souvenir in the form of a piece of clothing.

As the door closed behind them, Travis turned off the television and sat down in the chair Matt had vacated.

The other members of his band, James and Paulie, were asleep in their bedrooms. It wasn't often their living quarters anywhere were this quiet, and he planned to savor it.

"You look positively pensive, my dear." Lili paused in packing and turned to him. "And more than a bit out of sorts. Not like you. Furthermore, lately both Joe and I have noticed you're quieter than usual. Something bothering you?"

"Thinking of home and the house I've got under construction back there in the woods." He drew a deep breath. "The construction foreman texted me this morning to say they got the foundation finished and the frame up. In a few days they'll start putting on the logs."

"Your dream house." Lili sat down to smile at him. "I'm glad you've been sensible and planned for your future. I think your brother-in-law set a good example of how to have a good life after the music business."

"Marrying my sister and settling down on the family farm has surely agreed with him. And now they have a great kid…Katie Rose."

"So what's troubling you?" Lili wasn't about to let him off the hook so easily.

"Truth is I'm more than a bit homesick for my family and the farm." He ran a hand through his dark, curling hair. "And lately some of Annie's publicity stunts…" His voice trailed off as he shook his head ruefully.

"I admit she's been getting a bit over the top. She's a pushy woman, but I believe that's why she's such a topnotch agent. All part of the business, I suppose." She heaved a sigh.

"What I wouldn't give for a bit of peace and quiet, a chance to stop and relax, really relax. When I took over from Jake, I thought this would be the ultimate…hit recordings, mega shows, lots of money. Now…"

"Now it's beginning to pall." She came to perch on the arm of his chair and put a motherly arm about his shoulders. "Truth be told, sweetie, for all your talent and charisma, you're a country boy at heart."

"You got that right. Jake handled this stuff a whole lot better than I do. He was way smoother at being friendly with fans without being too familiar. I sure don't have that talent. Generally I feel like running away from them and hiding out. You know what I'd love to be doing right now? Riding at a nice, smooth gallop down the trail beyond the barn on our farm, back to my house in the woods, on my gelding, Midnight Brandy."

"Well..." She stood and put her hands on her hips, looking down at him. "We're headed for the Calgary Stampede, where there will be almost as many horses as people. I'm pretty darned sure you can find someone out there who will lend you a horse long enough to satisfy at least some of your cravings."

"Hey, yeah." He drew himself up in the chair. "Yeah, sure. I'll borrow a horse and go for a nice, long gallop. Thanks, Lil. You're one smart cookie."

"Don't forget your family will be there. Seeing your sister and that niece you keep bragging about, never mind performing with your brother-in-law, will perk you up no end, too."

"It will be great to see the folks again. I'm still finding it hard to believe Jake came out of retirement to go back to being Jordan Brooks, the guy who was the number one country singer just six years ago."

"He was lured." Lili went back to packing. "When the organizers offered to donate a goodly chunk of the proceeds of ticket sales to programs for at-risk teens, he was hooked. You've always said Jake—or Jordan or whatever you call him—has a passion for helping young people in trouble."

"He does. His seventeen-year-old brother Kevin died in a car accident. Drugs and alcohol were involved. Jake was away at university at the time. He's always blamed himself for not being there for Kevin."

"Well, then." Lili finished putting the last garment

into the suitcase and snapped it shut. "Cheer up, my boy. I know you don't like big cities. We'll be out of this one shortly. Then it's westward-ho."

"Westward-ho?" Travis grinned at her. "What's that mean, and where did it come from?"

"An old Zane Grey novel. You're much too young to know about such stories. There's nothing quite like a good, old-fashioned western yarn. You should read a few. They'd help you relax. Now get a move on. There's a lot to do to get this circus back on the road."

****

"Hey, Travis, look at this!" Jessie and Matt burst back into the suite. Jessie was waving a magazine. "Hot stuff or what!" He thrust it into his friend's hand.

"What the hell…!" The cover took Travis's breath away.

"Oh, my." Lili peered around his shoulder. "Travis, that isn't at all like you."

"No, it sure as hell isn't." He stared down at the colorful image of himself with Lanie Lanson, the singer who'd been opening act for his shows for the past month. Smiling smugly as she stood with her arms around his neck, wearing skin-tight jeans and a blouse designed to reveal as much cleavage as publicly allowed, she had her hips thrust against his belly, her head thrown back as she cast a sly, seductive gaze up at him. A headline blared, "Country Couple of the Year?"

"That photo shoot was rotten." Anger suffused him. "I didn't want to do it, but Annie insisted. To add insult to injury, Lanie was included. That woman never missed an opportunity to drape herself over and around me, with that miserable photographer never missing an opportunity to take a shot. As soon as I saw the results,

I ordered Annie to destroy them. She promised she would. Not the type of image she wanted me to portray, she said. Apparently she didn't get hold of them, or didn't really want to. There'd better not be any more with the article." He thumbed through the glossy pages until he came to page thirty-eight. "Shit! Another one!"

"Watch your language, my boy." Lili was quick to reprimand, but her lips tightened as she gazed at the center spread. "Well, at least, there's only one other photo of you two together," she said. "This one looks photo-shopped. I'm sure a lot of people will recognize it for what it is. It could be worse."

"Worse? I don't see how!" Travis flung the magazine onto a chair. "That damned thing is probably on newsstands all across this country and the USA."

"You both could be naked." Jessie chuckled.

"Yeah, right, smart guy."

"I think you'd better read the article." Lili retrieved the publication. "Make sure there's nothing libelous in it."

"You go for it, Lili." Travis headed into the bathroom. "Right now I need a cold shower before I confront Annie about this piece of garbage. I hope my family never sees that cover. I can only imagine what Shelby could say, never mind Katie Rose."

\*\*\*\*

When Travis emerged from the bathroom, Lili, seated in a chair by the window, looked up over her reading glasses and heaved a sigh. She was alone. His band members had all retired to bedrooms to nap.

"Well?" Barefooted and wearing a charcoal sweatsuit, he sank down onto the couch opposite her and ran a hand through damp curls.

"Nothing libelous, but a whole lot of innuendoes regarding you and her and your so-called relationship. It's obvious the reporter relied on Lanie for material. There's a lot of 'Travis said' in it, most of which I'm quite sure you didn't."

"I suppose it really could be worse." Cooled down by time and his shower, Travis heaved a deep breath. "If I had a serious lady friend, I'd have a whole lot of explaining to do."

"You certainly would."

"You know, Lili, I'm getting pretty darned fed up with this kind of thing. I'm starting to look like what my sister once called Jake when she said he was a counterfeit cowboy. And she was right...when she first met him. Until she took on the job of teaching him for a movie he was starring in, Jake had never ridden a horse. I think it's time I showed folks that I'm not a phony on the cover of a trashy magazine. Yeah, I know it's time."

He picked up the TV remote and surfed through channels until he found a ball game. As he settled down to watch, Lili's face crinkled into a frown.

"Travis, what are you planning?"

"A little publicity stunt of my own."

Chapter Two

"Look!" Emma grabbed Etta's arm. They'd been going through a rack of shirts and blouses in a store in a Calgary mall. "Over there, walking toward the door. It's Frasier!"

"What?" Etta followed her sister's stare. Still recovering from the red-eye flight from New Brunswick, she had to struggle to focus. "Are you sure? He's about the right height and build, but there have to be hundreds…thousands maybe, of tall, broad-shouldered, dark-haired men in Calgary. With those ratty clothes, long hair, and scrubby beard, he could be any derelict."

"It's the way he has to appear. That's his cover. He might disguise himself all he can, but I'd recognize the way those hips move anywhere…not to mention that stellar butt. Come on. We're going to follow him."

"Emma, I don't think…" Etta tried to protest, but her sister was dragging her toward the entrance.

On the sidewalk, Emma paused until she again fixed her gaze on the man she believed was her husband. With Etta still in tow, she began to push through the crowd in pursuit.

"We mustn't get too close," she hissed, although he was out of earshot ahead of them. "Frasier is an expert at knowing when he's being followed."

Etta didn't reply. It was too late for protest. Her

sister could be as persistent as a bloodhound when she was on the scent of something she wanted. All she could do now was follow along, try to prevent her from getting into serious trouble, and hope the man ahead of them was not Frasier MacKenzie.

After several blocks, the shopping district changed into streets of shabby hotels and taverns. The man supposedly her sister's husband turned into one of the former.

"Ah-ha!" Emma paused, triumphant. "So that's where he's staying. Come on."

"Emma, look at that place. I don't think…"

"Stop thinking and move it." Emma started off. When Etta didn't follow, she swung back. "Or are you letting me go alone?"

"No…no." Etta's words reflected her resignation.

The lobby stank of stale smoke and—Etta wrinkled her nose—God only knew what else. She paused to gaze around the dilapidated, dirty room while Emma made straight for the desk.

"Yeah?" At her approach, a scrawny man in rumpled clothing, who looked as if he hadn't shaved or washed in days, looked up from the tabloid he'd been reading.

As Emma leaned across the desk toward him, Etta turned away. She couldn't bear to hear or watch. Emma had a way of inveigling her way into whatever place or situation she wished. Any attempt she might make to halt her sister would be pointless. Stopping Emma Prescott-MacKenzie when she was determined to get her way was like attempting to block a runaway train.

A man in jeans, black leather vest open over a hirsute chest, entered the lobby. He paused to give her a head-to-toe appraisal.

"You new around here, baby?" Leering at her, he rolled a toothpick in his mouth.

"I'm waiting for my boyfriend." From somewhere, she didn't know where, the answer came, sharp and nasty. "So buzz off."

"Sure, sure." He held up his hands. "But if he don't show, I'm in room ten."

With a sneering backward glance, he headed up the stairs.

*Oh, God, Emma, let's get out of here!*

Seemingly in response to her silent plea, Emma had turned away from the desk and was heading toward her, a smug expression on her face.

"Come on," she said. She held out her hand to reveal a key. "Room eight."

"How did you…?" A sinking feeling enveloped Etta's gut.

"Money and a sexy smile. Now move it. This isn't the type of lobby one hangs out in."

She headed for the stairs. Etta hesitated only a moment, giving a resigned sigh, before she followed.

\*\*\*\*

Glancing furtively about, Emma inserted the key into the door of room eight.

"Etta, you stay out here and keep watch." She whispered as the lock gave. "If anyone approaches and tries to get in, stop them."

"How?" Exasperation boiled over. "Wrestle them to the floor?"

"You'll think of something. You *are* my twin." The door squealed on unoiled hinges as Emma swung it inward. Through the opening, Etta saw Frasier

MacKenzie bolting out of the bathroom, a ragged towel about his hips his only covering. His right hand held a revolver leveled at them.

"Emma!" The gun dropped to his side.

"Frasier!" She dashed across the room to leap onto her husband, wrapping legs and arms around him. The towel fell to the floor and the .38 went behind her back as his arms flexed around her. It was like the cover of a cheap thriller.

*Oh, my God, Emma!*

Etta covered her eyes with one hand, fumbled for the knob with the other, and pulled the door shut on the scene.

*How is it possible for that woman and me to be even remotely related, never mind twins!*

Heaving an exasperated breath, she leaned against the dirty wall and prepared to act as lookout.

*Please don't let Mr. Hairy Chest Leather Vest show up. Please, please, please! Think about something pleasant…the Travis Masters show, Travis Masters…*

"Hi, cutie." The odor issuing from him made her turn before she actually saw him. Grinning over blackened teeth with gaps in front was a creature in filthy jeans and a torn sweatshirt. "Waitin' for someone?"

"Yeah, my boyfriend Bruiser the Bat is gettin' the key for this room at the desk. You must have heard about him. He's the guy who put three dudes in the hospital last week. The police have been hasslin' him ever since, so he's not in a good mood. If you've got a clue, you'll move on."

He paused, staring at her. Finally, with a guffaw, he moved off down the corridor and into a room near the end. Relief flooded through her body.

*I sounded like dialogue from a really bad detective novel...or genuinely Emma's twin. Hurry up, Emma. For Heaven's sake, hurry up!*

Chapter Three

"Okay, let's go." Her face glowing as she buttoned her blouse, Emma MacKenzie emerged from the room. She pulled the door shut behind her. "The sooner we get away from here, the better."

"Oh, so *now* we have to get away fast." Etta glared at her twin, nerves worn thin from a half hour of fending off squalid men who'd passed along the corridor.

"We don't want to blow Frasier's cover." The words were a hissed whisper.

"We! *We!*"

"Okay, *I* don't want to. Come on." She gave her sister a nudge toward the stairs. Together they hustled down the steps and out into the hot sunshine of the street.

"Now, let's get back to that shopping." Emma squared her shoulders and smiled.

"Oh, fine. Back to shopping just as if nothing had happened. Just as if we hadn't run your husband to ground in this fleabag of a hotel. Just as if you hadn't left me on lookout while you…while you…"

"Stop fumbling for words, Etta. While I had morning delight with my sexy husband. Don't be such a prude. Heaven knows you don't fudge about it in your books."

A swing in her step, she set off down the street

toward the shopping district.

"I do not use inappropriate language in my books." Etta started after her. "They're all rated 'sweet.' But maybe…"

"Yes?" Emma paused and turned to her.

"Maybe you should check your blouse. It's buttoned all wrong."

"Okay, okay." They stopped while Emma made the adjustment.

"What did Frasier have to say?" Etta couldn't resist asking.

"Well, at first he was too surprised to speak, and then for a while, he was too busy. Oh, for heaven's sake, Etta, don't go blushing. After that…"

"After that?"

"Well…" She finished with her blouse, and they continued on down the street. "He sort of told me not to do anything like that again."

"*Sort* of told you?"

"Okay, okay, warned me. Actually said there'd be consequences."

"Consequences? What consequences? Emma…"

"Hollow threats. You'll recall he warned me off his previous case. All that happened then was that he ended up asking me to marry him."

"After you were both nearly murdered by drug dealers. Emma, for goodness' sake, Frasier is in an extremely dangerous profession. For your own safety, he doesn't want you involved."

"I'm well aware of what my husband does for a living. If I lacked the courage to face up to it, I never would have married him. Now, here's the mall. Back to our mission of getting a top that will draw Travis

24

Masters' attention like iron filings to a magnet."

Reluctantly, Etta followed her sister inside. The last thing she wanted was a pair of skin-tight jeans and a flaming-red tank top with sequins, but she knew if Emma had her heart set on dressing her up like a cowgirl hooker, protesting wouldn't help.

*I've brought my own jeans and plaid shirt. Emma may force me to buy something outlandish, but when it comes time to dress for the show, she can't push me into anything I don't want to wear.*

As she walked behind her sister across the foyer, she spotted a magazine store with a rack of the latest publications out front. She stopped short. On the cover of one, Travis Masters' likeness had been captured holding a gorgeous blonde she recognized as country music singer Lanie Lanson. The woman, in jeans that looked painted on and a top revealing a whole lot of breast, had her pelvis thrust against him suggestively.

*Wow! Hardly what I expected from a shy country boy. Guess I was wrong about him. Still...*

Unable to resist the temptation, she headed over to the store. Emma, unaware that her fellow shopper had left her wake, continued on across the mall.

Etta picked up the magazine and read the lead headline.

"Travis Masters and Lanie Lanson...Country Couple of the Year?"

*More and more mistaken. Lanie Lanson is hardly the type of woman I'd expect him to be romantically involved with.*

"What are you doing?" Emma had returned. "We haven't got all day. The concert is tomorrow, you know. I want to get this shopping done so we can watch some of the events this afternoon. What's this you're reading?" She snatched the magazine from Etta's hands. "Oh, God, what trash! As if a man who looks like Travis Masters and gives reluctant interviews would take up with something obvious like that!" She started to shove the publication back into its rack. Etta snatched it away from her and went up to the cashier.

****

Etta didn't remove the magazine from its plastic bag until her sister had gone into the bathroom to take a shower. As soon as she heard water running, she curled up on one of the hotel room's twin beds and rushed to page thirty-eight.

She was only a few paragraphs into the article when she realized that ninety percent of the quotes were from Lanie Lanson. The photos, aside from the one on the cover and another accompanying the article that appeared contrived, to her professional eye, were separates of Lanie and Travis. His participation in the interview, to the perception of a former magazine writer, had been minimal. In fact, she decided as she threw the publication onto the bed, it was a portrait of Lanie Lanson with just enough references to Travis Masters to draw the attention of his many fans.

"I forgot my conditioner." Emma, wrapped in a towel, burst dripping out of the bathroom. "Good God, are you actually reading that trash? Etta, a fan magazine!"

"I know, I know. I was curious. After all, Lanie Lanson is the opening act at the Travis Masters' show. I always like to get a bit of background on performers and events I'm going to attend."

"Maybe once when you were a magazine writer."

Emma plunked her bottom on the bed beside her sister. "Now you're behaving like a silly groupie who's thirsting for any and all information about her hero, no matter how ridiculous. Take it from me"—she stood and headed for the dresser—"Travis is exactly what he appears to be, a sweet, decent country boy perfectly suited for a sweet, decent romance writer like you." She snatched up a bottle and headed back into the steamy bathroom. "Throw that trash into the garbage and get on with your amorous fantasies about him."

As the door shut behind her sister, Etta took one last look at the article. With a sigh, she threw it into the wastepaper basket.

*A major fantasy shattered.*

****

At the Calgary Stampede, Emma and Etta found seats in a midsection of the grandstand and settled down to enjoy the afternoon's events.

"Would be nice if we knew some of the riders personally," Emma said. "Someone we could really cheer for."

"Well, since we're from the opposite side of the country, it's not likely we'll be acquainted with any of them."

"Still, it would be nice." Emma adjusted first her sunglasses, then the snow-white Stetson she'd purchased earlier that day. "I like to put my heart into things…like this morning." She winked at her sister.

"*Really.*"

"I wish you'd let me buy you one of these hats." Emma touched the brim of hers. "It would help you get into the spirit of things."

"I'm doing just fine, thank you. Look, the first

event is about to start."

Although she didn't know any of the participants, Etta found the saddle bronc riding exciting and was often on her feet, cheering on the participants. As the competition drew to a close, the announcer's voice boomed over the PA system with additional zeal.

"This afternoon, folks, we have a major surprise. Our final rider is a late entry, none other than the star of our show tomorrow evening. All you ticket holders better be keeping your fingers crossed he doesn't get dinged up. Let's have a big hand for Travis Masters, riding Whirlwind!"

As the crowd burst into wild response, Etta's stomach clenched. Travis Masters in saddle bronc competition? Surely he couldn't be a real cowboy.

*Oh, God, don't let him get injured or…killed! This has to be some crazy publicity stunt!*

With the crowd whistling, yelling, and clapping, Whirlwind and his rider burst from the chute. The horse leaped into the air. It came down stiff-legged to swirl into a move that Etta guessed had earned it its name. Through it all, Travis Masters managed to remain on top.

Although the ride lasted only a few seconds, to Etta it seemed forever before the pickup riders rode close to the bronc to allow Travis to get off. He slid over the back of one of their horses and hit the ground on his feet. As he walked to the sidelines, he ducked his head and raised two fists in the air. The crowd went wild.

"Go, Travis!" Emma waved and yelled. "Wow, that was an adrenaline rush!"

Etta dropped back onto the bench, too weak with relief to comment more than, "If he'd gotten injured, our pricey tickets would have been worthless."

\*\*\*\*

At six a.m. the following morning, Etta rested her forearms on the top rail of the fence surrounding the Rangeland Derby track. This arena of the Calgary Stampede grounds was designated for what were known as chuck wagon races, but at this hour she watched, fascinated, as a group of riders exercised and trained their horses. The men working their mounts in the early morning sunshine were, she'd been told by a man who'd paused for a moment to talk to her, the outriders, the cowboys who raced behind the chuck wagons, required to keep within a definite distance of them in order to qualify and possibly win.

Impressed by the demonstration of expert riding, Etta didn't notice the man who came up behind her, leading a saddled horse, until he spoke.

"Some great riders out there."

Whirling she faced a tall, handsome man in shabby jeans, a T-shirt that looked as if it had seen better days, a baseball cap, and sunglasses.

*Oh, God, no! It can't be. Not Travis Masters.*

Words tangled in her throat. She stared.

"You look like a woman interested in horses and fine riding. Otherwise you wouldn't be out here at six a.m. watching a training session."

His down-to-earth attitude soothed her. Words returned to her abilities, as did common sense. "Yes, I have been as long as I can remember."

*Of course this isn't Travis Masters. What would he be doing, dressed like a stable hand, out around the track at this time of the day? Some really good look-alike, that's all.*

"I take it you ride. Do you own a horse?"

"No to both. I've never had the opportunity."

"Well, we can remedy a bit of what you've missed right now." He swung into the saddle of the bay mare with what Etta recognized from years of watching equine videos as a smooth, fluid gesture. "Come on up." He kicked his foot—which Etta saw was shod in an expensive-looking cowboy boot—from the left stirrup and reached his left hand down to her. Fleetingly she noticed a jagged scar across its back.

"Oh, no, I couldn't…really."

*What is wrong with you, Etta Prescott? Even if this guy isn't Travis Masters, he's one handsome man. Furthermore, you'll be perfectly safe with him here on the Calgary Stampede grounds. That is, unless, like a character in one of your romances, he's about to gallop off into the sunset…or in this case, sunrise, with you.*

"There's an empty round pen right over there. I'll give you your first lesson. And don't worry. They told me back at the barn this old gal is certified bomb proof."

"Okay." She sucked in a deep breath, took his hand, put her sneakered foot into the stirrup, and swung up behind the sexiest man she'd encountered in a very long time…her brother-in-law Frasier excepted.

*Here's to bringing a fantasy to life. Here's to showing my twin I'm as up for adventure as she is. Here's to—*

"Put your arms around me." He interrupted her thoughts as he turned the horse away from the fence and across a short expanse of grass and dust. "You'll feel more secure."

*More secure…or ready to faint.*

Etta did as instructed, her head swirling with the unreality of the situation. The man was as hard muscled as any of her imagined heroes.

*Any minute now I'll wake up and discover this is all a crazy fantasy. He may only be a Travis Masters look-alike, but...Wow!*

He walked the mare slowly to the round pen, Etta trying to tell herself she wasn't savoring every minute of the ride, that it wasn't something straight out of one of her novels. The sensation of his body rubbing gently against hers, the fresh-from-a-shower scent of something definitely masculine...she could only hope he didn't hear or feel her heart pounding.

"Here we are." He stopped the horse. "Slide down."

"Okay." She drew her right leg across the horse's rump and dropped to the ground with a bump.

A lot more smoothly, he swung down to join her.

"Hold her while I open the gate." He held out the mare's reins.

"All righty." Swallowing hard, she took the leather into her hand.

*Oh, God, 'all righty'? I've never used that phrase in my life. This man has knocked sensible responses entirely out of my head.*

"Bring her inside." He'd opened the gate and stood waiting for her.

Etta stared at the horse that appeared so huge, and she froze.

"Come on, she's gentle as a lamb." His words loosened her trepidations.

She sucked in a deep breath and started forward. To her delight and relief, the horse walked behind her.

"See? Easy." He shut the gate after them. "I'm thinking this old gal has been around the block more times than you can count. It'll take a lot to spook her. Okay, now, on her left side, gather up the reins, get a grip on the horn, put your foot in the stirrup, grab the cantle, and…" His hand went unobtrusively to her bottom. "Up you go."

Etta found herself in the saddle.

*Luckily, I know what the horn and cantle are, from my research. But the way he put me up here…*

"There," he said. "Not so hard, was it? And off we go."

He took the mare's bridle, and Etta Prescott, who'd written over a dozen cowboy romances, was having her first horseback ride ever. Delight must have been obvious in her expression, because he looked up at her and grinned. "Great, isn't it? Wait until you get to lope…or best of all, flat out run."

"Oh, I don't think that will ever happen." She clung to reins and saddle horn with both hands.

"Don't sell yourself short. All you need is confidence. Take the reins in one hand. If you feel uneasy, hang onto the horn with the other. This old gal knows the drill, so all you have to do is touch the lines to one side of her neck or the other to let her know what way you want her to go." He released the bridle and stepped back. "Walk on," he said, and the mare moved slowly forward, keeping close to the sides of the round pen.

Etta's breath clumped in her throat, but after a moment, when the animal gave no indication of bolting or bucking or doing any of the wild things horses had done in her stories, she was able to breathe again.

"Relax, relax." Her instructor continued to walk beside her. "Enjoy it. That's what riding's all about." When the mare paused, he ordered, "Get on there, Dee." To his pupil, he advised, "Touch her sides easy with your heels."

Gingerly Etta did as he'd said. The mare began to move forward again, this time at a spritely walk. "Whoa!" Her heart seeming to leap to the back of her throat, Etta pulled on the reins. The horse stopped, snorted, and tossed her head.

"You were doing fine." He came to stand beside her left leg. "You put on the brakes too fast. You confused her, that's all. She's not going to take off at a mad gallop from the touch of a running shoe, but she does expect to get proper signals. Try again, and be confident you'll be okay. I'm right here."

She glanced down at him. A desire to impress him, to convince him she wasn't afraid, gushed over her. He might only be a Travis Masters look-alike, but he had all the charm of the sexiest of her fictional cowboy heroes.

"Walk on," she urged the mare, hoping her command sounded full of confidence.

The horse blew and moved ahead at her previous shambling gait.

After several more trips around the pen, he convinced her to urge the mare to a slow trot. Feeling secure by his in-control presence, she relaxed and savored the exhilaration of the moments.

As she was making her third circuit of the enclosure at a trot, she saw him glance at his watch.

"Do you have to be somewhere, at work, maybe?" She halted beside him.

"Not me, but I promised the guy I borrowed this old mare from I'd have her back at the barn in a half hour. Sorry."

"Not a problem." Her right leg scraped over the mare's hindquarters before her foot hit the ground harder than she'd planned. "It's been great. Thank you." She handed the reins to him. "Do you need help putting her in the stable?"

"I think I can manage." She caught a hint of teasing in the words.

Of course, he had to be wondering how this rank beginner could be of any assistance.

"Well, anyhow, thank you." She stepped back to open the gate as he gathered up the reins and swung into the saddle.

"Glad you enjoyed it." He touched the brim of his baseball cap before applying his heels to the mare's side and swinging her away into a gallop that left Etta lost in admiration of his ability.

*Who is he? Maybe one of the outriders for the rangeland derby? No, if that were the case, he'd have been out in the ring practicing with them. Probably he's simply a stable hand who's a great—at least in my opinion—rider. But he is wearing those fancy boots...*

Remembering what her sister had told her about high school kids who often had no money for lunch after spending hundreds on designer running shoes, she shrugged. Probably he was like those teenagers. Probably he'd spent every cent of his minimum wage paycheck, maybe even two, on them. Those boots were likely some kind of status symbol among his peers.

As she headed back to their hotel, a shadow of disappointment fell over the thrill of her early morning adventure. He hadn't asked to see her again, hadn't even inquired about her name or given her his.

*Put all that nonsense aside, Etta Prescott, and deal with this little adventure for the most it can ever be…a scene in one of your western fantasies.*

\*\*\*\*

"Travis, where on earth have you been?" Lili Farrah, in robe and fuzzy slippers, stepped out of the room she occupied with her husband next to the band's suite to confront Travis as he shoved the entry card into the door.

"Out. Lili, did you do a stint as a cop in your past?" He swung to face her.

"No, just a long career of dealing with rehab patients that required sleeping with both ears alert and one eye open. Where were you at six a.m.? You should be sleeping, what with that big show tonight."

"Doing what you suggested back in Toronto. Riding."

"Not another bucking bronc, I hope? After that stunt you pulled yesterday…"

"Definitely not a saddle bronc. Just a nice, gentle old mare my niece could ride."

He pushed the door open and stepped inside, Lili close behind him. She crossed the room to close the bedroom doors before she turned on him.

"Well, young man, the next time you decide to do anything like this, I'd appreciate your letting me know. I heard you leave, but by the time I got my robe, you were already in the elevator. I couldn't very well follow you in my night clothes. I worry about you, you know. You and all the boys."

"I know, Lil, and we appreciate it. You and Joe

have been like parents to us since Jordan left." He crossed the room and began to make coffee at the machine on a table. "I just had to get away, to relieve some of the tension."

"And that crazy ride yesterday afternoon didn't help? Travis, are you having some kind of twenty-something crisis?"

"No, Lil." He poured water into the machine and punched the button to start it brewing. "That bronc riding stunt was to give Annie a taste of her own publicity foolishness. This morning was purely for pleasure."

"Travis, what is it?" Lili moved to stand in front of him, hands on her hips as she looked up at him, eyes narrowing. "There's more, isn't there?"

"Don't talk so loud. You'll wake the guys."

He turned away from her to try to extricate coffee from the machine halfway through its brew cycle.

"Tell me, young man, or I will wake your buddies, and they'll question you without mercy."

"Okay, okay." He took a sip from the quarter-filled cup and grimaced as the hot liquid burned.

"I met someone out there. A girl."

"Oh, yes?" Lili followed him as he crossed the room to take a seat on the couch.

"That's it. She and I talked, I let her have a ride on the mare I'd borrowed from the stables, and then I came back here. End of story."

"Travis." He looked up at her standing in front of him and was reminded of his third-grade teacher, a woman he'd never managed to fib to or fool.

"Okay, okay." He gazed down into the coffee cup in his hands. "She was...different. She didn't have a clue who I was. She has a genuine love of horses. When I saw how star-struck she looked, staring at the old mare, I offered her a ride. She'd never been on a horse, and when she got up there, she looked like a kid on the best Christmas morning ever."

"And?" That third-grade-teacher kind of expression remained intact.

"And what?" Travis avoided the woman's eyes.

"Was she pretty, pleasant, what?" She sat down beside him.

"Yeah, real pretty. And from what I could tell, without a drop of makeup. She had hair the color of a field of ripe wheat."

"And probably with a nice little shape in a pair of jeans and a plaid shirt."

"T-shirt."

"So I take it you're hoping to see her again. What's her name? Where is she staying?"

He stared over at her. "Aw, hell!"

"Watch the language, young man. Why the cuss word? Don't tell me you were too smitten to ask her name?"

"Yeah, well, you got that right. Shit!"

"Again, language." She stood and went to the coffee machine. "And I take it you didn't even get one of her boots?"

"One of her boots?"

"The cowboy equivalent of a glass slipper. I'm saying you let your Cinderella get away without a trace."

Carrying her filled cup, she shook her head and quietly left the suite.

*Jerk!* Travis downed the rest of the half-brewed

coffee in his cup, got to his feet, and went back to the machine. No sense economizing on the stuff. Trying to get some sleep in the room he shared with James would be next to impossible, what with the drummer's snoring, never mind visions dancing around in his head of that woman with stars in her green eyes over her first ride on a horse. And who, thanks to his stupidity, he'd probably never see again.

****

Eight stories below, Etta found the room she and Emma were sharing was empty. Although her sister had been sleeping when she'd left, she wasn't surprised to find her gone. Emma, like herself, was a person to be out and about early.

*Probably went to get breakfast.*

Her stomach rumbled. She could do with something to eat. Early morning adventures with a mysterious, handsome cowboy must have whetted her appetite. The coffee shop downstairs could offer a remedy. No need to change from her jeans and T-shirt. Calgary during Stampede week wasn't a place for dressing up…unless it was in fancy cowboy gear. She headed for the elevator.

Turning a corner on the ground floor, she all but ran headlong into her twin.

"Etta, where have you been?" Emma clutched her by both forearms. "I've just had the most amazing experience."

Typical. Emma was always having amazing experiences. But why now? Now, when she was bursting to tell her about her own adventure… Etta heaved a sigh. Might as well listen. Stopping her sister in full storytelling mode was next to impossible.

"Amazing experience?" Etta acquiesced as her sister pulled her into a secluded corner of the lounge.

"Yes, yes! When I woke and found you gone, I decided to go down to the coffee shop and have breakfast. Who do you suppose I met there?" She pushed Etta onto a couch and perched down on its edge beside her, green eyes sparkling.

"I have no idea, although given the fact that any number of celebrities are supposed to be in town…"

"Shelby Masters-Brooks!" The name came out in a gust. "Travis Masters' sister and Jordan Brooks's wife! She and her five-year-old daughter were having breakfast. Fortunately, the place was so crowded, there wasn't a single space left…except at their table."

"Oh, Emma, you didn't!"

"Oh, Etta, of course I did. That's a major difference between you and me. I seize every opportunity, you sit back and wait for things to happen." She shifted into a more comfortable position. "Anyhow, I did have an in. You'll remember that her husband is Jake Brooks, formerly known as Jordan Brooks, number one country singer only six or so years ago, and we now work together back home at Carleton High School in the guidance department. Well, the short version of what happened is this. She recognized me right away. We've met at a few school activities. We had a nice chat. Shelby is a lovely person, and her daughter is a darling. She invited us to sit with her and Katie Rose—that's her daughter—right up on the bleachers near the stage at the show tonight! Isn't that wonderful?"

"Emma, you didn't by any chance mention I'm a big fan of her brother's, did you?" Etta stared at her sister.

"Well, I might have hinted at it...and that this trip and the concert were birthday gifts. Actually, you might get a chance to see the man offstage. Not only does his family have rooms here, he and his band are staying in the penthouse suite of this very hotel."

"Oh, my God, Emma, please, please tell me all this is some kind of uncanny coincidence. Please tell me you didn't know Travis Masters, his band, and his family are staying at this hotel. Please tell me you didn't do anything underhanded or even illegal to get us rooms here."

"Etta, Etta, calm down. Of course I wouldn't do anything that's against the law, especially since my darling husband is an enforcer. I simply took the opportunity at lunch one day in the school cafeteria to have a chat with Jake. I'd seen the advertisements about his coming out of retirement for a single performance here in Calgary to benefit at-risk youth. In the course of that conversation, he mentioned the hotel where he and his family would be staying. Of course, it didn't take a mental giant to figure out that his brother-in-law and his band would be staying here as well. After that, it was just a matter of money changing hands to get us rooms here."

"You bribed people!" Etta leaned forward to press her fingers to her temples.

"Relax. It's done every day. Nothing illegal about it. Now, come on. We've got some serious shopping to do. Today we're out to purchase cowboy boots. When in Calgary during Stampede week, do as the Calgarians do."

"I don't need to buy boots!" Her mind raced back

to the expensive-looking boots her mysterious cowboy had worn. "At the moment, I'm starving."

"Oh, for heaven's sake! Okay, okay, we'll go into the coffee shop while you stuff yourself with an egg on a bagel or something. Then we're off to buy footwear suitable to our present location."

As soon as they'd seated themselves in a booth, Etta ordered breakfast, while Emma asked for coffee and a muffin. Awaiting their order, the latter looked across the table, eyes narrowing.

"By the way, where did you get to so early this morning? I can't imagine you've met up with some handsome cowboy and were off to a booty call. With your romantic notions, it would take a promise of happily ever after to get you anywhere near spending a night with a guy."

"I'm comfortable with my romantic notions, thank you very much." Etta adjusted the condiments on the table before looking up at her sister. "And who are you to talk? You were the femme fatale of the Carleton High teaching staff and had a reputation of being unattainable, until you found your hero in Frasier MacKenzie."

"Okay, okay, so I was choosy. I'm not sorry. Frasier is exactly what I want in every way…except for his frequent and extended absences." Her green eyes took on a wistful look, making Etta sorry she'd challenged her.

"I'm sorry, Emma. That was thoughtless of me."

"Forget it." She smiled across at her twin as the waitress brought their food. "You're right, and you're also right to hold out for your own special hero. Believe me, it's worth it. Now back on topic." As the waitress moved away, she leaned across the table toward her. "Where were you?"

"I went down to the Stampede grounds to look at the horses." She turned her attention to the pancakes and sausages on her plate.

"And did you see any…horses?" Emma broke her muffin in two and began to butter, her focus on her sister.

"Yes."

"Oh, for God's sake, Etta! That cat in the cream look screams that there's a whole lot more to the story."

"Fine. While I was watching the outriders practicing for the chuck wagon races, this drop-dead handsome man rode up on a lovely horse. We got talking, and he offered me a ride. I climbed up behind him, and we went to a round pen where he let me ride on my own. Then he said he had to take the horse back to the stable and headed off toward the barns."

"Etta, this sounds like a scene out of one of your books. You aren't having me on in retaliation for my getting us into this hotel, are you?"

"No way. I would swear on a Bible. At first I thought he was Travis Masters. Then I realized it couldn't possibly be, not at six a.m. out in the stable area wearing really scruffy jeans and a baggy T-shirt."

"A delusion brought on by too many dreams of the guy. Understandable. Never mind. Are you going to see him again?"

Etta stopped, a piece of sausage half way to her mouth. "I…don't know."

"You did give him your name and tell him which hotel you're staying at?"

"No."

"Aw, Etta! You can't even recognize when romance comes calling. But no matter." Emma shrugged as she returned her attention to her muffin. "Probably just some stable hand exercising a horse. You don't want to get involved with a saddle tramp."

"Now who's sounding like something out of one of my books?"

Chapter Four

"Come on, come on!" Emma pulled Etta along by the arm. "Those passes Shelby gave me entitle us to the best seats in the place...top of the bleachers right by the stage."

"Okay, okay." Etta stumbled over the rough terrain behind the concert area. "But if one of us breaks a leg, neither of us will be enjoying Travis Masters."

They arrived at the bleachers and headed up to take their seats among those already in their places. The field in front of the stage was jammed with spectators—thousands, Etta conservatively estimated. Travis Masters definitely was a big, big star.

Hastened by her sister's hand, Etta followed her up to the topmost bench. A pretty chestnut-haired woman seated there smiled and shifted to the right to allow the twins space beside her. A golden-haired cherub of a child dressed in a pink cowgirl outfit sat beside her, swinging matching boots above the floor her legs couldn't reach.

"Great crowd," Emma said. "Your brother and his band definitely can pack 'em in."

"Travis is pretty popular," she replied. "Even though I almost cost him his chance to make it, a few years back. I wasn't big on the lifestyle involved, and I'm still not."

"Shelby, I'd like you to meet my sister Etta. She's

44

one of your brother's biggest fans. Etta, this is Shelby Masters Brooks, Travis's sister and wife to Jordan—or, as he's known now, Jake Brooks. The super cutie by her side is their daughter."

"A pleasure." Shelby Brooks held out her right hand. "It's always nice to meet someone who enjoys Travis's music, especially someone from our home town."

"Hello." Etta accepted the introduction and the handshake.

"Hi." The child wriggled off the bench beside her mother and trotted around her to hold out a small hand. "I'm Katie Rose."

"Nice to meet you, Katie Rose."

"Uncle Travis and my daddy are great together," the child continued. "Wait until you see them."

"Katie Rose," her mother admonished, "you've been told not to talk like that." Shelby looked over at the twins, shaking her head. "She's a bit precocious.".

"Mommy uses that word when she thinks I've said too much or the wrong thing." The child leaned close to Etta to whisper, "I'm not sure what it means, but I don't think it's real bad."

"No, it definitely isn't." *What a charmer.*

"'Evening." A tall, handsome man in jeans, cowboy boots, Stetson, and plaid shirt with shoulders out to there, followed by a pretty blonde, greeted them. "Excuse us, ladies. I think our seats are on the far side of you."

"Uncle Ross!" Katie Rose squealed, dashing as well as space would allow past the seated women to hold up her arms. The big man swept her up.

"Howdy, Miss Katie Rose. Don't you look pretty

tonight!" The man was grinning broadly.

"Hi, Aunt Jessi," the child said, to acknowledge his companion.

"Hi, Katie Rose." The lovely young woman Katie Rose had addressed as Aunt Jessi smiled at her, then caught at the man's arm. "Ross, honey, we don't have to push our way along. We can sit here just as well." She indicated a space beside Etta.

"Not tonight, darlin'." He held the child with one arm and swept off his Stetson with his free hand. "Katie Rose and I want to be as close to the action as we can get. Apologies, ladies."

Etta, Emma, and Shelby moved their legs aside to allow the couple to bypass them and take seats beside the one Katie Rose had occupied next to her mother. With an impish expression as she looked up at Ross Turner, the child retook her former position.

"Ross and Katie Rose have a history," Shelby explained to Emma and Etta. "He saved her life…twice. Now they're quite a pair. That little cowgirl outfit she's wearing is a gift from him and his wife Jessi. Katie Rose insisted on wearing it tonight even though I'd been given to understand it's intended for her appearance at a pony show coming up back home. And I should further explain that Ross and Jessi aren't her blood relatives. Katie Rose simply has a penchant for addressing any adult she likes as uncle or aunt."

Conversation came to an abrupt end as the MC stepped out onto the stage and was greeted by a deafening roar from the crowd.

"Simmer down, folks," the man dressed in cowboy garb yelled. "I know you're all dyin' to see Travis Masters and his brother-in-law Jordan Brooks in this once-in-a-lifetime show, but first let's have a nice round of appreciation for a rising star and the opening performer of the evening, Miss Lanie Lanson."

The crowd subsided into a more controlled applause as Lanie Lanson, black hair swinging down her back to her waist, skin-tight jeans hugging her hips, and a sleeveless plaid shirt cut low to reveal a fair bit of cleavage, danced across the stage, wriggling in a way that brought wolf whistles and shouts from the men in the audience.

"There's one of the reasons I'm glad Jake is no longer part of the country music scene," Etta heard Shelby tell Emma above the roar of the crowd.

"I agree. My husband was once into this kind of lifestyle. A rock band. I'm delighted he's out of it…at least I think he's out of it," Emma yelled back. In answer to Shelby's puzzled look, she shrugged and returned her attention to the stage.

After several numbers that included a lot of sensuous dancing and leaning forward toward the audience to allow her shirt to gap open even more, Lanie Lanson left the stage, blowing kisses and shaking her bottom.

"Wow!" Emma exhaled as the singer disappeared from view. "I wonder how many males in the audience listened to the lyrics."

"Now, ladies and gentlemen, the moment you've all been waiting for." The MC was back at the mike, holding high both hands. "Together for this one special performance…Travis Masters and Jordan Brooks!"

The crowd went wild. Glancing over at Shelby, Etta saw the woman close her eyes and, shaking her head, lower it. This definitely wasn't a part of Dr.

Shelby Masters-Brooks' life that she relished.

The two men sang and danced around the stage, bringing the roars of appreciation from the crowd to a deafening level. Etta lost herself in the excitement and yelled and clapped as loud as she could at the end of each number.

Finally, after an hour and a half of nonstop entertainment, the MC took the mike and held up a hand for quiet. "As a finale, folks, Travis and Jordan have worked up something pretty darned special."

As he spoke, Etta saw the man introduced to her as Ross Turner scoop Katie Rose up into his arms and make his way, cleared by security guards, to the stage.

"Ross, what…" Shelby, on her feet, tried to protest but they were gone, with fans closing in behind them.

In front of the roaring crowd, Ross hoisted Katie Rose up onto the stage to her father.

"Ladies and gentlemen, let's have a nice hand for former world champion bull rider, the rock star of rodeo, Mr. Ross Turner, and Jordan's daughter, Travis's niece, Miss Katie Rose Brooks."

The crowd went wild as Ross doffed his hat to them, then slid away from the stage.

Jordan placed his daughter on the stage, and she trotted over to stand beside her uncle. Raising his hands, her father made a bid for quiet.

"Katie Rose and Travis and I have worked up a little number I hope you'll enjoy. Take it away, guys."

Amid the thunderous appreciation of the crowd, Katie Rose, singing along with the famous pair, danced between her father and uncle, small pink cowgirl boots keeping perfect time and never missing a step, seemingly as smooth and polished a performer as the two men on either side of her.

"I'll kill those two!" Shelby cried. "I warned them about including Katie Rose in any of this!"

"But Shelby, you have to admit, she's absolutely adorable!" Emma yelled.

"Well, I guess she is." Defeated by her child's amazing performance, Shelby acquiesced. "But"—her tone picked up—"her daddy and uncles, which includes Ross, are all in for a dressing down when I get them alone."

****

As fans began to leave the concert area, Shelby held a sleepy child in her arms and waited for the place to clear out. Etta, Emma, Jessi, and Ross Turner remained with her.

"Ross, I don't think I had a chance to properly introduce you," Shelby said to the man on her right. "Etta Prescott and Emma MacKenzie, meet Ross Turner and his wife Jessi. Ross, as the announcer made sure everyone knew, was a world champion bull rider before he retired to be a rancher. Jessi is famous for her success with injured and traumatized horses. Etta and Emma live in Carleton, New Brunswick."

"A pleasure, ladies." Ross held out a big hand. "Jessi and I spent a bit of time in your neck of the woods last fall...not far from Shelby and Jake's farm. Real romantic place, isn't it, Jess?" He swung an arm about his wife, grinning.

"I guess." She smirked back. "Got you to propose, didn't it?"

"Sure did. Married this past Valentine's Day. Now we're hopin'—"

His words came to an end as Jessi nudged him in

the ribs and interrupted with, "Enough, honey. Right now, I'm thinking we should invite these ladies from Carleton to the party out at my parents' ranch tomorrow evening. Travis, his band, and a bunch of people who work for them will be there, as well as some of our friends and neighbors. Shelby and Jordan are coming."

"Sure, right." Ross was all-out pleased by the suggestion. "Where are you staying? I'll have someone pick you up. Buses don't run out our way, and a cab would cost you as much as your plane fare from New Brunswick."

"Oh, we couldn't..." Etta tried to protest, but her twin's elbow found her side and silenced her.

"We'd love to. What time should we be ready?" Emma smiled.

"Five o'clock."

\*\*\*\*

"Emma, this is crazy! You shouldn't have accepted that invitation. Ross and Jessi were only being polite."

"Oh, come on! Don't be such a spoilsport. This has to be something out of your wildest fantasies. A party with Travis Masters? Come on, girl. Live the dream!"

They were standing in their hotel lobby, dressed in cowboy boots, jeans, and plaid shirts...what Emma had deemed proper attire for a party at a ranch and what made Etta feel as if she were dressed for a masquerade party. She wasn't any kind of cowgirl. The footwear made her feel as if she were about to slog through snow or ice. She'd never worn boots in summer.

"Maybe no one will come." She glanced around the lobby. "Maybe it was just an aside remark, and they've forgotten."

"Cowboys never forget."

"How would you know?" Etta put her hands on her hips and cast an exasperated stare on her sister.

"I read it in one of your books."

"You actually do read my books? I thought you said they were too fairytale-ish."

"Of course I read my sister's books. Anyhow, as a school district employee, I'd never use such an unacceptable word as fairytale-ish."

"Okay, okay, whatever term you used. Nevertheless, I'm astonished…"

"Look! That tall hunk wearing a black Stetson. He just came in, and he looks enough like Ross Turner to be his brother. Come on. Maybe he's the person sent to collect us."

"Emma…" Etta tried to protest, but she was being dragged toward the desk, where she heard the newcomer asking for Etta Prescott and Emma MacKenzie.

"See!" Emma hissed as she continued to pull her twin forward. "I told you…cowboys never forget." Aloud she called out, "We're Etta and Emma. Did Ross and Jessi send you?"

"That they did. 'Afternoon, ladies." With a wide grin, the man doffed his hat. "Chase Turner, Ross's brother, at your service. My truck is right outside, if you're ready."

"Ready and rearin' to go," Emma replied.

*Oh, God, why did Emma always have to be so bright and bubbly, so outgoing? This is downright embarrassing. And what was that she was saying about using unacceptable words? Rearin'? Really!*

As they came out of the hotel, Etta saw a dusty black king cab pickup at the curb, a woman in the passenger seat.

"Parked illegal, I guess." Their escort smirked. "But so far no ticket. Hop in the back seat, one in each side. Our boy, Jordan, is in the middle in his kid's seat. Oh…" He paused before going around to the driver's door, as the woman put the window down to smile out at them. "This is my wife, Janet. Janet, these are Etta Prescott and Emma MacKenzie. Shelby tells me they're twins."

"Pleased to meet you," she said. "Twins?" Her eyebrows raised.

"Fraternal," Emma was quick to explain. "Therefore, no similarities beyond those of sisters…and even then, in the personality department, it's a stretch. Etta, get in. I'll run around to the other door."

Inside, they were confronted by a handsome baby boy in a safety seat. As the twins took their places on either side of him, he glanced first at one, then the other, a smile brightening his cherubic face.

"Hello, Jordan Turner," Emma greeted him. "You're one fine-looking lad."

The baby chuckled.

"Typical man." Janet Turner turned in her seat to cast a rueful grin at the passengers. "Loves to be complimented by the ladies."

"Now, now, darlin'." Her husband started the engine and glanced into the mirrors. "When you got it, you got it."

Janet Turner shrugged off his teasing with a wink at the women as her husband pulled out into traffic. Etta found herself relaxing.

*I like these people. I hope the rest of the afternoon goes as smoothly.*

\*\*\*\*

The drive out of Calgary through sun-brightened rolling country fresh in summer greens, its landscape dotted here and there with white-faced cattle and sleek horses, thrilled Etta. At last she was in genuine cowboy country. Leaning back, she drew a deep breath and let delight in its ambience envelope her. She had to give her sister credit. This was turning out to be an amazing trip.

As they came into view of the ranch house and outbuildings, Etta suppressed a gasp of delight. It was something right out of one of her stories—rambling log house, big red barn and outbuildings, surrounded by what looked like acres and acres of hayfields and pastures with horses grazing contentedly in the late afternoon sunshine. It was all too good to be true. She had to be dreaming.

Her bubble of delight burst as Chase turned the truck into the ranch yard. The people and activity in the yard and on the veranda nearly overwhelmed her. She fought an urge to beg Chase to turn the truck around and take her straight back to the hotel. The crowd gathered for the party was much bigger than she'd anticipated. There must have been at least fifty people assembled around the house, coolers of drinks on the veranda, and a huge fieldstone barbecue smoking lazily up into the warm July afternoon. All the partygoers were dressed as if they'd stepped out of one of her books.

"Here we are," Chase announced as he parked his truck with a variety of others on the verge of the ranch yard. "Make yourselves at home. No need to be shy."

He climbed out and opened the door for Emma.

"Thank you, kind sir." She gave him one of her coquettish smiles that Etta knew from experience had the power to melt the heart of the most reserved male.

"Not a problem, ma'am." He grinned as she passed him with a swinging walk that made his gaze follow her.

"Chase…Jordan?" His wife, catching his interest, brought him back to the moment with mention of his child and a jerk of her head.

"Yeah, yeah, right, darlin'." He reached inside to free his son as Etta climbed out on Janet's side.

"Come on, Etta." Chase's wife took her arm with a smile and drew her toward the partying crowd. "Ignore my husband. He's totally besotted with me but still has to stare at anything that catches his eye. I assure you, he's got all he can handle at home." She winked at Etta.

"You got that right, baby." Chase, with Jordan in his arms, caught up to them.

"My sister has a way of attracting male interest wherever she goes," Etta said. "It's always been like that. Everybody loves Emma. But don't let her fool you. She's absolutely and devotedly married. It's just her way." She watched as her twin inserted herself into the crowd, making herself acquainted with everyone she encountered.

"Some women have that certain quality about them," Janet replied. "Come on, meet the gang."

For the next few minutes Etta struggled to remember names: Bob and Laura Turner, Ross and Chase's parents; Jack and Joan Wallace, Jessi's parents; the members of Travis's band and road crew; and a middle-aged couple who apparently travelled with them, bus driver Joe Farrah and his wife Lili. And that didn't include a myriad of friends and neighbors. Everyone good-naturedly accepted her and Emma into their company. One person she didn't see among the group was Lanie Lanson. She'd expected the singer to be there, especially after seeing that magazine cover and reading the associated story. She was relieved. The woman exuded far too much blatant sex appeal to be someone around whom Etta would feel comfortable.

And then the big moment. Jordan Brooks came out of the ranch house, carrying a tray piled high with steaks. Behind him, weighted down with an oversized cooler, came Travis Masters.

*Am I really here on an Alberta ranch with the two men who have dominated country music for years? Please, please don't let me wake up and find it's a dream.*

"Hey, folks, get ready to chow down!" Jordan called as he stopped beside the smoking barbecue.

"You cookin', Jake?" Ross Turner taunted.

"You've got to be kiddin', my man. I burn everything I put near fire. No, the honors go to our hosts Bob and Laura. I've been told there's no one who can touch them when it comes to cooking up a steak."

A cheer of agreement went up from the crowd. Etta barely heard it. Frozen in staring at Travis Masters as he put down the cooler and threw back the lid to reveal its contents of well-iced beer, she'd become oblivious to her surroundings. When he looked up and saw her, he stopped twisting a cap off a long neck and stared. Her breath clogged in her throat.

*He looks as if he's been hit by lightning. Oh, God, no! He's coming this way. He's smiling. He looks so much like that stable hand I met on the stampede grounds. Please, please let him go on past. Please let him be looking at someone behind me.*

"Hello." He paused in front of her, wet bottle in hand. "Cinderella?"

"What?" The word came out in what sounded to her a ridiculous squeak.

"Cinderella. The girl from the round pen. The girl whose name I was too dumb to find out. I didn't get a glass slipper...or even a running shoe, to help me find her again. You are her, right?"

"I guess...yes." His left hand holding the bottle had the jagged scar down its back that she remembered from the cowboy who'd given her a riding lesson.

"Nice to see you again." He extended his right hand. "I'm Travis Masters."

"I know." She was only vaguely aware of accepting his offer, too astonished to feel any of the famous tingle she'd so often written about that occurred when her hero and heroine made their first physical contact.

"And you're...?" He was looking into her eyes, strangling speech in her throat.

"Et...Etta Prescott. My name is actually Henrietta, but everyone calls me Etta." *Oh, damn, I'm stuttering...and rambling. Get a grip, Etta, get a grip. Tell yourself he's only another good-looking guy.*

*Not exactly.* The disconcerting thought rattled around in her head. *He's Travis Masters, number one country singer, and you're quite possibly his biggest fan.*

"You met everyone?" He waved his bottle around to indicate the crowd.

"More than whose names I can keep straight." This

time she managed to speak coherently.

*Calm down, calm down. Ignore the fact of who he is. Imagine he's only a nice person you happened to meet at a barbecue. You can do it. You're good at imagining.*

"Hey, Travis, come and lend a hand," his brother-in-law Jake Brooks hailed him. "There's more food and drink to bring out of the house."

"Sorry, duty calls." Travis gave a resigned shrug. "See you later."

\*\*\*\*

The rest of the early evening was a mix of food and drink, with the music of Travis Masters, Jordan Brooks, and their band wafting from a state-of-the-art sound system. Because Travis and Jordan/Jake had decreed this was a holiday for all the musicians, there would be no live performances.

Etta, once she began to relax, fell into the spirit of the party. Travis Masters' family and friends were generous, outgoing people who welcomed her and Emma as if they were long-time acquaintances. By the time dancing began around a bonfire, after the remains of the huge barbecue supper had been cleared away, she allowed herself to become fully immersed in the experience and was enjoying it immensely.

A pang of regret suddenly hit when she watched Emma claimed in the first of the dances, some kind of western two-step. She knew her twin, for all her outward vivacity, wasn't happy. Emma Prescott-MacKenzie loved her husband with all her heart and soul, but the couple had been forced to lead separate lives for nearly a year because of Frasier's work. And while his wife supported his objectives in catching drug dealers—she worked with too many kids damaged by illegal substances, in her job as guidance counselor, not to see the importance of his job—Etta understood Emma longed for the day when they could settle down, have a real life together, and start a family. She might pretend this seeking him out across the country was a lark, but Etta knew the truth. Her twin missed her husband acutely.

*I'll never let myself get caught up in a relationship like that. When I find the right man...or he finds me...we'll be together forever and ever.*

A smirk pulled at her lips. *Dream on, Etta Prescott. When you find the right man. You're not Emma. You're too shy to attract anyone you'd be ready to fall in love with. If Prince Charming appeared on your doorstep, you wouldn't have the gumption to invite him in.*

"Etta?" His voice made her start. Looking up from where she was seated on a lawn chair, she saw Travis Masters standing beside her, holding out a hand. "Dance?"

*Talk about Prince Charming appearing right in front of me...*

"Well..." *Damn it, Etta, stop stuttering.* "I'm not sure how to do this one."

"It's easy. Follow me. Come on." He wiggled his fingers, world-famous grin in place.

"Okay." As she struggled out of the low lawn chair, she all but upset it and herself. He caught her by a hand and righted her.

*Good for you, Etta. Embarrass yourself all you can.*

"Those chairs are only good if you plan to stay in

them all day and then roll out at night." He chuckled. Her discomfort vanished with his words.

They danced the next two dances, so vigorously there was little opportunity to talk. Etta was amazed to discover she could follow the steps and find it fun.

As the music stopped after the second number, Katie Rose struggled through the crowd.

"Uncle Travis, Uncle Travis!" She caught at his hand. "You promised to put me to bed, remember? Mommy, Daddy, and I are staying here for the night, so…"

"That I did." He cast Etta a rueful glance before looking down at the child.

"Uncle Travis will be gone tomorrow," the child explained to Etta. "I won't see him again for months and months." She held her arms wide to indicate a vast amount of time.

"Come on now, kid." Travis caught her up in his arms, grinning. "Call it weeks, not months, and it won't seem so long."

"But you will be back for Christmas, won't you?" She clasped his face between her hands, forcing him to look into her eyes. "Promise."

"I promise. Now, will you let go? You're crushing my cheeks."

"Okay." Giggling, she planted a loud kiss on the left side of his face. "Please take me to bed. I'm really sleepy."

"Okay, okay. Excuse us." He nodded to Etta. "Uncle duties call."

"Of course. Good night, Katie Rose."

"Good night, Etta. Hope you get to be Uncle Travis's girlfriend. I like you."

"Katie Rose." With a rueful shake of his head in Etta's direction, Travis started toward the house, carrying the child.

Precocious certainly did describe that little imp. Watching them go, Etta smiled. Her uncle would make a great father some day.

*Damn it, where did that last idea come from? He gave me a riding lesson out of the goodness of his heart and danced with me twice. There's no need to go building a future around it.*

\*\*\*\*

Etta found herself in demand for the following dances. In the light from the fire, the ranch yard was filled with fun and camaraderie, and she was loving it. Furthermore, it would prove excellent fodder for her books.

When she finally sat down to enjoy a cold drink and a rest, Travis returned. He was wearing a Stetson.

"Sorry that took so long," he said. "First I had to wait until Shelby gave her a bath, and then her stuffed pony got lost. Finally she demanded I sing her to sleep."

"I think you're very special to her, and she wants to keep you with her for as long as possible, seeing as how you'll be heading out on a long tour."

"We are. We leave for New York City in the morning. After that, we're off to Europe for concerts in five cities. Later, I'm not sure. We'll have to wait and see what our manager, Annie Wyse, has in store for us."

"An exciting life."

"At times. At others, these past few months in particular, it's downright tiring." His tone reflected his weariness. He revived as he caught her by a hand. "Come on. I've got a surprise for a fellow horse admirer."

He pulled her to her feet and took her striding beside him toward the big red barn she'd noticed on her arrival. Lights glowed from its windows. Inside, he paused and held out a hand to indicate a pair of horses tied and saddled in the walkway.

"The big bay is Ross's horse, Wrangler, and the little palomino is one of Jessi's rescues. She calls her Maisy." He untied them and gathered up their reins. "Ross and Jessi tacked them up for us while I was getting Katie Rose bedded down. Come on, we're going for a ride."

"What!"

"It would be a shame to waste all this moonlight."

*Don't look at me like that! How can I say no when you're looking at me like that?*

"You know I don't ride. You know…" She followed him as he led the horses out of the barn. "You know—"

"Nothing to worry about. Jessi's been using Maisy to teach kids to ride. She's assured me the little mare is gentle as a lamb."

"Lambs cavort, kicking up their heels and—"

"Trust me." He paused to look down at her. "I'd never risk putting an inexperienced rider on a horse that was less than bomb proof. Take the reins and stick your foot in the stirrup. It'll be easier this time. You're wearing boots."

*Thanks to Emma. Okay, here goes. Like he said, it would be a shame to waste the moonlight.*

She gathered up the reins he handed to her, stuck

her foot into the stirrup, and made an attempt to spring into the saddle. It didn't come off well. Once again his hand on her bottom propelled her up onto a horse.

"There you go." He went to the bay and swung into the saddle. "Just to give you further reassurance, I've got a lead rope on Maisy." He held it up. "There's a nice trail back of the barn and out across the meadow. It'll be perfect."

He nudged his mount into a walk. The little palomino followed.

As they headed around the barn and down a trail that led across the rangeland, the sensation of unreality once again overwhelmed Etta. Could she possibly be going on a moonlight ride with the man of her most romantic fantasies? Not even Emma could have arranged it any better.

"Come on, Maisy." He urged the mare up beside his horse with the lead rope. "This lady and I would like to ride a bit closer." He glanced over at Etta before continuing, "Wouldn't we?"

"Yes." Emboldened by his unassuming attitude, she agreed as they came abreast.

They rode in silence for a few minutes, Etta enjoying the magic of it all...the moonlight, the vast stretch of meadowland, and most of all the presence of the man beside her, whose company was becoming moment by moment more comfortable, more companionable. She relaxed, giving herself over to the beauty of the night, the magic of the setting, and the reassurance of his company.

A full moon lighted their way, casting long shadows out from horses and riders. The night air, still and soft, scented with newly mown hay, cast a gentle spell over the moment. Wrangler shook his head, jingling his bridle. From somewhere in the trees along the edge of the field, a coyote howled. Etta Prescott was living a scene out of one of her books, and she wanted it never to end.

"What do you do for a living, Etta?" he asked as the horses walked along together.

"I'm…" she started to reply, then hesitated. Would he laugh or scoff when she told him? "I write western romance novels," she said.

"Hey, a writer." From what she could see of his expression in the shadow cast by his Stetson, he was sincerely impressed. "Great! I think writers are like wizards. They conjure stories out of thin air. We have one in our band…Paulie…he writes great songs and lyrics. Without him, we'd never have had as many tunes that sell as well as some of ours have."

"My stories aren't great literature." Encouraged by his response, she continued, "I simply enjoy writing them and hope they give pleasure to readers. I use the pen name Vanessa Dean."

"That's exactly how I feel about our music." He halted the horses to look over at her. "We're not classical or opera, but I think we give folks a bit of relaxation and fun. At the end of a long day, that's what hard-working men and women need most."

"That's exactly how I feel about my writing." His thoughts mirrored hers. He understood, even recognized a kinship between his work and hers.

"Well, then, seems like we're two people who have found their groove, know its value, and feel comfortable in it, right?"

"Right."

"How would you feel about breaking into a trot? I'll be right beside you, lead rope in hand."

"Okay."

They jogged along for a while before Travis returned their pace to a walk.

"Enjoying the Stampede?" he asked. She liked his companionable tone.

"Very much. There was one saddle bronc rider yesterday that was especially impressive."

"Yeah, well, that was a crazy thing to do with a big show coming up." He focused on the reins in his hand. "My manager-agent had just gotten a picture of me on the cover of a fan magazine, a picture I didn't approve and I sure as hell didn't like. I was trying to get back at her by scaring the beejeebers out of her that I wouldn't be able to perform last night."

"I think I saw that magazine." She looked off across the rangeland, the image of the man beside her in the arms of a sexy woman throwing a pall over her pleasure.

"Too many people probably saw it." Disgust registered in his words as he scoffed, "Country couple of the year, right!"

"What did Lanie Lanson think of it?"

"I don't know and I couldn't care less."

"That's an astonishing attitude when the article implied she and you…"

"*Implied* is right." Annoyance colored his tone. "There's never been anything between Lanie and me and never will be. She's not my type, by a long shot. It's getting late. We'd better head back to the barn."

As they turned back toward the ranch buildings, something inside her plummeted. She shouldn't have pressed the subject of Lanie Lanson. It had destroyed the ambience of their perfect time together. When they reached the barn and Travis swung to the ground, she hesitated to join him. She didn't want it to end.

"Need help?" He held up a hand.

"No, no, thanks, I'm fine." *Damn, stumbling over words again*. She dragged her right leg over the patient mare's rump and dropped to the ground. Feeling confident after her ride in Travis's presence, she went to the mare's head and reached up to scratch behind one of Maisy's ears. The little horse blew softly and nuzzled up to her.

"She's lovely," she said, delighted at the animal's gentle affection.

"She is a pretty little thing, even if a bit on the small side." He was gazing over at her. "Jessi told me she was scared of her own shadow when she came to her for rehabilitation. Now she's perfect for kids…or ladies."

"I'd love to own a horse like her someday." Etta rubbed Maisy under her forelock and hated the idea of parting from her…and Travis.

"Too bad we didn't have more time," he said as he took the reins from her and led the two horses into the lighted barn. She was relieved that his tone had returned to his former one of affability. "I'd like to teach you to ride."

"I'd like to learn." She followed and watched as he tied both animals in cross ties. "Can I help you unsaddle them…or anything?"

"I'll be okay." He scratched Wrangler's head under the animal's forelock. "If we had time, I'd show you how to put them up."

"Time!" Etta glanced at her watch. "It's almost midnight. Chase said he'd drive my sister and me back to our hotel at midnight! I have to go." She started to turn away, but swung back. "I feel guilty, leaving you with all the work of putting away the horses and equipment."

"I'm an old hand at it. It will only take a few minutes. No great amount of rubbing down to do…they never broke a sweat."

"If you're sure."

"I'm sure. Go catch your ride."

"Thank you for a lovely evening."

"My pleasure. I enjoyed it."

With a disheartening sense that one of the best experiences of her life had come to an end, she headed out of the barn. She was crossing the darkened space between stable and the brightly lighted dooryard when she heard footsteps running after her. By the time she'd swung about, Travis had caught up with her.

"Etta." Her name sounded wonderful in the soft, warm night.

He drew her into his arms, and suddenly Etta Prescott was being kissed by the man of her dreams. Could anyone still be on earth and feel this ethereal? Surely the ground disappeared from beneath her feet, surely she was floating into a dimension too wonderful to be real. His mouth covering hers, his tall, muscular body warm against hers in the soft, sensuous rangeland summer's night…she had to be dreaming.

And then he was drawing back from her, holding her out at arms' length, looking down into her face.

"Go, Cinderella." The words were soft, a verbal caress.

For a moment she stood mesmerized. Then, realizing she had to break out of the spell, that she had a ride to catch, she whirled and ran, stumbling through the darkness, toward the lighted dooryard.

"Etta, where on earth have you been?" Her sister greeted her when she arrived in the circle of light. "It's after midnight. Chase has been waiting."

"Sorry." Etta struggled to contain the wild crash of emotions raging through body and brain.

*Travis Masters took me riding in the moonlight. Travis Masters kissed me!*

"Etta, what is it?" Emma drew her sister deeper into the firelight. "You look positively…glowing. What have you been up to?"

"I'll tell you when we get back at the hotel," she hissed as Chase Turner approached, truck keys in hand.

## Chapter Five

As the partygoers dispersed from the back yard, Travis sat alone in the darkness on the steps of the ranch house's front veranda. He needed time alone to reflect. It had been a great night, and Etta Prescott had been the biggest part of it. Pretty as a picture, she'd behaved like a lady through and through, he decided, as he remembered the way she'd politely thanked him for the evening. If that wasn't the behavior of a lady, he didn't know what was. Thoughts of his time spent with her sent a nice, warm feeling washing over him.

When he remembered that kiss in the moonlight, it gushed into the hot zone. But she hadn't lingered over it, hadn't made a move to make more of it...not like a lot of women he'd met in his travels, women determined to make the most of their time with a country music star. No, when he'd released her, she'd moved off—run, actually—to catch her ride. He hadn't met a woman like her in a long, long time. Exactly like her, not ever that he could remember.

She even loved horses. A grin curled his lips as he pictured her holding the little mare's head, shyly falling in love with the animal. Could she get more perfect? Leaning back on his elbows, he looked up into the star-studded summer sky and knew he had to see her again.

Another thought crossed his mind. Maybe she wouldn't want to see him, not the real him, anyway.

Maybe she was tied up in his image. His image! Damn it, what really nice girl would want to get seriously tangled up with the person he'd appeared to be on the cover of that fan garbage?

His thoughts came to an abrupt end as a sports car careened up the drive.

*What in hell…?*

It skidded to a stop near the steps, and Annie Wyse bolted out. Wearing one of her power suits, this time navy in color, she strode toward him on stilettos. Half way, she turned an ankle on the uneven ground and cursed.

"You're late." Travis decided to attempt damage control before his agent broke into the tirade he knew was coming. "Party's pretty much over."

"It nearly was over for you forever, yesterday afternoon!" The words barked out in the quiet of the night. "I just heard about it. I knew I should have stayed in Calgary to keep an eye on you! Going to New York yesterday to check out your next venue was *my* mistake. How could you be so crazy? Riding a saddle bronc! I was raised on a Texas ranch, I know about horses, and I damn well know how dangerous that event can be. Furthermore, you're not a bronc rider. You trained nice little western pleasure horses, a far cry from something like Whirlwind, a first-class professional at unloading even experienced riders. What got into you, for God's sake?"

"That damned fan magazine cover and story, that's what." Travis stood, towering over her thanks to his natural height and being on the first step. "I told you I didn't want any of those pictures published, that I wanted them destroyed."

"I thought they were." Her tone moderated. "Look, Travis, in this day of digital photography, it's next to impossible to completely eradicate anything. All you have to do to fix it is push your image as the shy country boy harder."

"Well, maybe that's what I was trying to do when I went into that bronc riding contest...damage control for those sleazy photos."

"Okay, okay." After working around Annie for six years, Travis recognized the signs. Realizing she was pushing him too hard, she was backing off. She wasn't about to lose a major source of her income. "I let a nasty bit of publicity slip past me, and you did a stupid thing in riding that bronc. Touché. Moving on." She looked into the backyard, where the family was clearing away the remains of the party. "Think a country gal might still be in time for a steak and beer?"

\*\*\*\*

"Tell me!" Once the sisters were alone in their hotel room, Emma caught Etta by an arm and pulled her down to sit on a bed beside her.

"Tell you what?" Suddenly reluctant to describe to her twin those magic moments with Travis Masters in the moonlight, afraid recounting it would somehow ruin the perfectness of the memory, she struggled to sound casual.

"Oh, come on. Since when have you ever been able to keep anything from me? You know I'll keep digging until I get it out of you."

"Okay, okay." Etta heaved a sigh she hoped sounded bored and indifferent as she stood and sauntered into the bathroom. "I went riding with Travis Masters...in the moonlight...and he kissed me."

Once inside the bathroom, she swung shut the door and locked it. Leaning back against the closed panel, she let a smug little smile curl her lips as she listened to her sister's entreaties to "come out this instant and tell me all about it!"

**\*\*\*\***

Etta awoke to a knocking on the door. Looking across at the other bed, she saw her twin also struggling out of sleep.

"Delivery for Etta Prescott and Emma MacKenzie," a voice informed them.

"Coming." Emma stumbled out of bed, pulled her robe about her, and headed groggily to the door. Opening it, she faced a delivery man balancing two long white boxes in his arms.

"Etta Prescott?"

"Here." Etta, wrapping a robe around her, came to join her sister.

"Sign." He thrust a recording device forward.

After she'd scrawled her name in the window, he handed her one of the boxes.

"I'm Emma MacKenzie." Without waiting for him to make the inquiry, Emma reached for the other container. "It's for me."

"Sign first."

"Okay, okay." She scribbled before grabbing the second package.

"Ah…" With an outstretched hand, the young man stalled her as she started to close the door.

"Fine. Give me a minute." Emma laid the box on her bed and picked up her purse from the nightstand. "There. Okay?" She handed him the tip.

"Fine. Have a great day, ladies." The door shut on

his words as Emma tore open her box.

"A dozen red roses." She stared inside. "From Frasier, I've no doubt. An apology for the way he threatened me the other morning. Or maybe a thank you." She winked at Etta. "And yours?"

"A dozen red roses too." Etta had lifted the cover and extracted the card, heart pounding. She hardly dared guess whom they might be from.

"Ah-ha! Frasier!" Emma had yanked her own enclosed card from its envelope, a smug expression coming over her face as she read aloud, "Love you, my darling Emma." She paused a moment, looking down at it, before she swung on her sister. "And yours?"

"From Travis." Heart pounding with delight, Etta fought to sound casual.

"Wow!" Her sister jerked the card from her fingers and read, " 'To Cinderella, all my best, Travis.' Etta, what does he mean, *Cinderella*?"

"That's between him and me." Etta snatched her sister's card. "You didn't quite finish reading yours, sister dear. 'Love you, my darling Emma. Now please go home!!!' Gee, there are a lot of exclamation marks. He must really want you back in Carleton."

"He just wants to make sure I'm safe." Emma reclaimed the small rectangular piece of cardboard. "He knows I'm my own woman and that an entire page of such nasty little punctuation marks won't make the slightest difference in what I decide to do. Now let's get packing. Our flight leaves at noon."

"There's no way we can take these with us." Etta stared regretfully down at the long box. "They'd never survive all the way to New Brunswick. Much as I hate to leave them to housekeeping, I don't see any other practical solution."

"So how about a memento?" Emma pulled a single rose from her bouquet. "We'll take the cards and each press a flower in one of the books we plan to read on the plane."

"I suppose." Her acquiescence reflected her reluctance.

"Oh, come on, Etta. You've got the man seriously interested. I'm guessing there will be another box of these beauties waiting for you when we get home."

****

"Where have you been? I've been looking all over for you. Our flight leaves at noon." Six-inch heels tapping a staccato, Annie Wyse strode up to the hotel newspaper and magazine kiosk to glower at Travis. Perusing a book he held in his hand, he stood in front of a rack of paperbacks.

"Picking up some reading material." He tried to hide it against his chest.

She snatched it away from him. "Oh, my God! *Cowboy's Country Bride* by Vanessa Dean? Really, Travis, I hope you weren't seduced by that little blonde writer."

"Writer? What writer?" He struggled to feign ignorance.

"Don't try that on me, chum. Ross Turner told me all about how you got him and his wife to saddle horses for you to take her riding last night. He said you were gone for quite a long time. I immediately did a Google search on my phone and found out exactly who she is. Turns out she's Etta Prescott, who writes this tripe"— she held up the book—"under the pen name of Vanessa Dean."

"So? It's not a crime to enjoy the company of a pretty woman."

"It is in your case, sweetie. I'm not about to lose another top star to a darling little country girl."

"She's not a country girl. She's…"

"Never mind the terminology. She's one of those…nice girls like your sister, to whom I lost one of my greatest discoveries. Jordan Brooks turned into Jake Brooks in your sister's hands and dropped out of the music business like a stone from a 747."

"Whose idea was it to send Jake to learn to ride at my sister's farm? Who stooped so low as to steal our prize stud to force Shelby to take him on out of financial need? I'd say what happened served you just about right, Annie Wyse."

"Okay, okay, maybe I didn't foresee what was about to happen when I threw two attractive people together virtually on their own for nearly two months. But I learn from my mistakes. I'm not about to let it happen a second time."

"I've met other women out on the road. Why the deep concern about this one?"

"Because this one is in the same category as your sister. Sweet, smart, caring…all the things that can lead a man like you into a long-term relationship. And that, sweetie, is not what I want."

"Yeah, well, I'm still calling the shots where my future is concerned, Annie." Travis snatched the paperback away from her. "If I want Etta Prescott in it, I'll have her…if she'll have me." With a defiant glance, he headed for the cashier to pay for his purchase. Half way there he paused. He turned and went back to the bookstand to grab a second Vanessa Dean book. With a triumphant smirk at his manager, he headed back to the counter.

"I give up…for now. Just don't be late for our flight. You can read that stuff once your bottom is firmly seated on Flight 672 headed for NYC."

He paid for the pair of books but refused the bag the cashier offered. Keeping *Cowboy's Pride* in his hand, he stuffed the other paperback into his jacket pocket.

As he started across the lobby, he turned it over in his hand and stopped abruptly. Smiling up at him from the back cover was a golden-haired woman he barely recognized. Etta Prescott glamorized up to be Vanessa Dean could have been a movie star…or another version of the Lanie Lanson phenomenon.

*Ah, damn!*

\*\*\*\*

"Etta, why won't you tell me what happened between you and Travis last night?" Emma stuffed a pair of jeans into her suitcase and struggled to force it shut. "If you want it kept secret, you know I'm good for it."

"I know you are." Etta paused on her way from the closet, a shirt over her arm, to give her sister a hug with the other. "It's just that…"

"It's just that what?" Emma looked at her. The suitcase, freed, popped open.

"I know you'll think this is stupid, but at least for now I want to keep it to myself." She continued to where her valise lay open on her bed. She folded the shirt, put it inside, and closed the lid.

"I don't think it's stupid at all. Some of the moments I've shared with Frasier are for us alone." Her sister went back to fighting with her suitcase, this time managing to force it shut and snap the lock. "They're to be held and hugged in your heart."

"You do understand." Etta smiled over at her.

"But if you ever want to share, I'll be all ears." Emma tossed her a teasing look as she pulled her luggage from the bed.

"I don't see that happening any time soon, but I'll keep your offer in mind."

A determined knocking at the door stopped Emma as she dragged her suitcase across the room toward it.

"Who can that be?" she asked as Etta went to answer it. "More flowers? Really, Frasier is just too romantic."

"Good morning, miss." A tall, uniformed officer of the Royal Canadian Mounted Police faced Etta as she opened the door. "We've come to escort you to the airport."

"What!?" Emma whirled to face the man.

"Are you ready to leave?" He ignored the outrage transforming her face. "There's a car and driver waiting out front."

"Oh, this is too much!" Emma flounced across the room to stare out the window, arms crossed tightly, shoulders defiantly back. "Frasier MacKenzie, I'll kill you!"

"Let me help you with your bags." The officer crossed to the bed and took Emma's suitcase in one hand, Etta's in the other. "Can you manage your carry-on luggage?"

"Come on, Emma." Etta picked up her small case and purse. "We can't fight the RCMP. Frasier simply wants to make certain we get safely to our flight.

Anyhow, it's a free ride to the airport."

"Argh!" Her sister turned back to face her twin and the officer. "Damn it, okay. Let's go. But…" She turned on the man, green eyes sparking in defiance. "Don't think this is the end of it."

"I'm sure it isn't, miss." Unperturbed, the officer left the room and waited for the twins to follow him.

At the curb, a squad car waited, engine running, another officer at the wheel. Their escort deposited their luggage in the trunk before going to hold the rear door open for them. As they were whisked through Calgary traffic, Etta suppressed a chuckle when she glanced at her sister's bellicose expression. Sergeant Frasier MacKenzie may have bested his wife on this occasion, but he would be in deep trouble the next time he got an opportunity to visit with her.

At the airport, grabbing her purse and carry-on, Emma attempted to bolt out of the police vehicle. Their escort was faster. He'd jumped from the passenger seat to open the door for her.

"Thank you, officer." Head held high, Emma pushed past him toward the trunk. "Please allow us access to our luggage."

"Definitely. Constable," he called to the driver, "crack the trunk."

The cargo space opened. Before Emma could stop him, the officer had grabbed the handles of both suitcases and was pulling them out.

Etta couldn't help admiring the policeman and enjoying the look of chagrin on her sister's face each time he bested her. *This guy is fast. A criminal would have to be a super mover to get ahead of him.*

"Corporal Willis and I will see you safely aboard

your flight," he said as the other officer joined him and took the suitcases from his superior officer.

"Not necessary." Emma made a last-ditch effort to retrieve her luggage. "We'll be perfectly all right."

"Just to be sure." He jerked his head toward the entrance. "After you, ladies."

"Aren't you illegally parked?" Emma pointed to the patrol car.

"One of the perks of being in law enforcement. No one will ticket a police vehicle."

Emma's attempt at escaping the officers foiled, she strode into the terminal, head held high, shoulders defiantly back. Etta followed, suppressing a grin. It was good to see her usually unstoppable sister not get her way once in a while.

Inside, the officers saw to the checking of their luggage and accompanied them to the gate from which their flight was scheduled to depart. Emma acquiesced to it all until the pair sat down beside them.

"Oh, God!" Emma hissed into Etta's ear. "They're going to wait until our flight leaves. We look like public enemies number one and two. What can Frasier MacKenzie be thinking?"

"Thinking he knows his wife. Thinking she might choose to abort her plan to return to Carleton today and make another attempt to visit him. Cheer up, Emma. Hardly anyone here in Calgary knows us. Furthermore, once we're on the plane, people won't be concerned when they see that the officers didn't accompany us aboard."

"Okay, maybe. Apparently there is nothing we can do about it." With a resigned shrug, Emma opened her carry-on and took out a book. "May as well relax." As she opened the paperback, a crushed red rose fell onto the floor. Her hand swept down to retrieve it and place it back between the pages.

"Where is the card?" Etta scanned the floor.

"I didn't keep it. I wasn't particularly fond of those exclamation marks." Her twin shrugged off the inquiry.

"What are you reading? Hey, that's one of my books." Etta looked at the cover.

"You do spin some decent tales. Now please be quiet and allow me to escape our present untenable circumstance in one of your yarns."

"Okay, okay." Etta settled herself more comfortably on the hard seat and reached into her carry-on.

"What's that you're reading?" Emma glanced over at the paperback Etta took out.

"Nothing. A bit of research." In an effort to avoid her sister's prying eyes, she randomly opened to a page midway through it. A rose and card fell out. As she shoved them back inside and hurriedly closed the book, Emma's hand shot out and managed to turn it to the front cover.

"*Western Riding*," she read. " 'Learn to ride like an ole cowhand in six easy lessons' Etta, really?" She gave her sister a belittling glance.

"Like I said, just a bit of research." Heat rose up her neck as she realized one of the officers was looking at her and her choice of reading material.

*Probably a former member of the Musical Ride, probably having a genuine struggle to maintain that poker face. Can this day get any more embarrassing?*

Then she saw him. Entering the terminal with the members of his band and a bunch of people she recognized as part of his troupe was Travis Masters. Beside him, strutting her stuff in skin-tight jeans, transparent white blouse, and high-heeled cowboy boots that were never intended for riding was Lanie Lanson. The singer pulled off the Ray-Bans she'd been wearing and gazed about.

*Oh, please, please, don't let him notice me with this police escort.*

She tried to scrunch down in the seat behind the officer's broad shoulders, but he'd turned in her direction. He paused for a moment, then came striding toward her, expression brightening with recognition.

"Etta," he called as he approached.

Instantly the officers were on their feet, facing him.

"You know this gentleman, Miss Prescott?" The policeman stepped between her and Travis.

"Yes, definitely. He's...a friend." She stood.

"Very good." He moved aside to allow Travis to approach her.

"Etta, what's all this?" Travis waved a hand to indicate the two men. "Are you okay? Not in any kind of trouble, are you?" His face crinkled into a puzzled frown.

"No, no. These gentlemen are...friends. They've been kind enough to escort us...to make certain Emma and I get off all right."

"Oh." His mystified expression revealed he in no way understood, as he wet his lips and shifted from one foot to the other. "Well, then, fine. I'll be going. Maybe we'll meet up again some time."

"Yes, maybe." She felt something she believed was her heart sinking like a stone, but forced a smile and watched as he turned and headed back to his troupe.

"Hurry up, sweetie," Lanie Lanson called. "Our flight is on the tarmac. Hustle your cute little buns over here."

As the group headed off toward the far end of the airport, Etta sank down onto the seat beside her sister.

"Damn you, Frasier MacKenzie!" she hissed.

****

"Etta, I'm so sorry." Emma turned to her sister as the plane reached cruising altitude and leveled off. "Count on it, my husband will pay when I get my hands on him!"

"Emma, please. The last thing I want to do is cause a rift between you and Frasier. You two are so much in love and so perfect for each other." Etta struggled to downplay the incident in the airport. "What happened between Travis Masters and me was a moment…a bright, never-to-be forgotten moment. It's over, and I thank you for a birthday gift right out of my wildest fantasy. Now I'm going to take a nap."

As her sister emitted what sounded like a half-exasperated, half-wistful sigh, Etta closed her eyes and pretended to go to sleep.

"Rest assured, my darling twin, this isn't over…not by a long shot." Emma's words brought an apprehensive wave washing over Etta. What was her sister plotting now?

****

"Where's Paulie?" Travis came out of the bathroom into the New York hotel suite he and his band occupied and looked around. With a towel around his hips, his dark curls wet, his nerves taut with only three hours before the show at Madison Square Garden, he wasn't in the mood for anything to go wrong.

Memories of his recent encounter with Etta Prescott at the Calgary airport exacerbated his agitation. She'd been the last person he'd thought might be in trouble with the law, but there she'd stood, between two tall, broad-shouldered officers, offering the flimsy excuse that they were friends. Friends, right! In full duty uniforms. Damn and double damn! Just when he thought he'd met the perfect girl…

"Not back yet." Matt brushed past him toward the shower. "Leave any hot water for me, boss?"

"We're not exactly in a backwoods cabin," Travis snapped. "Of course there's hot water."

"Okay, okay, just joking around. Jeeze, man, you're wound up way too tight." Matt slammed the door behind him.

*Calm down, just calm down.* Travis sucked in a deep breath and headed into one of the bedrooms to get into the clothes Lili had laid out for him. She always picked the band's clothes for performances. Tonight was no exception. She'd done it before she and Joe had headed out for an early dinner.

He paused to pick up one of the Vanessa Dean novels he'd left on the dresser and stared down at the glamorous face staring up at him.

*Man, it's hard to believe this is Etta Prescott. She looks so different in real life. Painted up like this, she reminds me of Lante.*

He threw the book into a chair and pulled open a drawer to find underwear.

\*\*\*\*

"Anybody know where in hell Paulie is?" Barefoot and wearing only jeans, Travis asked the question for the second time as he entered the living room area, where Jessie was slumped in a chair watching Michelle Layton in her soap opera role. Matt dozed on the couch. James was thumbing through a music magazine.

"Not a clue, Trav," Jessie replied dismissively. Michelle, wearing a dress that revealed a generous amount of cleavage, held his attention.

"James?" Travis moved to stand over the broad-shouldered drummer of their group. Two-hundred-pound James was a person whom Travis had always thought of as a gentle giant and the one member of his band he felt confident would never hedge with him.

"We went out shopping this afternoon." The drummer wet his lips as he looked up at him. "Paulie said he'd heard of a place here in Manhattan that had the fanciest cowboy boots in the world. He wanted to get a pair."

"So did you?"

"Yeah." James stuck out a foot encased in hand-tooled leather.

"Did Paulie?"

"Yeah."

"And then?"

"What do you mean, Trav?"

"Don't play dumb with me, James. Paulie didn't come back here with you. Where did he go? Come on, man. I haven't got all day! We're due to leave for the Garden in an hour."

"He went…with her." James pointed to the black-haired woman strutting across the television screen. "He told me not to say nothing, Trav. Said he'd be back in lots of time for the show."

"And you believed him? Damn it, James, you know how she tried to seduce him away from us in

Nashville. You might have guessed she'd try again when we came onto her home turf where that bit of trash is filmed. You know what can happen to Paulie if he gets in with the wrong crowd!"

Dragging his fingers through his thick, black hair, Travis began to pace the room.

"This is just dandy," he muttered. "The biggest show next to the Stampede, and Paulie has to screw it up. Paulie and that bitch!"

The door to the suite opened, and the keyboard player/song writer stepped in. Keeping his head down, he made an attempt to cross the room toward the bedroom without speaking. Travis caught him up by the arm.

"Look at me, Paulie—damn you, look at me!"

When he did, Travis heaved an exasperated sigh. "Ah, sweet Jesus, you're high. I don't need a crystal ball to tell me where you got the stuff."

"I'll be fine tonight, Trav." Paulie weaved slightly. "Just let me get a shower and a coffee…"

"You're damn right you'll be fine." Travis dragged him across the suite to the second bathroom. "I'm going to soak you in ice water until you're sober as a judge, then pour a gallon of coffee down your throat. Guys, not a word of this to Lili and Joe when they get back. And definitely not to Annie. She's in the hotel and will be coming up to make sure we're ready for the big night. Jessie, stop ogling that damned woman and listen up."

"Okay, okay." Jessie clicked to another channel as the soap ended. "But Trav, you have to admit she's one hot chick. Don't blame Paulie too much for falling for her."

"Argh!" Dragging Paulie, Travis headed toward the shower.

\*\*\*\*

"Damn, we got through it!" In his dressing room at the Garden, Travis, sweat drenched and feeling limp as a rag, leaned against the wall.

"Sure we did." Matt, who'd followed him inside, grabbed a towel to wipe his wet face. "Paulie's a pro. He wasn't about to let us down."

"Travis, why in God's name didn't you tell me!" Annie Wyse burst into the dressing room. "What would inspire you to go on stage with Paulie under the influence? I met him just now heading out a side door. He's shaking like a leaf in a hurricane! Have you lost your mind?"

"No, I haven't." Travis struggled for calm under his agent's attack. "We had a big show to do, I sobered him up, and he made it, didn't he? So what's the big deal?"

"He could have wrecked your squeaky clean image. He could have ruined the whole damned farce of it!"

"Well, he didn't. As for me and my band being squeaky clean, that's hardly a farce. We're good guys. One of us just fell from the wagon."

"Okay, okay, so you pulled it off this time. Don't ever, ever let it happen again." She swung to leave, but the door opened to admit a distressed-looking Lili.

"Have any of you seen Paulie? I haven't been able to find him since he left the stage."

Chapter Six

"Where in hell is he?" Travis paced the length of their Manhattan suite for more times than he cared to count. "It's been three hours since anyone has seen him."

"We should call the police." Lili, in a chair by a window, looked out into the lights that never seemed to go out, her husband on its arm beside her.

"Take it easy, honey." Joe gave her shoulders a squeeze. "He's a young man in a big, exciting city. He's probably out seeing the sights."

"I think we should call the police." His wife wasn't about to be so easily pacified.

"No way." Annie leaned against a bedroom door jamb, a glass of scotch in hand. "Reporters in this town have one eye on the police and the other on their computers. If they caught the least hint that one of our band members is missing, suspected of drugging out, we'd be ruined."

"Our? We?" Travis swung on her. "With you, it's all about image, publicity, money, isn't it! We're talking about Paulie, a friend, one of the finest musicians I've ever met. I don't give a damn about all you hold near and dear. I'm calling the police."

"Travis, no, wait a bit longer." She caught him by an arm as he reached for his cell. "Just a bit longer." Her tone had turned soft, cajoling.

"Okay." Her words hit home. He knew the kind of publicity that could be generated by news of Paulie's trouble. He also realized what it could do to the band members who relied on the group to make a living. "But only until daybreak."

"Daybreak." She cast one of her warmest smiles up at him. "Still the sweet country boy at heart."

Not about to be seduced further, Travis headed for the mini fridge and grabbed a beer.

****

"Sun's coming up." Travis pulled himself upright on the couch and reached for his cell. "I'm calling…"

The suite landline rang. He lunged for it and got there before Annie.

"Yes, this is the Travis Masters suite, Travis Masters here." He listened, a sick feeling further engulfing him at each word. "Yeah, sure, of course. We'll be there right away."

He replaced the receiver and turned to the group staring at him.

"Well?" Annie, at his side, seized his arm.

"That was the police. Paulie was hit by a cab late last evening. He's in the hospital, in critical condition." The words came out mechanically, robot-like.

"Oh, my God!" Lili snatched up her purse. "Let's go. Which hospital, Travis?"

****

"It's definitely time we put some serious thought into what comes next." Lili, her husband's arm about her shoulders, faced the four young men and Annie Wyse back in their hotel suite late in the afternoon. "We've been given a reprieve, in that the doctors say Paulie will survive. But as all of you heard, he'll need a long period of convalescence. I'm proposing"—she drew a deep breath and looked up at Joe, who gave her a nod of support—"that we take a hiatus, that we…"

"Hiatus!" The word coming from the agent was a shriek. "Hiatus, my ass! We've got a huge European tour coming up— We're booked to leave Wednesday!"

"Right now, nothing is more important than Paulie and his recovery." Travis stepped in front of her, hands on his hips. "Cancel the tour. We're heading home to the Maritimes."

"You tell her, Trav!" Matt was quick to back him up. "We need a rest."

For what seemed to Travis like hours but probably only seconds, Annie stood staring up at him. Finally, with a disgusted guffaw, she strode toward the door.

"All of you signed contracts, don't forget! Quitting isn't so easy."

The door slammed behind her.

"Well, now that's settled"—Lili picked up her purse—"Joe and I will be heading back to the hospital. We'll keep you posted on Paulie's condition. Try to get some sleep…all of you."

\*\*\*\*

"Damn it, Travis Masters, let me in!" Annie, Lili, and Joe had been gone only minutes when the banging started at the hotel suite door.

"That would be sweet Lanie." Smirking, Jessie stood and went to the door.

"Damn it, Travis Masters," she repeated as she pushed Jessie aside and strode across the room to confront him. "What do you mean by cancelling the European tour? What gives you the right—"

"Annie told you, I guess." He remained calm.

*Isn't there anything Annie won't do to make me change my mind? Well, this time she's way off base. Setting this witch on me is one very big mistake. Hell, one of the perks of cancelling the trip is not having to deal with Lanie Lanson.*

"Yeah, Annie told me." Her face, under its heavy makeup, was turning an ugly shade of dark red. "Look, you backwoods bumpkin, I'm not one of your simple-minded fans! You can't go throwing me out like a bit of garbage. This tour is my chance to make it big on the international scene, and I won't let you ruin it."

"I don't recall signing a contract with you."

"Not signed yet. Annie was in the process of drawing one up."

"Guess I missed that bit of information." *Keep your cool, man. She's going to storm out of here in a few minutes, and you might never have to see her again.* "Anyhow, Paulie's been in an accident. We couldn't go without a keyboard guy."

"Don't give me that crap, Travis. This is New York City. Keyboard players are a dime a dozen. You can pick one up in any dive."

"Not one like Paulie."

"So you're determined to ruin my career and that of your band as well." She looked around at the others. "Are you guys just going to sit there and let this half-assed cowboy destroy your lives?"

"Hey, who are you calling a half-assed cowboy?" Jessie, always the first to take offense, was on his feet, his expression bellicose. "Didn't you see him ride at the Stampede? Furthermore, Trav has more talent in his little finger than you have in your entire body, bitch!"

"Hey, hey!" Travis was on his feet. "Both of you cool it. There'll be no European tour, and that's it. Lanie, if you're as talented as you believe you are, you shouldn't have a whole lot of trouble hooking up with another band heading across the pond. Now…" He took her by an arm and guided her to the door. "I suggest you leave. We've been up all night and need some sack time. Good luck. I wish you the best."

He held the door open for her.

"Yeah, right, I just bet you do."

Head held high, she strode out of the suite as fast as her high-heeled cowboy boots would allow.

"What a certifiable bitch," Matt muttered after Travis had closed the door.

"Yeah, well, maybe, but I'd appreciate it if you watched your language." Travis dropped into a chair and heaved a gigantic sigh.

"Okay, okay." Matt headed into a bedroom. "I'm going to sack out."

The other band members muttered agreement and followed his example. Travis remained alone in the living room. He needed time to unwind.

Out of seemingly nowhere, Etta Prescott flashed into his mind. She'd be in Carleton now. When he went back there, would he see her? Should he see her?

He shook his head ruefully. Why couldn't he put the woman out of his thoughts? After what he'd witnessed at the Calgary airport, she had to be bad news. There'd be other women in Carleton, women he'd known and dated when he lived there six years earlier. Nice women, women with no mystery hanging around them, nice women he'd known since they were kids together. Nice women, he reflected on second thought, who were probably either married by now or had a significant other.

In an effort to erase Etta Prescott's image, he turned his thoughts to his house, the log house he was building in the woods on his sister's farm. To call it a dream house was just a tad too girlie, but that was in fact what it was. It was a place he'd fantasized about building since he was a kid and which he now had the financial means to make a reality. It would be great to see how it was coming along.

He pulled out his cell. Time to make plane reservations to New Brunswick.

## Chapter Seven

Etta rubbed her hand across her forehead and stared at the computer screen. In spite of the peace and quiet of Loon Lake, in spite of Beau's placid company, she was finding it next to impossible to get on with the manuscript she'd started before she and Emma went to Calgary.

Nothing seemed to fit or flow. The hero, a swashbuckling cowboy with an eye for the ladies, wouldn't come to life as her characters usually did. His swaggering, lusty personality didn't fit with the plot, with the kind of man she needed to fulfill the heroine's needs. Leaning back in her chair, Etta Prescott reached for her cup and took a drink of cold coffee.

"Yuk!" She set it aside and looked down at Beau. "How long have I been sitting here trying to force a square peg into a round hole, boy? Fresh coffee is definitely needed."

She stood and went to the percolator on the sideboard. As she set about making fresh brew, Beau jumped up to place his front paws against her thigh.

"Okay, okay. We'll leave the coffee and we'll go for a walk. You've been patient. You deserve to get out and sniff rabbit trails."

Five minutes later, they were walking down the trail that led from the two cabins to the secondary road. Their path through a tunnel of the bright green leaves of lofty maples and birches revived Etta's spirit. Her thoughts wandered back to Alberta and that night of magic with a man she'd never forget—his shy grin, his unassuming manner, his love of horses, his amazing voice. By the time she and her dog turned back toward the cabins, she knew exactly what had to be done. Eager to get her ideas into the computer, she broke into a trot.

"Come on, Beau!" she urged the basset who seemed determined to sniff every blade of grass along the way. "That arrogant hero just bit the dust. A nice, down-to-earth guy has taken his place."

Once back at the cabin, with a Travis Masters CD playing softly in the background, Etta Prescott became Vanessa Dean and began to write a story about a blue-eyed hero with the power to melt any woman's heart with a quiet sex appeal so natural it couldn't be resisted. With her fingers dancing over the keys and a smile tipping her lips, she found words flowing like a mountain stream.

By the time she paused to rest, an entire chapter had appeared. Satisfied, she stood, stretched, and went to make the fresh coffee she'd abandoned for their walk.

"I think this Trevor Manners is the best, the very best hero I've ever conjured up, Beau." She leaned her hips against the cupboard and looked at the dog stretched out on the couch while she waited for the coffee to perk. "Only problem is"—she drew a deep breath—"all he'll ever be for the rest of my life is a bit of fiction."

She wandered back to her desk and shuffled idly through some of the pages she'd printed off.

"But I need something more to bring this story to life." She reread a page featuring horses and riders. *Doesn't ring quite true. There's nothing like hands-on experience...I found that out in Alberta. Maybe...*

****

"Shelby? Dr. Masters? Etta Prescott here." Etta's fingers tightened on her cell as she addressed the woman on the other end of the call.

"Oh, hi, Etta. Nice to hear from you." Her voice, bright with friendliness, dissolved Etta's nervousness. "You had a good flight from Calgary?"

*This won't be so bad...I won't sound foolish...or conniving...I hope.*

"Yes, very good, thank you. Shelby, I was wondering..."

*Damn it, I'm faltering. Just get on with it, girl.*

"Yes? What can I do for you?"

*Still friendly, still welcoming. Here goes.*

"I write cowboy stories, and I'm coming up short on actual equine-type research and experience, and I was wondering..."

*Oh, God, I can see my editor flinching at that sentence strung together by "and's."*

"And maybe you'd like a little hands-on knowledge...like riding lessons here at the farm?"

"You're a mind reader, Doctor. Sure you didn't study psychology as well as veterinary medicine?" A wave of relief washing over her, Etta relaxed.

"Quite sure. When would you like to have your first lesson? I have an opening tomorrow at two p.m."

"Perfect. I'll be there. Thanks, Shelby."

As Etta finished the call, she heaved a sigh. Shelby hadn't revealed that in any way she suspected her of asking for riding lessons because of Travis. She was crossing the room to pour herself a cup of coffee when another thought stopped her in her tracks. Shelby and Emma had gotten along like the proverbial house afire. Had Emma somehow guessed that she, Etta, might want to take riding lessons after that magic night in the moonlight with Travis? Had she and Shelby gotten together to play it cool when she called?

No, that kind of thinking was pushing the envelope way too far. Not even her scheming sister could manage such a feat. Anyhow, Travis Masters was probably in Europe, so busy with his tour he hadn't had the time or the inclination to give Etta Prescott a second thought. He'd told Katie Rose he wouldn't be back until Christmas or thereabouts. She'd make sure her lessons terminated no later than mid-November…just to be safe. She couldn't bear the thought of his finding her at the farm and thinking she'd contrived to meet up with him again.

****

"You're doing fine, Etta," Shelby called across the arena. "Now kiss her into a lope."

"Really? You think I'm ready?" Etta, understanding Shelby meant to make the kissing sound that would break Candy into a canter, felt her gut tighten. Three weeks into her lessons, Etta had gained confidence in the saddle. Nevertheless, she hadn't expected Shelby to move her ahead so quickly.

"Definitely."

Bracing herself and taking courage from Shelby's reassuring presence, she puckered her lips and drew in her breath. Beneath her, the mare broke into a rhythmic stride.

*I'm doing it—I'm actually doing it! I'm galloping on a horse just like a heroine in one of my books! Wow! What a rush!*

Then, as the mare rounded a corner to head back toward Shelby, she saw him. Standing beside his sister, hands on his hips, handsome as ever in jeans and chambray shirt, was Travis Masters.

*Oh, God, no! It's too early. He's not supposed to be here.*

She lost the rhythm of the cantering horse and nearly left its back sideways as she rounded the next corner. Somehow she managed to regroup her focus sufficiently to ride up to the watching pair. Reining to a halt with a soft "whoa" she forced a smile.

"Hello," she said.

"Hello yourself." He nodded his approval. "Lookin' pretty darned good."

"Really?" In spite of her embarrassment, his assessment delighted her.

"Really."

"Your sister is an excellent teacher."

"Agreed, but you've come a long way from the woman I had to have on a lead rope to take her riding in the Alberta moonlight."

"Thanks." She swung down and gave the mare a pat on the neck.

"Etta, I have a patient due in a few minutes," Shelby said. "Think you can unsaddle Candy, rub her down, and put her in her stall?"

"Certainly." Etta had never done the entire operation on her own but wasn't about to let Travis see her deficient after he'd praised her prowess.

"You run along, Shel." Travis jerked his head in

the direction of the house. "I'll hang around in case Etta needs any help."

"Thanks, little brother. I'm confident she'll do just fine. Still, it's not responsible to leave a student on her own."

She flashed a smile at both of them before striding off toward the house.

"Let me." He took the reins from her hand. Leading the mare, he headed into the barn.

"I can do it." The words came out sharper than she'd intended.

"I'm sure you can or Shel wouldn't have left the chore to you." When they were inside the building, he slipped Candy's bridle off to replace it with a halter and put her into the crossties. "But I've been on the road for months, and I've missed this old gal. Sorry if I stepped on your toes." He moved back. "Unsaddle her. She's all yours."

"Are you here for a visit?" Keeping her back to him, she asked the only question that came to mind as she moved to release the girth.

"A rest, more like. We cancelled the European tour."

"Oh." She pulled the saddle and blanket from the mare. At a loss for more words, she carried the gear into the tack room and put it away as Shelby had taught her. When she came back out into the corridor, she carried brushes, rags, and a hoof pick.

"The guys and I were all pretty bummed out after the Stampede and New York. Our agent has been setting us up one devil of a schedule. We needed a rest." He sat down in a plastic lawn chair by the wall.

Silence followed as she worked on the mare.

"You realize you're staring?" Finally she could stand it no longer. She spoke as she ran her hand down Candy's front left leg and raised the hoof to clean around the mare's shoe.

"Sorry. I'm thinking…"

"Thinking what?" She straightened up to face him.

"Thinking you've come a long way with horses since this summer in Alberta. Good for you. The woman I met outside the rangeland derby track in July could hardly find the confidence to take the reins of an old, broke-to-the-bone mare. Now look at you, cleaning hooves."

"Thank you." She moved to Candy's left hind leg and repeated the cleaning process. His praise made her think she might swell with pride at any minute.

"I was also thinking about the last time I saw you. You and your sister were escorted by a pair of RCMP officers. Was there a reason…one that you care to give me?"

Her hand froze in lifting the mare's hoof. Carefully she replaced it on the floor. Straightening, she stood with her back to him.

"No."

"Okay."

"I would if I could, but I can't." She swung on him. "All I can say is that neither Emma nor I have done anything criminal."

"Witness protection program? No, no"—he was quick to contradict himself—"you wouldn't have been with two *uniformed* cops."

"Will you please stop questioning me…and making wild guesses?" She struggled against snapping at his persistence. "I've already told you all I can."

"Fine." The annoyed skepticism in his tone made her heart sink. He didn't believe her. But why should he?

He stood and headed on down through the barn to enter the stall of the big black gelding Shelby had told Etta belonged to him, a horse named Midnight Brandy. With a queasy feeling in her gut, Etta returned to grooming Candy. Before she had finished, he brought the big gelding out into the walkway and tied him in another pair of crossties. With calming words for the restless horse but none for her, he saddled up and led the horse out of the barn. Once outside, Etta watching him with peripheral vision, he swung into the saddle and turned his cavorting mount toward the trail behind the barn.

Travis Masters had written her off as trouble. He couldn't allow a relationship with a woman who appeared to have a dubious past tarnish his good-boy image. Their relationship, if it had ever truly been one, had definitely ended. Etta moved to where she could watch him ride away and decided, contrary to what her editor would have said, a person really could feel a heart sinking.

****

*Damn the woman!* As Travis rode away from the barn, his emotions were a chafing muddle. *Just when I thought I might be getting her out of my mind, she shows up here…here where I came to get away from a collection of females and the trouble they're causing me. Michelle, Lanie, Annie, and, worst of all, Etta Prescott. The other three are just plain manipulating pains in the ass. But that woman back at the barn… Hell!*

In an effort to dispel the memory, he touched his heels to the gelding's sides and felt a reviving rush as the animal broke into a smooth canter. He rode down the trail into the trees. He could hear the sounds of construction.

Slowing Brandy to a trot, he turned down a trail that looked as if it had recently borne the brunt of some heavy equipment. A warm sense of satisfaction began to replace the turmoil of feelings that had been racking him.

*So Bob and the boys are hard at it. I probably should have waited until they let me know most of it is up, but man, I'm champing at the bit to get a look.*

He walked Midnight Brandy into the rough clearing beside a brook that danced and sparkled over rocks in the autumn sunlight—and saw it. His house.

The sight of the big log structure taking form filled him with satisfaction. Two-storied, over eighty feet in length, with a veranda stretching around the front and sides of the lower floor, a balcony projecting from the side of one of the upper-story rooms to give a view of brook and forest, it was exactly as he had envisioned it when he'd hired an architect to work out the details…except for the group of workers swarming over and around it.

"Hey, Travis!" A tall, brawny man came down the steps and waved. "Didn't expect to see you here, man." As Travis walked his gelding toward him, the work foreman wearing a white safety hat over his suntanned face paused and waved a hand back toward the emerging structure. "What do you think?"

"Looks A-1, Bob."

"Well, get down and come inside. Mind you, it

looks way too big and hollow now, but with the right furniture…"

Travis swung from his horse and tied the reins to the veranda railing.

*Yeah, with the right furniture chosen by the right woman…*

Etta Prescott's image lighted up in his mind as he made his way up the steps.

*Damn, I've got to get that woman out of my head!*
****

"Shelby?" Etta tapped on the kitchen door. "Are you busy?"

"Always, but come on in. We'll chat while I make supper. How about staying? Chicken pot pie. I make a darned good one."

"Thanks, but I really have to be getting back to the lake and my dog." She stepped into the sunny kitchen. "Shelby, I won't be taking any more lessons just now. Maybe in the spring…"

"What? Why? You're doing so well. Winter riding isn't a problem. We use the closed arena all year round." She paused a moment, then continued more slowly, "This isn't because Travis came home, is it? I was hoping you two would hit it off. Things seemed to be going so well in Alberta."

"I'm just really busy with my writing. I've promised my editor two manuscripts by April."

"I'm glad your work is in demand." She rubbed her hands on her apron. "But I understand. I'll miss spending time with you during lessons. "

"As will I. If you don't mind, I'll make one last visit to the horses before I leave."

"Sure. Feel free. Grady is in town picking up

medication for my practice. Jake and Katie Rose have gone to pick up eggs at a farm down the road. Travis will keep you company."

"He's gone for a ride." She opened the door. "I'll toot my horn when I leave."

****

At the barn, she changed her mind about going inside. She wasn't anxious to say goodbye, even temporarily, to Candy. Instead she wandered around behind the structure to the pasture.

*Strange. Not a horse in sight.*

Leaning on the top fence rail, she noticed her old watch had slipped around on her wrist. As she tried to straighten it back in place, the bracelet let go. It dropped to the ground inside the enclosure.

"Oh, no!"

Kneeling, she stretched her hand through the bars but couldn't reach it. With an exasperated sigh, she stood. She couldn't leave it there. The next time horses were put in the paddock, one of them would surely trample it. She scanned the pasture. Nothing in sight.

She unlatched the gate, opened it enough to allow her to go inside, and headed for the watch. She was stooping to pick it up when she heard hooves thundering behind her. Straightening, she saw Midnight Black heading toward her at a full gallop. He must have been in the trees at the far end of the field.

*Oh, God!*

She made a dash for the half-opened gate, slipped in manure, and fell. The stallion skidded to a stop a few feet in front of her. Snorting and whinnying, he rose on his hind legs.

Closing her eyes and shielding her face, she

waited, frozen in fear, for those iron-clad hooves to rain down on her.

Suddenly, above the horse's clamor, she heard singing. Someone...Travis, singing.

Hooves dropped to the ground beside her. The horse's angry cries diminished to blowing snorts. She opened her eyes to see Travis inside the gate. He was singing as he slowly approached the stallion. Breath seized in her throat, she watched as he eased out a hand to take the animal by the halter. The big animal shook his head at first contact, then nuzzled up to the man.

Still singing, Travis led Midnight Black away from her. With a jerk of his head he indicated Etta was to get out of the pasture.

Scrambling to her feet, she obeyed. Once on the other side of the fence, she turned back to the man and horse. With another gesture, Travis indicated she was to close the gate.

She hesitated. Although the horse seemed under control, she didn't want to leave Travis trapped with the creature.

Another more emphatic shake of the man's head told her he brooked no refusal of his request. Feeling heartsick, she swung the gate shut.

She watched as, still singing, he released the stallion and, turning his back to the animal, headed toward the pasture entrance. Midnight Black followed him, bumping the man's shoulder with his nose as they walked.

*Please, please don't let anything happen. Please.*

When Travis stepped out of the pasture and latched the gate behind him, a gust of repressed breath rushed from her lips.

"Go on, get!" He stopped singing and turned to the horse. "I'm all through serenading you for today."

With a snort, the stallion swung away and raced off across the field.

"What were you thinking?" Travis turned on her, a scowl creasing his face. "Shelby must have warned you never to go near Midnight Black. She wouldn't have allowed you around the barn otherwise."

"My watch fell into the pasture." Realizing she still clutched it, she opened her hand.

"You risked a serious accident for that?" He stared down at the old timepiece with the broken leather strap. "Lady, you are lacking in common sense."

"I didn't know the stallion was in the field. I looked for him." She fought to keep the hurt of his outrage from erupting into an emotional outburst. "He must have been in the trees down by the brook. This watch is special to me."

"Yeah, well, it would have to be damned special." He was angry, angrier than she'd ever seen him. "You could have gotten killed. Just goes to show how little you do know about horses. Luckily, Black is partial to country music, or you'd likely be on your way to Carleton in an ambulance. Now, climb into your vehicle and get the hell out of here."

Mustering what dignity she could, she turned and strode off toward her Jeep.

*What right does he have to get so angry? I made a mistake…a mistake anyone could have made.*

She was almost to Carleton, tears trickling down her cheeks at intervals, when the reality of what had happened came to her. He'd been overcome with fear when he'd seen her predicament, and as so often happens as an aftermath, relief had propelled him into anger.

She pulled a tissue from her pocket and blew her nose. He'd been afraid she'd be injured—or worse. He cared, really cared for her.

Or did he? Maybe he would have behaved the same for anyone endangered by the stallion. Maybe he was only concerned about his family farm's liability in the event of such an incident.

*Stop speculating, Etta Prescott. You and Travis Masters have no future together…at least not until I can explain those police officers with Emma and me at the Calgary airport…and that won't be for months, maybe years.*

She blew her nose again.

*It doesn't matter that he was miffed or why. When life throws you a lemon, make lemonade. This incident will make a great scene in my manuscript…the hero rescuing the heroine from a wild stallion. It will make a perfect final chapter.*

*Final chapter…*
\*\*\*\*

*What in hell…?*

Travis rode into the farmyard to see a sleek black sports car parked near the barn.

As he approached, a woman emerged wearing form-clinging jeans, knee-high ebony boots, and a black leather jacket.

*Oh, God, not her.*

The recognition made him halt his horse. He didn't want to get any closer to Michelle Layton than necessary. Bad enough he'd had to go for a long gallop to clear the image of Etta all but being trampled by

Midnight Black. Now this.

The woman wasn't about to grant him that choice. She strode toward him, perfectly made-up face screwed up into a mask of anger.

"Okay, cowboy, where is he?"

She stopped at Brandy's left shoulder and glared up at him.

"Where is who?" He feigned ignorance.

"Paulie, of course. Don't play dumb with me. I went to the hospital in New York to find out when he was going to be discharged, and surprise, surprise, he was gone. Of course, since I wasn't family, I couldn't get any information. They wouldn't believe me when I told them I was his fiancée. So I decided to come to the guy who definitely knows where I can find him."

"Sorry, Michelle. Like the hospital, I'm not free to divulge that information." He nudged his horse to move past her, but she caught the animal's bridle. Midnight Brandy snorted and cavorted, knocking her sideways. She stumbled and landed on her bottom in a puddle left from the previous night's rain.

"You did that on purpose, Travis Masters!" She scrambled to her feet to glare up at him, slapping at her behind. "Do you know how much these jeans cost?"

"Send me a bill." He nudged Brandy again, and the horse trotted on to the stable entrance.

As he swung to the ground, he glanced over his shoulder in time to see the woman getting into her car. The motor roared as she whirled the vehicle around, tearing up sod. He watched as she gunned down the lane, past the farmhouse, and out onto the highway.

"Nasty bit of work, that one, right?" He rubbed Brandy's snout. "I'll have to be on my guard every minute now that she's back in the area. No way is she going to get to Paulie, not if I can help it."

His thoughts went back to the incident earlier in the day. When he'd seen Etta fallen in front of the stallion, something in his chest had banged like a sledge hammer against his ribs. He still didn't know how he'd managed to keep his cool, to start singing right off.

*The woman might love horses, but what she doesn't know about them would fill more than a few of her books. She needs a whole lot more lessons to be anywhere safe around them, but after I got stupid and yelled at her, I doubt she'll want to come back to the farm. Crazy for her to go into that field after that ratty watch.*

He paused in pulling the saddle and blanket from Brandy. *It must be a special watch, maybe a gift from a former boyfriend...some guy with less taste in jewelry than I have. Wonder who he was? Aw, what the hell. It doesn't matter. I'm not getting myself any more involved with the woman.*

He finished stabling his horse and headed up to the house.

"Got any food for a hungry man?" He stepped inside and sniffed an appetizing aroma issuing from the oven.

"Chicken pot pie and apple crisp for supper, but it's not ready yet." His sister turned from the sink where she was peeling apples. "How about Katie Rose's favorite...cookies and milk?"

"Now there's a treat." He went to the cookie jar on the counter and took out a handful.

"Etta left in a hurry." She went back to her work.

"Guess she had to get back to her book." He'd

decided on the way up to the house not to tell anyone about the incident at the pasture. He knew any accident or near accident on the farm distressed Shelby. Anyhow, no one got hurt. All was well.

"Annie Wyse called while you were down at the barn," she said without looking up from her work. "She said you're either not answering your cell or you have it turned off. I'm guessing you're avoiding her."

"You didn't tell her I was here?" He took a tall glass from the cupboard and headed for the refrigerator.

"No, but she's convinced you are. She said she'd be here tomorrow to talk sense into you."

"Hell!" Travis dropped into a chair at the table and stretched long legs out beneath it.

"And that sexy singer called. Lanie Lanson. Something about not being able to hook up with another band and that you'd better do something about it. She was nattering on about a verbal contract."

"Shit!"

"Travis, you know my view on four-letter words, especially with Katie Rose often within earshot."

"Sorry, but this is one miserable turn of events. I can't stay here with all three of those vipers on my trail. You've got to help me find a hideout, Shel."

His sister paused, knife and apple in hand, as she stared out the window over the sink.

"Hmm. Let me think. It seems to me I've heard of a secluded cabin that's for rent, about a forty-five-minute drive from here. How does that sound?"

"Exactly what I need. Do you have the number of the person managing it? I can't get away soon enough."

"The place is at Loon Lake. I'll have to call Emma MacKenzie to find out who's in charge of letting it.

She's the person who told me about it." She put apple and knife aside, dried her hands on a towel, and reached for her phone. "Give me a minute."

"Sounds good. If you can make a deal, I'll talk to Grady about arranging a truck swap. If I'm going to make this hiding-out business work, I'll have to ditch that fancy rig I rented. It's far too easy to trace."

Chapter Eight

Beau pulled himself to a sitting position on the hearth rug and howled. At her desk by a window in her Loon Lake cabin, Etta paused in her writing and turned to see the basset getting to his paws and waddling toward the door.

"What is it, Beau?" She knew from experience the dog could catch sounds long before she did. She got up and followed him. Then she heard it, too.

A vehicle was coming up the trail. Who? Certainly not Emma. Although whatever form of transportation was approaching muttered and groaned, she knew it wasn't her twin's car. Her sister's old compact had a distinctive roar and rattle all its own. So an unknown person.

Remembering Emma's run-in with drug dealers in the area the previous year, she picked up a length of pipe from the counter before opening the door. She'd found it in the generator shed the first time she'd gone down to refuel the apparatus and decided it would make a decent weapon if the need ever arose. Clutching it in hand, she stepped out onto the veranda.

A rusted green half-ton truck drove slowly into the area in front of her cabin and stopped. As the driver, wearing sunglasses and a baseball cap, cut the engine and swung out, she gasped.

*Oh no, it can't be! Not here! Not driving that*

*rescue from a wrecker's ball...*

"Etta?" Travis Masters stopped and stared up at her.

"Yes." The word came out as unexpectedly as a burp and just as genteelly.

"This is a surprise. When Shelby told me about this place, she couldn't have known you'd be here."

"Shelby?" Words were still coming out one at a time, her astonished thoughts incapable of more.

"Yeah. Your sister told Shelby she knew of this great place for me to unwind and hide out from the world."

"Emma told Shelby about these cabins?" Coming out of shock, Etta began to think rationally. "My sister told your sister about Loon Lake?"

"Yeah."

"Oh, God!" Heat rose up Etta's neck to suffuse her face. She covered it with her hands.

"What?" He pulled off his sunglasses and squinted up at her.

"Don't you see? This is a setup. My sister engineered it."

"You think?"

"I don't think, I know." She lowered her hands. "Look, Travis, you're welcome to stay in the other cabin. Rest assured I won't bother you. I've got reams of work to do, and Beau hardly ever barks. It'll be perfect peace and quiet. I assume that's what you're looking for, or you wouldn't be up here."

"What about you? Is that what you want? Peace and quiet?"

"Yes, of course."

"Good, then we understand each other. I'd better

111

start moving into my cabin and get my groceries unpacked. A lot of that stuff doesn't last long without refrigeration. I thought this place was mine." He indicated her cabin. "Now I realize I'm in cottage number two. You wouldn't happen to know if the power has been turned on?"

"It has. The property manager was up yesterday. He said the cabin had been rented. I just didn't expect..."

"Me?"

"Yes."

"Driving this?" He jerked his thumb at the truck.

"Well...yes." She avoided wrinkling her nose at the distinct smell of manure issuing from its cargo bay.

"Necessity. If I'm going to hide out, I can't use a rental. Too easy to trace. So I made a trade with Grady. You must have met him...the hand at our family farm. Seems his last cargo was manure."

"Seems so."

"As soon as I get settled, I'll find a hose and do some odor control. Can't have my vehicle offending you or your buddy." He indicated Beau standing beside her, head back, nose twitching as he appeared to savor the smell.

"It's okay, really."

"It's the neighborly thing to do." He climbed into the truck and started the engine before glancing back at her. "By the way, you can put the lead pipe away. I don't plan to do anything that will make you want to take a swipe at me."

He drove the few yards to the second cabin and stopped again. She watched as he got out and began to remove grocery bags and luggage from the back seat.

Turning, she strode into her cabin. She dropped the pipe on a table near the door and sank into a chair.

*Emma Prescott-MacKenzie, I'll kill you. And I'll never, never again act as lookout while you have a rendezvous with your oh-so-sexy husband.*

Beau, with hound curiosity, remained on the veranda to watch their new neighbor unpack.

\*\*\*\*

"Beau, where are you?" An autumn twilight was favoring Loon Lake with a spectacular sunset over mountains and water when Etta stepped out onto her veranda to summon her dog. "Supper…"

"Over here." Travis's voice made her turn toward his cabin. Seated on the veranda steps beside him was Beau. "He came to pay a welcome visit. Care to join him?"

She hesitated. *Don't get any further involved with the man. He'll be here for only a couple of weeks, a month at most, and then he'll be gone again. After what he saw at the Calgary airport, with what he must be thinking or at least wondering, he's not about to want to have anything more to do with me. He never tried to contact me afterward, and he could have. His sister knows where I live…thanks to my sister.*

*But,* a small, silent voice wickedly suggested, *why not simply enjoy his company? He's a nice guy, someone you won't need a steel pipe to keep at bay.*

"Okay." She headed over to join them. He stood at her approach.

"Come up on the veranda. There are a couple of lawn chairs, more comfortable than these steps. How about a beer?"

"Okay."

*Etta, stop repeating yourself. You're a writer, for God's sake. You're supposed to have a decent vocabulary.*

By the time he came out of the cabin with two sweating longnecks, she'd settled herself in one of the chairs and resolved to treat him as casually as he was treating her.

*But, oh, my, he's looking at me, smiling, handsome beyond the legal limit…*

"Great sunset, isn't it?" He handed her a bottle and settled into the chair beside hers.

"It is. This is beautiful country. Our family used to come up here in the summers when we were kids. That's why Emma came back when she needed a place to stay with her Pug. It's not easy to find an apartment that will take dogs."

"Is that why you came here…because of him?" He indicated Beau, stretched out at their feet.

"Partly, but also because it's the perfect place to write…at least for me." She found she was relaxing, enjoying a normal conversation as they had on that evening ride at the Turners' ranch. "You said you're here for a rest?"

"Yeah, mostly."

"I thought by now you'd be in Europe—New York, then across the pond for a big tour, if I remember your itinerary correctly."

"Yeah, well, stuff happened, plans got changed." Focusing on it, he ran his thumb up and down the bottle.

*He doesn't want to discuss it. Fine, we'll leave it there.*

She took a drink and looked off across the lake.

There definitely were things she also didn't want to explain. Mainly one, but it was a biggie.

"You ever do any canoeing?" he asked.

"Actually, quite a bit when my family stayed up here."

"Property manager said there should be a canoe hidden in the long grass down by the dock. Thought I might take it out, go for a scoot around the lake."

"He was right. I know where it is. Have you canoed previously?"

"Enough to know how to handle a paddle." The subject ended without an invitation to come along, and with an abrupt change. "What made you choose a basset hound as a pet...or companion, or whatever you want to call it? Not exactly a guard dog for a lady living alone up here."

"When I decided to move up here, Emma decided I needed a dog. At first she thought I should take her husband's German shepherd, Scout, but..."

*Careful, Etta. You were on the verge of a major slip. Scout is a trained RCMP dog.*

"But?" Travis was obviously interested, too interested for her comfort. She had to come up with a plausible story.

"But, as you probably know, German shepherds are large dogs that require a lot of exercise. What with my planning to spend most of my time writing, I wouldn't be able to give him the proper care. So Emma and I decided to leave him with a friend of Frasier's who lives in the country, at least until such time as they build a house and have a suitable home for him."

"Still no explanation why a basset."

"Okay, okay. Once Emma and I had decided

against Frasier's dog, we went to the local SPCA. There were so many lovely dogs there needing homes, it broke my heart, but Beau with his long ears and big, soulful eyes won me over. I was hooked."

"Got ya. Understood. Sometimes a person and an animal just connect. Like Midnight Brandy and me. Have you always been a writer?"

"Always?" His sudden changes of topic caught her off guard, and for a moment she fumbled for a reply. "I believe so. I began writing stories as soon as I could read and handle a pencil. I studied journalism in college. After graduation, I worked for a magazine until the people and the pace started to get to me. I'd always wanted to write romance fiction, and I'd managed to accumulate a small savings account, so I gave up my apartment and moved into my parents' basement. I wrote my first novel there. Sooner than I expected, I found an editor and publisher who really liked my work. I've been doing it ever since, with enough success to put food on the table, keep a roof over my head, and manage to maintain a pre-owned vehicle. What about you? Did you always want to be a country music superstar?"

"I began playing a guitar and singing when I was about ten or twelve. Shelby wasn't a fan of my having a career in country music. She's a nose-to-the-grindstone type, but after she met Jake, he talked her into letting me pursue my dream. He's a great brother-in-law. I couldn't ask for better. What about your sister? She's married, too, I've heard. Do you like the guy?"

"I'd better be going." She stood and placed her beer bottle on the veranda railing. "I'll leave you to settle in."

His asking about Frasier startled her. She had to get away before she revealed anything she shouldn't.

"Hey, sorry. I shouldn't have asked. None of my business. Don't rush off."

"I have to get back to work."

"Sure." He got to his feet. "Thanks for the company."

"Thanks for the beer. Come on, Beau."

She believed he watched her as she and her dog went down the steps and across the short distance to her cabin. In her stories, she'd often written that the heroine could feel the hero's gaze on her. Now she knew it was true. At her door, she paused and turned back to wave good night, but he'd already gone inside.

A chill enveloped her as she entered the living area. He'd been friendly, they'd seemed companionable as they'd enjoyed the sunset, but then he'd asked about Frasier.

Pulling off her clothes as she went, she headed into the bathroom and a shower. Would she ever be able to tell him the truth about the scene at the Calgary airport? She suspected Emma hadn't told Shelby about the incident when she suggested Travis take the other cabin at Loon Lake. Shelby Masters-Brooks definitely didn't seem the type of woman who'd let her brother get mixed up with someone who had a dubious past.

\*\*\*\*

In his cabin, Travis likewise was also heading into the shower, thoughts of Etta Prescott whirling around in his head.

*Damn it, I wish I hadn't seen her at that airport, escorted out of town by the RCMP. I've tried to come up with innocent explanations but can't find a single one. And why did a casual mention of her brother-in-law send her running off? Is he in some way tied in with that scene? Is he some kind of master criminal and the law is keeping a close watch on his wife in hopes of her leading them to him?*

*Stop it, you fool.* He reined his thoughts. *Master criminal, like hell. Now she's got you building fantasies. Damn, damn, damn!*

He stepped into the flow of water and began to sing, as he always did. Only this time, he discovered the words included those of a classic country song... "We can't go on together with suspicious minds."

\*\*\*\*

"Beau, come back! Beau!"

Travis woke the following morning to the baying of a hound and a woman's frantic calls.

"Ah, hell!" He tumbled out of bed, rubbing his temples. *Peace and quiet, right.*

Grabbing his pajama pants, he pulled them on and headed, barefoot, for the door.

"Beau, Beau!"

Her cries were fainter now. Was she chasing that hound into the woods?

Coming out onto his veranda, he looked in the direction of her calls. Apparently she'd gone straight into the bush, not down the trail. Fog hung over land and lake, blocking from sight everything beyond a few yards.

"Etta!" he bellowed. "Etta!" His voice echoed eerily in the mist.

No reply.

*Damn it, I'll have to get dressed and try to find her and that long-eared dog.*

He headed back inside.

\*\*\*\*

As he came back out onto the veranda, dressed in boots, jeans, shirt, and jacket, he saw her.

Emerging from the bush beyond her cabin between lake and vehicle trail, she looked as if she'd been through a war. Her hair had tangles of twigs entwined, and her face was smudged with dirt. She wore mud-splattered pink flannelette pajamas. No dog accompanied her. When she looked up and saw Travis, her expression struck a pain in his heart. The farm boy in him understood what it was to lose an animal companion.

"Can't find him?" Trying to sound casual, he came down the steps.

"No." She shook her head, looking down at her wet, dirty, once-fuzzy slippers. A burdock was stuck to one toe. "He chased a rabbit. I followed him for a while, but then I couldn't hear his baying anymore, and I lost him."

"Don't hounds have some kind of homing instinct…like carrier pigeons?" He hoped he was finding the right words. "Think I read about it once in one of Shelby's books."

"I don't know." Pushing tangled hair back from her face, she looked up at him. "I don't know much about the breed."

"We'll organize a search." He had to turn away. With tears brimming in those fantastic green eyes, she was getting to him, this disheveled girl standing dejectedly in the mist. "Sun's trying to come out. It'll soon burn off the fog. That will make visibility a whole lot better. You go up to your cabin and change into hiking clothes. You said you knew about that canoe beached down by the dock. We'll use it to circle the lake. That's the best way to cover a lot of territory."

He started to stride toward the shore. When he heard no sound of movement, he swung. She was standing where he'd left her, tears trickling down through the dirt on her face.

"Hey, it will be all right." He fought the urge to go back to her, to take her into his arms. "I know animals, and trust me, your Beau isn't stupid. He'll be fine. Now"—he toughened his tone—"get a move on. You need a hot shower and dry clothes."

"Okay, sure." Although the words came out shakily, she nodded and headed for her cabin. He bit his lower lip and started off again.

"Travis?" His name stopped him once more.

"Yeah?"

"Thank you."

The sound of her footsteps scurrying up the steps of her cabin and a door opening and closing spared him a reply.

\*\*\*\*

The canoe looked water worthy, he decided after he'd examined it. A couple of paddles lay in its bottom. He straightened from his perusal, put his hands on his hips, and looked out across the lake becoming visible through a soft curtain of fog the rising sun was turning to gold.

The surface lay still and glinting in the increasing light. A pair of loons appeared as if by magic out of the mist, talking in chuckles. Along the water's edge, as far as he could see, deciduous trees had turned to their autumn hues of yellow, orange, and red, set off by a deep green backdrop of pines, spruce, and cedars.

Shelby had been right. This was the perfect place to get his head back on straight, to find the real Travis Masters after a half dozen years of being something he'd desperately longed for and now wanted to put behind him. Hopefully, those three witches wouldn't find him.

His thoughts strayed back to the previous evening on his veranda, watching the sunset with Etta.

*Don't go there, man. You don't want to get involved with any more women, especially one with some kind of crazy mystery hanging around her.*

With a shrug, he forced himself out of his reflections, untied the canoe from its moorings, and shoved it out into the water. Later he could put his thoughts in order. Right now he had a hound to find.

****

By the time she arrived on the shore, he'd made a fast trip to his cabin to make coffee and, wearing a life jacket, was standing with a travel mug in his hand. A second one he'd placed on the front seat with a lifejacket.

"Climb aboard," he said indicating the forward bench. "Have you got a dog whistle?"

"Yes, but Beau isn't the most obedient of creatures."

"Still, if he's tired and getting hungry…"

"You're right. He might respond."

"We'll go up along the right side and circle around." He waited while she climbed aboard, put on the life jacket, and took up her paddle. Once she was settled, he shoved the canoe out into the lake and jumped aboard.

"You don't have to do this." She swung from the waist to face him. "You came to Loon Lake to rest, not chase a dog through the woods."

"I came up here to take a break, not vegetate. Canoeing is one of the best forms of R&R I know. You don't have to paddle. I can handle it. Drink your coffee."

"Thanks, but I want to do my share. It is *my* dog we're searching for."

The mist burned off in a warm autumn sun, water and forest became more visible. When a buck deer came out of the woods and lowered its antlered head to drink, Emma pointed.

"So lovely," she breathed when the animal finally turned and walked back among the trees.

"Etta, look!" On the bank something brown was moving among the alders.

"Beau!" Etta had to stop herself from standing up in the canoe. "Beau!"

"Paddle." He dipped his oar deep into the water to send their craft sweeping forward.

They were nearly to shore when the brown creature slid smoothly into the water and swam away.

"Beaver." Travis paused, resting his paddle across the gunwales. "Must be building a dam on one of the brooks that flow into the lake. Sorry, Etta. I thought it might be your dog."

"So did I." She leaned back and rotated her shoulders. "It was about his size and color. An easy mistake."

"So let's get going." He back-paddled out into the lake. "We're only half way around. Still lots of territory to search."

\*\*\*\*

At noon, they returned to the dock.

"I'll take another turn around the lake later." Travis secured the canoe to a post. "He hasn't been gone long. Don't give up."

She heaved a deep sigh as she removed her life jacket. "I won't. And Travis…" She looked down at him as he bent to secure the craft. "I really appreciate all you've done."

"Not a problem." He fought to sound casual, but the pain in her eyes was making it difficult.

He watched as she headed for her cabin, steps lagging.

*Damn it, I have to find that foolish dog!*

\*\*\*\*

Seven hours later, he screwed the top on a thermos and stuffed a flask of brandy into his jacket pocket. Alone, he'd canoed around the lake in the last light of day and still no sign of the dog. Now the unpleasant probability had to be faced, but he didn't want Etta to do it alone. Bracing himself, he headed out into the cold rain and buffeting wind that had begun at dusk.

"Etta." He knocked softly on her cabin door. "It's Travis."

The door opened onto an Etta whose expression was one, for an instant, of hope, dissolving into disappointment.

"You didn't find him." She stepped back to allow him to enter. "I saw you going off in the canoe earlier. I thought maybe…"

"I didn't ask you to come with me. I decided it best you stay here in the event he came home. By now he'd be tired and hungry and…"

"Yes." She indicated a chair beside the hearth where a fire crackled. Its warmth felt good after his time on the lake in the rapidly cooling evening and mizzle. Hot days, cold nights. Typical at this time of year in this area. "If your jacket is any indication, it must be really coming down out there."

"I've brought something for you." He held out the thermos. "My brother-in-law Jake recommends this for tough times. Take a seat, and I'll serve it up."

He placed the container on the kitchen counter while he shrugged out of his jacket and hung it over a chair by the fire. In the cupboards, he searched until he found a pair of mugs. He placed them on the table, screwed the top from the thermos, and poured hot, sweet tea into both.

"Here." He handed one to her. "But hold on a minute." He went to his jacket and removed the flask. "Brandy." He held it up. "Just the thing for a time and a night like this." He poured a generous dollop into her cup before adding a more modest amount to his.

She looked up at him for a moment before gingerly lowering her mouth to the mug. And flinched.

"Too strong?"

"Actually, I believe it's just what I need."

"We'll keep looking. In the morning…"

"That's kind of you, but we both know there's not much hope. What with bears and coyotes and such in the woods, and now this miserable night…" She drew a shuddering breath.

"Dogs are survivors. They've been known to come home over all odds. What about Lassie?" He struggled for an analogy.

"Lassie?"

"Lassie…you know, the book and movie, *Lassie, Come Home*."

"Those are fiction." She looked up at him, slightly exasperated, then continued, cautious interest in the words, "How long did it take Lassie to come home?"

"Well…" *Damn it, caught.* "I never actually read the book or saw the movie…but she must have. I saw a rerun of the TV series when I was a kid, and she was home."

"Thanks"—he saw her lips twitch with a hint of amusement—"for trying to give me confidence, even if you haven't firsthand knowledge to back up your theory."

"Look, Etta, I think I should sleep over here tonight—on the couch—in case Beau comes home and you don't hear him at the door." *I can't leave you looking so forlorn and hurting.*

"I appreciate the offer, but…"

"This isn't some kind of stupid come-on." He hoped she saw the sincerity in his expression. "I understand how you feel. I lost a cat when I was a kid…looked for her for days."

"And did she come back?"

"No." The admittance came out soft, almost a croak, as memories of his long-held fractured hopes returned. "Probably I should have shut up after my Lassie story."

"Maybe you should have."

"So what do you say?" He brought his tone up to normal.

"About what?"

"My sleeping on your couch."

"Travis, I…"

"Come on, Etta. You can trust me. I'll even make coffee in the morning. I've gotten pretty good at it in all the hotel suites and rooms I've lived in over the past few years."

"Okay." With a resigned sigh, she finished her drink and stood. "If you're going to be out here near the door, I'll lie down on my bed. I am tired."

"You do that. See you in the morning."

As he watched her head into her bedroom, shoulders slumping, something inside him lurched.

*Get yourself back here, dog. That woman needs you.*

He glanced at the door to the veranda. No need to lock it any more than he locked the one at his own cabin. A home invader would have to be pretty desperate to come all the way up here.

He looked at the couch. *May as well get comfortable.*

He'd removed his shirt and pulled his T-shirt over his head when Etta's voice made him turn back toward the bedrooms.

"Here's a quilt—" She broke off, her gaze falling on his bare chest.

Feeling like a fourteen-year-old confronting his first date, he clutched the T-shirt to his chest.

"Thanks."

"Good night."

"Good night."

*Damn it!* He threw the shirt aside and dropped down onto the couch. *When did I get so shy in front of a woman? Sure as hell not out on the road with Lanie and her like.*

He lay down and pulled the quilt over him. *Man,*

*this smells good.* He buried his nose in the softness. *What does she wash her laundry in? Or maybe it's essence of Etta. Or maybe I've been living around sweaty guys too long. Damn it, man, go to sleep before you get any more crazy ideas.*

****

He woke to the sound of a vehicle lumbering up the trail, then a door slamming. As he struggled to a sitting position, the cabin door burst open, and Emma MacKenzie, a Pug at her heels, burst inside.

"Etta, it's…" She didn't finish. Instead, her mouth gaped open as she stared at his bare chest. "Oops, sorry."

"Emma!" Etta burst out of the bedroom in a disheveled jogging suit, her hair a tangle of curls. "I'm so glad you're here. I was going to call you to come and…"

"I seriously doubt it." A sly grin curled her sister's mouth. "Come on, Bruise. We know when to make ourselves scarce."

"No, no, no!" Etta crossed the room to catch Emma by an arm. "You don't understand! Beau went missing yesterday. Travis and I searched and searched, but we couldn't find him. Travis offered to spend the night…on the couch…in case Beau returned in the night and I didn't hear him."

She indicated the crumpled quilt as Travis snatched up his T-shirt and pulled it over his head.

"Oh, no, Etta! I'm so sorry." Emma was instantly all sympathy. "What can Bruiser and I do to help?"

"Not much, I'm afraid. I'll go out looking again this morning. You can tag along, if you like."

"Maybe Bruiser can find his trail. He found Ross's

dog Fox last fall when she got lost."

"I doubt very much if a bloodhound could track Beau after last night's rain." Etta headed across the room toward the coffee machine.

"I'll do that." Having struggled into his T-shirt, Travis strode to cut her off. "Remember, I promised last night."

As Travis busied himself making coffee, he caught Emma giving her sister a subtle thumbs up. Etta vehemently shook her head. Was it a simple denial that nothing had happened between them in the night, or was it some sort of secret signal between conspirators? Memories of the Calgary airport slithered back.

*Damn!*

\*\*\*\*

"Come on, Bruiser, try again." Emma urged the Pug around the area where Beau had vanished into the woods. "You can do it!"

Under foliage still dripping from the previous night's rain now glistening in morning sunlight, the little dog circled again and again, nose to the ground. Finally, he threw back his head and gave a dismal howl. Ears and tail drooping, he gazed up at Emma.

"Okay, you did your best. Come on, everybody back to the cabin. I plan to make us all a stellar breakfast."

"I'm not hungry." Etta heaved a sigh as she, her sister, Travis, and Bruiser turned back the way they'd come.

"You have to keep up your strength. As soon as we eat, we'll start looking again. Travis, how do you feel about a stack of blueberry pancakes? I brought the makin's with me." She gave him a nudge accompanied by a conspiratorial nod behind Etta's back.

"I could go for some." He took the hint.

At Etta's cabin, Emma insisted he and her sister stay on the veranda in burgeoning sunshine while she cooked. Bruiser stretched out beside them with a weary sigh.

"Little guy thinks he's a failure." Travis bent forward in his chair to pat the Pug's head. The response was a weak tail wag.

"He's not alone." Etta leaned back with a sigh of her own. "I should have known that as a hound Beau would be prone to chase rabbits. I should have…"

Bruiser lifted his head and sniffed the air. He jumped to his paws, issued his loudest howl, and raced down the steps.

"Bruiser!" Etta leaped to her feet. "Come back!"

"I'll get him." Travis cleared the veranda railing in a leap and was off and running in pursuit.

He sprinted down the trail after the Pug and around its first bend. He found Bruiser sniffing at something at the side of the road. A sick feeling in his gut, Travis slowed and approached. His breath caught in his throat as he saw what the Pug had found. Lying in the weeds and bushes was the basset hound. His eyes were closed.

"Ah, hell!" He knelt beside the dog. *Don't let him be dead, don't let him be dead!*

The dog's side moved slightly. *Breathing. Alive.*

"Beau, wake up!" He rubbed the dog behind one ear. "Come on, guy! Snap out of it."

Brown eyes opened a slit.

"That's it! Hang in there, guy. I'm takin' you home."

He shoved his arms under the hound. With a grunt,

he staggered to his feet.

"Man, you're a whole lot heavier than I thought. Lead the way, Bruiser. I want to get your friend home fast."

Before he'd gone more than a few paces, Etta rushed up to join them.

"Beau!" She stroked the head and floppy ears hanging against Travis's arm. "Is he…?" She looked up at him, hope and fear mingling in her eyes.

"Alive. Head on back to the cabin. I'll need someone to open the door for me. He's all I can handle."

Chapter Nine

In the cabin, Travis laid the basset on his dog bed near the fireplace while Emma hurried to add a log to the languishing embers.

"He's wet and cold and probably suffering from shock," she said, while Etta, concern crinkling her face, knelt beside the dog, stroking his long ears.

"Besides an ugly scratch along his side, he's covered with insect bites." Travis hunkered down to examine the animal. "And here's the reason he didn't come home." He held up a slender gold-colored wire hanging from his right hind leg. "He got caught in a rabbit snare, probably one left over from last winter's trapping. He must have gnawed himself loose. It's cut pretty deep into the flesh." He bent closer to examine it. "It will need to be removed surgically by a vet. And I know just the one."

"Yes, let's go." Emma was turning off the stove and the coffeepot. "Come on, Bruiser. Later we'll treat you as the hero you are once again. Right now, we have to get Beau to Dr. Shelby Masters."

\*\*\*\*

"More coffee?" Emma brought the pot out onto the veranda of the house at Ebony M Farm and asked her sister the question.

"No, thanks." She shook her head, staring down at the cup in her hand.

"Look, Travis might not be a licensed veterinarian technician, but I bet he's had lots and lots of practice assisting his sister over the years." Emma looked down at her sister. "Beau is in the best hands possible with him and Shelby. Now, how about some toast? You should eat something."

"Emma, stop fussing!" Etta was startled to hear herself snap. Then, "Sorry."

"No need to be. I understand. If it were the Bruise in surgery, I'd be a veritable Tasmanian devil. Right, Bruise?"

Bruiser, sitting in front of Etta, wiggled his tail and looked up at her, round eyes wide and bright.

"You've always understood me." Etta forced a smile at her twin.

"That's what twins are for." Emma placed the coffeepot on the floor and sank into a chair beside her. "Peaceful, isn't it?" She changed the subject by glancing around. "Smell that ocean breeze! Wouldn't it be great to live here!"

"I guess." *My enthusiasm for anything other than Beau's recovery couldn't be at a lower ebb right now.*

"I'm glad that wrangler Grady took Katie Rose down to the barn to ride her pony. She's a sweet kid, but I was afraid her chatter might be too much for you at the moment. Jake is usually here on Saturdays to look after her, I imagine, but today he's gone on a field trip with some of the high school kids. I overheard them planning it at school this week."

The door to the clinic opened into the living room. Etta vaulted to her feet as Shelby and Travis in scrubs came out onto the veranda.

"He's doing well." Shelby didn't wait for her to

ask. "But I'd like to keep him here for the remainder of today and overnight, to watch for infection."

"Yes, yes, of course, whatever you think is best." A huge weight lifted from Etta's mind. "May I see him?"

"It's best that you let him rest. He's sedated. The sound of your voice might rouse him, and that wouldn't be in his best interest right now."

"He's looking much better, Etta." Travis pulled off the cap that had been covering his hair. "Shelby's a great vet, and I'm not saying that because she's my sister. I've assisted her often enough to know."

"I'm sure."

"Another thing." Shelby rubbed the back of her neck. "Beau will have to be kept confined for a week or so. Do you have a pen?"

"No, but maybe I can make one out of the veranda. I'll buy a baby gate and…"

"No need." Travis responded. "The cabins are identical in all but one feature. I noticed it when I moved in. There's a pen with a dog door leading into it from the house at the back of my place. It's plenty big enough for Beau to move around and yet not overdo. We'll trade living quarters when we get back to the lake…if that's okay with you, Etta?" He looked over at her.

"You'd do that? You've just gotten settled in…"

"No problem. I'm good at throwing stuff into a bag and moving on."

"Thank you."

"Can you drive Etta back?" Emma asked. "Bruiser and I have to head home to our apartment. Cleaning, grocery shopping…lots of Saturday chores, you know. Luckily we followed you guys in my car. We won't have to trouble you for a ride."

*Will my sister never stop matchmaking? She couldn't be more obvious if she stuck a sign on me saying Desperately Seeking Romance.*

"Definitely." He smiled at Etta. "I drove her here, and I always see the lady I brought safely back home."

"You almost sound like a gentleman," Shelby teased. "Maybe all my efforts weren't in vain."

"Definitely not, sis." He planted a quick kiss on her forehead before heading back into the house. "I'll change and be right with you, Etta."

\*\*\*\*

"Sorry about the smell." He glanced over at her as they drove toward Carleton. "I still haven't hosed out the cargo space."

"I didn't notice it when we were on our way to your sister's, I was so upset. Now that lovely ocean breeze seems to be taking most of it away." Suddenly she chuckled.

"What?"

"I wonder if any of your fans would recognize you? I think those Ray-Bans and that baseball cap are not nearly as good a disguise as this vehicle."

"You're probably right. This antique came to the farm with Jake as part of his disguise years ago. Grady fell in love with it and has been using it ever since. I think he had a hard time parting with it, even temporarily, though I traded with him for a fancy, brand-new king cab. You know what I also think?" .

"What?"

"I think it's a perfect disguise for both of us. We look like a typical farm couple on their way into town to do some shopping and errands."

"I'd hope most farm women would be better turned out than I am." Etta looked down at the shabby jeans and sweatshirt she'd pulled on that morning. "I also think they'd have taken a shower and done something with their hair."

"Maybe, but I think you look fine just as you are."

The glance that accompanied his words made heat rise up her neck. Travis Masters was saying she looked just fine. Travis Masters!

"Now, how about breakfast…if the smell of this fine vehicle hasn't turned you off?" He returned his attention to the road ahead. "There's a restaurant on Main Street that makes a terrific seafood omelet."

"Okay." Although she would rather have gone back to the cabin and crawled into bed, she guessed he was hungry. "My treat. I definitely owe it to you. So far your plans for R&R up at the lake haven't worked out all that well. Beau and I have been a real pain, and now this cabin swapping… We'll try to do better."

"Hey, I needed a change of pace, and I'm getting it. Canoeing, hiking, and even getting to go back to the farm to help Shelby all qualify in that department. Furthermore, I'm eating and sleeping at decently regular hours."

"Are you sure you don't mind trading cabins?"

"What do I want with a dog pen? The only thing I have that in any way resembles a pet is my gelding, Midnight Brandy, and he's way too big for it. Here's the restaurant."

"Aren't you afraid of being mobbed by fans?" she asked as he maneuvered the truck into a parking space.

"Here? Naw. To folks around here, I'm just the vet's kid brother who used to train horses and shovel manure. Seeing me is no big deal."

"An artist is never appreciated in his hometown. Seems I read that somewhere once."

"Appears to hold true here. What about you? Are you afraid of being mobbed by readers? Vanessa Dean is probably a well-known author."

"I'm not all that well known, just a midlist writer who manages to eke out a living. Have you seen the glamour photos on the back covers of any of my books? A far cry from the actual item. I doubt anyone would recognize me from them."

"Actually I don't think they do you justice." He stopped the truck and turned off the engine. He pulled off his sunglasses and swung to face her. "I think the real thing is a whole lot better."

Leaving her too astonished to respond or even blush, he removed the key from the ignition and got out. When he came around to her side to open the door for her, she stumbled over the sill.

*Damn it, the man is sweeping me off my feet…and I don't think he's even trying.*

****

Although she hadn't thought she was hungry, Etta surprised herself by digging into the omelet and washing it down with several cups of strong, bracing coffee. When she'd finished, she glanced over at Travis. He was grinning.

"What?"

"Not hungry, right?"

"I didn't realize I was. Now, in spite of the coffee, I'm really sleepy."

"Me, too. I think a morning nap is what we both need." He stood. "We'd best head back to the lake."

"You go out to the truck. I'll pay the bill."

"No need. I'll take care of it."

"Please allow me. It will make me feel a little better in the face of all you've done for Beau and me."

He hesitated.

"Shelby would have a fit if she caught me letting a lady pay. As you've seen, she prides herself on having attempted to make me into a gentleman."

"And you have been, believe me. In this case, allowing a lady to relieve herself of a bit of her sense of obligation would be a totally gentlemanly thing to do."

"Okay, if that's how you feel, I'll wait in the truck."

As she waited at the counter for the bill, she watched him stride out of the restaurant into the bright autumn morning.

*Yes, you most certainly are a gentleman, Travis Masters, something way better than being a superstar.*

\*\*\*\*

"Think we should wait to swap cabins until after we've had a snooze?" Travis asked as she joined him in his truck. "Not much sleep and now a big feed leaves me ready for one whale of a nap."

"Sounds like a plan." She settled into the passenger seat.

"Okay." He started the engine and fastened his seat belt. "Feel free to doze off on the way back. You've had a rough couple of days."

"That also sounds like a plan." Closing her eyes, she settled back in the shabby seat of the old truck.

\*\*\*\*

Knocking wakened Etta.

"Etta? You up to swapping cabins yet?" His voice

137

reminded her of their plan, and she scrambled up from the couch where she'd been sleeping, a quilt wrapped around her.

"Sure." She rubbed her eyes and headed for the door.

A duffle bag and a suitcase beside him, he stood on the veranda in the lengthening shadows of late afternoon, handsome and appealing as ever.

"If you're still tired…" He looked at her.

*Oh, God, how rumpled I must look.*

"No, not at all. We should get it done now. Beau may be home tomorrow." She spoke as she headed back to the couch to sit and put on her running shoes. "I'll start packing my things."

"Can I help? I've pretty much got all my stuff gathered up." He indicated the bags.

"You're either a super-fast packer or you didn't nap very long."

"I'm able to pull up stakes in a hurry. I've had lots of practice."

"I'm sure." Etta finished with tying her laces and stood. "It'll take me a few minutes to get organized. Come in and start making yourself at home."

"How about I light a fire? It's going to be a cold evening. I've got one set up in the other cabin."

\*\*\*\*

Etta was placing the last of her belongings in Travis's former cabin when she noticed two books had slid out of one of his valises. She bent and picked them up.

*Cowboy and the Heiress* and *Cowboy's Country Bride*. He'd bought two of her books. She turned them over in her hands. Page corners turned down at various places told her they'd been read.

Embarrassment rushed over her. What did he think of her stories? Had he been shooting holes in her lack of horse knowledge? No wonder he was familiar with those ridiculous glamour photos on the back covers. He'd not only seen them, he'd purchased them.

She was still holding the books when he stepped into the cabin.

"You bought my books."

"No use denying it." He waved a hand to indicate the pair in her hands as he crossed the room to add a log to the fire.

"I suppose you scoffed to your heart's content at the happily-ever-after plots?" Her chagrin at her discovery bubbled out in sarcasm. "And no doubt you discovered lots and lots of errors in my knowledge of horses and riding."

"No way." He straightened and turned to her, blue-eyed gaze intense with sincerity. "I liked both books. They leave a reader with hope that things can turn out right, that the world isn't a completely nasty, hostile place…that there's love and caring if we're willing to make the effort to look for it. Now, how about a beer? I think we deserve one after all that moving. I have a couple of cold ones over in my new digs."

"I'll take a rain check. Still lots of stuff to put away." She had to stanch the moment. He was getting far too appealing.

"I'll hold you to it." He held out a hand. "May I have my books? I haven't finished reading *Cowboy's Country Bride*. I'm hoping that cowboy has enough sense to realize what a great girl Lizzie is before she goes off with that useless Jared. Won't be able to sleep until I find out."

She handed them to him, and he headed for the door.

"Travis?"

"Yeah." He paused and swung back.

"Seriously, did you find a lot of errors when I wrote about horses and riding?"

"Nothing a bit of hands-on experience won't fix. Actually…"

"Actually what?"

"I was impressed with how well you handled those parts, given that you'd never ridden before you wrote those stories. You could fool almost anyone into thinking you were an equine expert."

"Really!" The word came out in a gush of gratitude.

"Really." He turned away. "See you later."

****

An hour later, Etta sank down on the couch in her new living quarters and heaved a sigh. What a day! She was weary to the bone. That nap hadn't been satisfying. What she needed was a good night's sleep.

Her stomach rumbled. Oh, good heavens, supper or dinner or whatever you chose to call it—she'd have to find something to make a sandwich. She didn't have the energy to do more.

"Etta?" He knocked lightly on the door. "Hungry?"

"You must be a mind reader. I was trying to conjure up a plan for dinner."

"Problem solved. Come with me."

"Travis, really, I'm too tired to go out anywhere."

*Listen to yourself, Etta Prescott. You're turning down a dinner invitation from Travis Masters? You must be weary to the point of stupidity.*

"I figured as much. I'm inviting you over to my place."

"You found time and energy to cook?"

"Come and see."

She stood and followed him. When he swung open the door of his cabin and indicated she was to precede him inside, she stepped in to a faint smell of cooking. The table was set with a pair of TV dinners and two glasses of ice water.

"Elegant, right?"

"Definitely elegant for someone as hungry as I am."

"Come on." He led the way and pulled out a chair for her. "I'm not sure how long this microwaved stuff stays hot."

*He's so comfortably unsophisticated for someone who's traveled the world, who's performed for royalty...so I've been told. Never mind that the man gives me palpitations every time he looks at me. Who wouldn't fall in love with him? Oh, God, where did that come from?*

Dismayed, she glanced across the table to where he was taking his seat.

*Thank goodness he can't read my mind.*

"Dig in." He picked up knife and fork. "Bet this is the first time you've had a date with a TV dinner and a glass of ice water."

"It is." She pushed her fork into the mashed potatoes. "It's unique."

"No doubt you're a writer." He focused his attention on the dinner. "Only a writer would come up with a word like that to describe this combo."

"Well, it is. I appreciate your thoughtfulness."

\*\*\*\*

"I *can* make coffee." He stood as they finished their food and went to the counter. "How about having it in front of the fire? Cream and sugar?" He poured two cups from the percolator.

"Black, please." She joined him to take one of the mugs before heading for the couch.

"Me too." He sank into a chair to her left. "Back home on the farm, I used to dose it. Double, double, that was me. But after a few months on the road, I started taking it black, hoping it would keep me awake. Habit stuck."

"Do you still enjoy your work?"

"Good question. Lately I've been asking myself that one a lot." He heaved a sigh and stretched out long legs toward the fire. "It was a rush at first...crowds cheering and all that. Now there're more than a few times I find myself wanting to be back home on the farm, for peace and quiet with the horses and my family."

"I'm fortunate. I'm doing what I love in the environment that suits me."

There was a silence broken by the snapping of a log in the fire. When he spoke again it was hesitantly.

"Etta, about that day at the airport in Calgary..."

"I know it looked suspicious, but as I've said, I can assure you neither Emma nor I did anything criminal. It was simply a safety precaution. I wish I could explain further, but I can't."

"So you don't trust me?" He stood and went to replenish his cup, annoyance in his words and stiff movements.

"It's not that." She fumbled about for an explanation that would satisfy him. "I can't tell you more because it's a matter of life and death that I keep it secret."

"Life and death?" He swung back to her, splashing coffee over the rim of his cup. "Whose life, whose death? Etta, is someone after you?"

"Not me." She put her mug on an end table and stood. "Not Emma. That's all I can say. I'd better go."

She headed for the door, but he caught up to her and stopped her with a hand on her arm.

"Etta, you gotta know. This is real important to me. I like you…a lot…but I can't see taking this thing any further with a big ol' secret between us…especially one that you say involves life and death."

"I have to go, Travis." The expression in his eyes wrenched at her emotions, and she had to look away. "I've said all I'm at liberty to say. Good night."

She yanked open the door and fled into the darkness that had fallen while they ate. Feeling like a genuine Cinderella, she ran to her cabin and burst inside. With her back against the closed panel, she paused for breath, disappointment and anger flooding through her.

*Frasier MacKenzie, I hope someday you'll know what you've cost me.*

\*\*\*\*

"Etta." His voice drew her from making toast and coffee the following morning. He was at her door.

"Yes?" She made no move to draw the deadbolt or open it. Last night had left her with a resolve not to further torment herself with thoughts of Travis Masters. He'd said he wasn't about to let their relationship move any further ahead without an explanation, and since she couldn't give one, that was the end of it.

"I'm thinking we could drive over to the family farm earlier than the noon pickup time Shelby gave us for Beau, maybe go riding. It's a great day, weatherwise. What say?"

She heaved an exasperated sigh and went to open the door. There he stood, over six feet of him, one sexy creature in well-fitted jeans, chambray shirt, and denim jacket.

*Hard to resist or what!*

"I thought you said you wanted nothing more to do with me until I was willing to give up my secret." She hoped she sounded and looked stern and annoyed.

"I didn't exactly say that." He looked down at the toe of his boot. "I just said we can't get in any deeper until the air is clear between us. Since you've assured me you're not an ax murderer or a master criminal, I don't see any reason we can't be friends."

She hesitated. Did she want a casual relationship with this man who made her heart host a butterfly convention, whose kiss she'd never forget, the hero of her wildest fantasies?

"It's got the makings of a great day…sunny, warm, trees turning out their best colors." He focused a blue-eyed gaze on her.

"Travis, I'm just not sure…"

"We can go on a trail ride."

The man was definitely aiming at her Achilles' heel.

"Is that toast and coffee I smell?" He leaned to one side to look past her. "Man, I could go for a bit of breakfast."

"Come on in." Hoping reluctant resignation colored her words, she moved aside to let him enter.

"And maybe a couple of eggs?"

"I guess I do owe you a meal." She headed for the refrigerator. "How about some bacon to go with it?"

"Great. I'm not much of a cook. I guess last night's supper made that clear. Lady, you need that fireplace cleaned. I'll get at it while you rustle up some breakfast."

He picked up the metal bucket placed beside the hearth. Taking out the small shovel it contained, he began to move ashes into it.

She watched him out of the corner of her eye. A warm feeling spread over her. What would it be like to have him doing domestic chores around *their* house? What would it be like to share life with him?

"Breakfast is ready," she informed him as he returned from placing the covered bucket on the veranda.

"Looks great. I'll wash up and get right to it." He headed into the bathroom as Etta put two plates of bacon, eggs, and toast on the table.

"Man, am I hungry!" He rubbed his hands together when he returned and took a seat at the table. "Those TV dinners don't do much to fill a belly."

"A belly that has probably eaten in some of the finest restaurants in North America and Europe?"

"A few." He picked up a rasher of bacon and took a bite. "Mostly it's been fast food and room service late at night. I'd almost forgotten breakfast exists. That's one of the things I miss a lot. Shelby is a great cook. We always had meals on time, too. Now I can understand why Jake had such a mixed-up gut when he came to stay with us."

"And do you have a mixed-up gut?" She avoided looking at him as she concentrated on her toast.

"Sometimes. Not as bad as Jake had, but some days I can feel it coming on."

"But you're going to keep working with your band, touring?"

"I promised Jake when I took over the group that I would. The guys need me to keep the whole circus tied together." He shrugged and took a sip of coffee. "Some things are important, and you gotta hang onto them." He stopped for a minute before continuing, "Like a watch with a ragged wristband."

"You want an explanation as to why I ended up in the field with a cranky stallion in a crazy effort to save it?"

"Would be interested." He forked into an egg.

"It's the first award I ever won for writing." She avoided his eyes and continued with her meal. "Winning it made me realize what I wanted to do with my life."

"Then well worth a risk." He stood and went to get coffee.

"Are you mocking me?" Annoyance made her words come out with a harshness.

"Hell, no." He held the pot over her cup, and she nodded for him to replenish it. "When I was twelve or thirteen, I won a plaque with a guitar on it at a local talent competition. After that, there were no holds barred. I was going to be a musician. It's still on the wall in my bedroom at the farm. Now, we'd better eat up and get on the road. This fine morning is a-wasting."

\*\*\*\*

"I'm clearing up, no arguments." Travis stood and reached for her plate when they'd finished their breakfast. "I can do that much. You go and get dressed in something you can ride in. Those sweatpants would send you sliding right out of the saddle."

His assessment of her clothing made her embarrassedly aware of the jogging outfit she'd pulled on getting up that morning with plans to write until noon, when it would be time to pick up Beau. Images of Lanie Lanson in hip-hugging jeans and plunging blouse flashed across her mind as she went into the bedroom to change.

*No wonder the man only wants friendship. Frasier MacKenzie couldn't have ruined my chances any more than my own dowdy self.*

Maybe friendship wouldn't be so bad, she thought as she selected a pair of jeans. They had enjoyed their conversation over breakfast. He'd told her about how he'd come to take over his brother-in-law's band. She'd described her time of writing for a magazine, then making the decision to follow her heart's desire and write fiction. Two people with a passion for their work, two basically shy individuals who shunned the spotlight their careers could foist upon them. Yes, friendship with Travis Masters might work.

Another thought invaded as she pulled on a T-shirt and topped it with a hoodie. Friendship could work only if she stopped drowning in his blue eyes, if only his touch didn't send her senses into a swirl.

"Don't forget your boots…Cinderella." His voice from the kitchen brought her out of her daydreams. "Running shoes won't do."

\*\*\*\*

When they arrived at the Ebony M, Travis drove straight down to the barn.

"Beau…" She gestured back toward the house.

"When Shelby says a patient will be ready at noon, she means it, and not an hour or more sooner. There's no use trying to convince her otherwise. Come on." He stopped the truck and opened his door. "I want you to meet my boy. I think you'll like him."

"Shelby pointed him out to me when I was taking a lesson."

"Pointing him out isn't like introducing him."

He led the way around the side of the barn to a wide expanse of fenced pasture. Several horses were grazing out across its width. In a rainbow of equine colors, they looked sleek, well fed and cared for.

Travis put two fingers to his lips and whistled. One of the horses, a shiny black, raised his head, shook the flowing mane on his arched neck, and looked toward them. Emitting a shrill whinny, he started toward the gate at a dead run. Etta stumbled back, away from the rail. Big and powerful, he appeared perfectly capable of either leaping the fence or crashing through it.

As the horse slid to a halt in front of them, Etta gulped.

"How are you, boy?" Travis scratched the animal's neck while it rubbed its snout against his chest. He turned to Etta. "What do you think of Mr. Midnight Brandy?"

"He's beautiful, absolutely beautiful," she breathed, staring at the pair. "But he's so big."

"About average for his kind. Look. Here comes a smaller version…and a lot better mannered."

A sorrel mare had followed the gelding across the

field at a trot. She came to a halt a few feet back from the rail.

"You must know Miss Candy pretty well by now. You've probably been riding her since your first lesson. We use her for beginners. Like that mare you rode in Calgary, she's pretty much bomb-proof."

"Candy is patient…and extremely forgiving." As the animal approached slowly, Etta reached to pat the mare.

"Hey, are you guys going riding?" Etta turned at the child's shout to see Katie Rose racing down the lane. "Can I come with you?"

"Do you mind if we take the cowgirl along?" he asked.

"No, of course not, but I haven't ridden outside the area yet. If Katie Rose comes with us, you'll have two people to watch out for."

"Come on, Aunt Etta, it will be fun." Katie Rose caught her hand and looked up at her with appealing eyes. "If you and Uncle Travis don't take me, I won't get to go all day. Mommy and Daddy are too busy, and Uncle Grady has gone to town to pick up a mare—" She paused to glance over at Travis before leaning close to Etta and continuing in a whisper, "A horse that wants to have a baby with Midnight Black."

"Little pitchers have big ears." Travis's mouth quirked at a corner. "You might also note you've gained the cowgirl's approval. You've become Aunt Etta."

"Please, please, Aunt Etta." The child tugged at her hand. "Go riding with us."

"Yeah, please, Aunt Etta." Travis's eyes appealed to her.

Midnight Brandy chose that moment to throw up his head, snort, paw, and prance.

"I don't think…"

"Don't mind him." Travis waved a hand, and the horse half reared before racing off across the field to rejoin the other horses. "He'll be a handful today. He hasn't been ridden lately. See that big albino farther back in the field? I'll take him. He's a retired movie actor and so well trained even Jake can ride him, right, Katie Rose?" He winked at her.

"Yeah, even Daddy can ride him." She chuckled.

"Well…"

"And you don't have to worry about this kid." Travis caught the child up in his arms. She squealed in delight. "She's pretty good at handling her pony." He put her down and gave her a light slap on the bottom. "Run up to the house and ask your mom if you can come with us."

As the child raced away, he shouted after her, "Tell her to call me on my cell with permission."

He turned to Etta with a wry grin. "Not that I don't trust my niece, but when it comes to going on a trail ride, she's not above pushing the truth."

"You've got a way with children."

"I wouldn't be too sure about that. Most of my experience has been with Katie Rose, and I'm thinking she might be one of a kind."

Chapter Ten

Later, riding at a careful walk down a trail behind the barn on the docile Candy, Etta let the absolute happiness of the moment envelop her. Deciduous trees were turning their autumn hues of red, gold, and orange, the cool air fresh and clear with not a cloud in the sky. Ahead, on a white horse no less, rode the man of her fantasies. The day would have been perfect except for Travis's understandable inability to trust her.

"Uncle Travis, show Aunt Etta your house." Katie Rose's voice broke in on her musings as they came to a fork in the trail, the one leading off to the left gouged with the marks of heavy equipment.

*A house back here, what must be a half mile from the farm buildings?*

"I don't think a log cabin would interest her, Katie Rose." Travis shrugged off the child's suggestion.

He was building a cabin? A holiday getaway, perhaps? Curiosity brought out her response.

"I'd like to see it…that is, if it's okay with you."

"Okay." He turned the albino to the left.

"Yehaw!" Katie Rose slapped her heels against her pony's sides to send it into a shambling trot by her uncle.

"Katie Rose, behave." Travis's words were a mild reprimand. "If you're pitched onto your bottom, your parents will never let me take you riding again."

151

"Be cool, Uncle Travis." She laughed as she passed him. "Remember you said I ride like my mother."

"I said…" He urged his horse ahead to block her path. "I said," he repeated once they were both stopped, "you'll probably ride like your mother some day."

"Aw!"

"Now get back into your place in line. Remember I'm the boss of this trail ride."

"Okay, okay." Holding her pony stopped until Travis had resumed his position in the lead, the child glanced back at Etta and gave a resigned shrug. Etta suppressed a smile. Precocious should have been her middle name, not Rose.

Shortly, the trail opened into a clearing. As Candy carried her into it, Etta experienced a rush of astonishment. Reining in beside Travis and Katie Rose, she stared at the most impressive log house she'd ever seen. Log cabin indeed! Close to a hundred feet in length, two-storied, with a wide veranda stretching across its entire front and along both sides, it stood in a stand of mixed coniferous and deciduous trees. Fieldstone chimneys jutted from its roof. The structure faced a brook gurgling over and around rocks.

"Oh, my!" Etta breathed her awe.

"I knew she'd like it." Katie Rose jumped to the ground and held up a hand to Etta. "Come on, Aunt Etta. Climb down. You've got to see the inside."

"Do you mind?" Etta looked over at Travis. "I have the feeling this is something private and special."

"It is, sort of, but now that we're here…" He shrugged and dismounted. "Do you need a hand?"

"No, thanks, I'll manage." As she swung her leg over Candy's rump and bumped to the ground, his half-heartedness in sharing his house with her sent a chill coiling around her heart.

*He didn't invite me here. Katie Rose put him in a position where a refusal would be awkward and inhospitable. This place is obviously special to him. He's probably built it with a plan to share it with someone equally special. Someone who isn't me.*

Yet as they walked toward the house, she couldn't help enthusing, "This place is gorgeous. I bet it's that way in every season. Just enough evergreens to keep it from being bare in winter, leafy trees for shade in summer and autumn. That brook is the ideal finishing touch."

"You think?" He looked down at her as they reached the steps. Something she saw as appreciation brightened his eyes.

"I think."

"Okay, come on in."

\*\*\*\*

Inside, all was rustic log walls and oak floors. The kitchen area to the right had sparkling white appliances and an array of hardwood cupboards and shiny countertops. The remainder of the big space lay fallow except for a huge fieldstone fireplace along the left wall. Above, an open gallery ran around the back of the structure, with doors opening off it. Their booted footsteps echoed in the emptiness.

"Haven't gotten around to buying furniture yet. I don't have any expertise…or taste, I'm guessing."

"I have an idea!" Katie Rose danced around the room. "Marry Aunt Etta, Uncle Travis, and she'll help you pick out chairs and tables and stuff. I bet she'd be really good at it."

Heat rushed up Etta's neck. *Oh, God, in another second my face will be beet red!*

The next moment she stifled a chuckle. Travis had colored also.

"Come on, come on!" Katie Rose skipped up the half-log steps to the second story. "There're tons of bedrooms up here, and a couple of bathrooms, and a balcony on one, and"—she broke off as she cavorted along the railed gallery—"lots and lots of room for kids to play."

"Too bad that kid doesn't say what's on her mind." Travis shook his head.

"She's precious."

"She wants another kid for company." He started across the room toward the stairs. "She's been tormenting her parents to get her a baby brother or sister. Jake, joking around, told her maybe she should convince her Uncle Travis to get married so he'd have a baby for her. Ever since then, she's been on a mission." He paused at the bottom of the steps and swept out an arm to indicate the way. "Want to go up?"

"Of course."

The second floor, although devoid of furnishings aside from two fully equipped bathrooms, was equally empty. Four large bedrooms had wide windows that looked out into a beautiful forested area at the rear.

"It's amazing, Travis, absolutely amazing."

"I like it."

"Come on, come on!" At the far left end of the upper story, Katie Rose was holding open the door to what appeared to be a fifth bedroom. "This will be Uncle Travis's." She danced inside.

"Do you mind?" Etta looked up at him.

"Would it matter? Katie Rose has put herself in charge of this tour."

"Oh, my!" Stepping into the room, Etta gazed around.

Seeming vast, with its lack of furniture, the space was flooded with sunlight from garden doors that looked out onto a wide balcony across the end of the house. Another wide window faced toward the brook at the front of the house. The rear wall housed a fieldstone fireplace. To the right of it, an opened door revealed a bathroom larger than the previous two.

"Come and see the view." He threw open the doors and stepped out onto the balcony.

She followed him. From that vantage point, she could look out toward the brook on her left or back into the variegated colors of the trees to her right. Straight ahead, through the branches of evergreens, the trail leading to the house could be seen.

"Perfect."

"Glad you like it."

"Who wouldn't?"

"Uncle Travis, Uncle Travis!" Katie Rose burst in on the moment. "There's a whole family of rabbits out back. I saw them from the bathroom window in the second bedroom. I had to go in there to…you know. Come on, come on! Maybe we can catch one of them!"

"Katie Rose, you know better than that." He quieted her as she tugged at his hand. "You know it's not right or safe to capture wild rabbits. They wouldn't be happy in a cage. We'll take a look at them, and that's it. Understood?"

"If you say so, Uncle Travis." The words came with a defeated sigh. "But"—she brightened quickly—

"come and look. They're sooooo cute."

"No help for it," Travis said over his shoulder as he allowed his niece to tug him from the room. "She's obsessed with babies and rabbits."

Etta followed the pair into one of the bathrooms off a bedroom down the gallery, and they all peered out at the rabbit family.

"They're adorable, aren't they, Aunt Etta?" The child looked up her, blue eyes wide with joy. "I do love babies, don't you?" She gave Travis, standing beside them, a nudge and jerked her head toward Etta.

****

Back at the barn, Etta helped Travis put the horses away while Katie Rose worked on Pretty. Travis finished first and went to assist the child. When the horses were in their stalls and they started up to the house, Katie Rose broke into song, one of her father's hits, as she skipped along beside them.

"Pretty fine, cowgirl." Travis patted her on a shoulder. "Just don't get any ideas about going into the business. I think your mom has had her fill of country singers."

"Guess she has." The child stopped singing. "Not to worry, Uncle Travis. I plan to be a world class rider, then a vet like Mommy."

"Good for you. She'll be pleased."

At the house, they found Shelby sitting at the kitchen table, a cup by her right hand.

"Tea?" she invited as they entered. "I felt the need of something comforting this morning, and Jake is working at the school."

"Problem?" Travis went to take two mugs from the cupboard. "Patient?"

"Major failure." She rolled her eyes at Katie Rose.

"Did you lose someone, Mommy?" The child went to put a hand on her mother's shoulder, her voice soft with a sympathetic perception that amazed Etta. Truly an astonishing child. "Sorry." Katie Rose bundled her mother as best she could into her arms.

"Thank you, angel." Shelby allowed her daughter to hold her for a moment; then, blinking, she held her out at arms' length. "Now run upstairs and wash your hands so you can have some cookies and milk."

"Sure." The child started to move away, then turned back to whisper so audibly in her parent's ear there was no way the others could avoid hearing, "I got Uncle Travis to take Aunt Etta to the log house like you said I should. She really liked it. I did good, huh?"

Silence. Shelby glanced first at Travis, who stood holding two cups, then to Etta, who'd taken the teapot from the stove.

"Oh, oh." Katie Rose pulled a wry face as she glanced around at the adults. "Guess I'll go wash up." She scuttled out of the kitchen toward the stairs.

"Well." Shelby stood and watched her hands run down the front of her jeans. "You'll be eager to see Beau, Etta. He's well enough to go home today."

"Wonderful."

"You can go ahead to the surgery. I want to set out Katie Rose's milk. She has a habit of slopping it all over the place if she pours it herself."

"Okay."

As Etta paused in the living room to remove her hoodie, she overheard Travis hiss at his sister, "Stop matchmaking, understand?" She heard the kitchen door slam.

\*\*\*\*

"I forgot it was locked." Shelby joined Etta outside the surgery door and applied a key. "I don't want Katie Rose going in without me. She loves the animals, but as you can understand, it's not always a safe place for her. At the moment, a rabbit is one of my patients, so with her fetish for bunnies, I have to be extremely cautious."

"Of course."

"Etta, I'm sorry." Shelby paused before entering the facility to look at her. "I shouldn't have used my daughter to promote a romance between you and Travis. It's just that Emma and I feel you two are so perfect for each other, and we want you to be happy. I thought your seeing the log house would inspire you to visions of sharing it with my brother."

"I appreciate your thoughts and efforts, Shelby, but Travis has declared his desire to remain friends and nothing more. Anyhow, I'm sure he has someone in mind to share that beautiful house with him."

"Actually, my brother did a cart-before-the-horse thing in constructing it." She pushed open the door and strode inside. "He's always had a dream of having a log house out by that brook, so when his finances made it possible to build, he did. Finding someone to share it with apparently will come later in his plans. Now let's go and get your dog. He's doing well."

\*\* \*\* \*\* \*\*

Etta paused to draw a deep breath before she started up the steps to Travis's cabin as another spectacular sunset over the lake was being eclipsed by dark clouds. She'd never invited a man to dinner, and now here she was making her first attempt on country music's number one singing sensation.

In an attempt to reconcile her move, she thought back to his help when Beau had disappeared and then turned up injured. He'd also taken her riding on two, possibly three occasions if you counted their first encounter in Calgary. Furthermore, he'd already made dinner…of a sort…for her.

*I do owe him big time. Look at it this way, Etta Prescott. The worst he can do is refuse and leave Beau and me to eat beef stew for days on end. But…*

Remembrance of his ordering his sister to stop matchmaking flooded over her.

*He doesn't want anything to do with me. This definitely is a bad idea.*

She started to retreat but was stopped when Travis stepped out onto the veranda.

*Too late.*

"'Evening," he said. "Looks like we're in for rain…or snow. Were you coming over for a visit? Perfect timing. I was about to sit down to a beer."

"Actually, I want to invite you to dinner. Travis"— she looked up at him—"if you haven't already eaten or made something, would you like to come over for supper? I made a huge pot of beef stew. Beau and I will be eating it for a week if we don't have help. And"— she hurried on, not wanting him to misconstrue her invitation—"I'd like to do something for you since you were so kind and helpful when Beau had his crisis."

"Hey, that sounds great. I was about to pull another frozen dinner from the freezer. Give me a minute to wash up, and I'll be right over."

He turned back into his cabin. She headed back to hers, her heart beating a trembling tattoo.

*I'm a mass of weird feelings where that man is*

*concerned. And there's no basis for it. There's nothing between us…not really.*

Busily trying to convince herself that such was the case, she entered her cabin and looked at the table she'd carefully set for two. Much as she struggled to shove them aside, memories of that ride in the moonlight on an Alberta ranch and a stellar kiss in soft shadows held her in a thrall of nervous anticipation.

She rubbed damp palms up and down the thighs of her jeans.

*At least I didn't make the mistake of dressing up, of making this appear to be anything more than a casual dinner for a friend.*

A knock on her door made her jump.

*He's here. Oh, God, why did I invite him? He's a superstar. Travis Masters! I must have been crazy.*

She squared her shoulders and smoothed her white shirt. *There's no going back now. Breathe deep, smile, and answer the door.*

"Hi," she greeted him. "Come in."

"Thanks." He stepped inside, and she saw he was still wearing his usual garb of jeans and plaid shirt. *Good. He hasn't dressed up either.* He held out a six-pack. "I know I should bring wine, but this is all I have."

"Beer is fine." She took it from him and indicated chairs and the couch by the hearth. "Have a seat. It's turning cool. I lighted a fire. Dinner will be ready shortly, but we have time for a drink."

"Sounds like a plan." He bent to pat Beau, who had waddled forward to greet him, tail whirling. "How are you, guy? You're looking good…except for that bandage on your hind leg." He looked over at Etta.

"You took the cone off? Shelby put it on to keep him from tearing at the dressing."

"I know." She took two beers from the carton and placed the remaining four in the fridge. "But he was so miserable, I removed it. He's been a good boy. He hasn't touched the bandages."

"Just be careful. He doesn't need any more medical emergencies."

"I will." She uncapped the bottles and handed one to him. He took a seat on the couch, while she sat down in a chair to his left.

Beau jumped his front paws up beside Travis, tail still expressing his joy at the visitor.

"Okay if the guy gets up beside me?" He looked over at Etta. "No hard and fast rules about no dogs on furniture?"

"Definitely not. Beau and I spend most evenings curled up there together."

"Just you and Beau? No gentleman callers?"

Startled by his question as he hoisted Beau up beside him and avoided her eyes, she didn't answer immediately.

"Sorry." He straightened as Beau snuggled up next to him, leaning his weight against the man's shoulder. "None of my business."

"Probably not." From somewhere she managed to regain her composure sufficiently to reply with what she hoped was recognizable nonchalance. "But no, it's just Beau and I. Sometimes Emma comes to visit. Excuse me." She stood hastily. "I have to check on dinner."

\*\*\*\*

"That was a great supper…dinner, I mean." Travis

set aside his coffee cup as Etta removed the plates that had held their dessert of lemon pie. "Country boy in me still has dinner at noon and supper in the evening. The stew was terrific, and that pie...I never tasted a lemon pie like it."

"It's made from scratch with actual lemons." Etta put the last of the dishes into the washer. "Thanks for the appreciation."

"I wish you'd let me help clean up. I should be helping out some way, after you cooked that fine meal."

"You can put another log on the fire. I think we're in for a cold, wet night. I hear the wind rising, and rain is hitting the windows."

"A dark and stormy night." He stood and moved to do as she requested. "I'm a big fan of Charlie Brown...Snoopy in particular."

"As am I. That beagle does spout some funny stuff and even a bit of sound philosophy at times."

"You gotta love that hound." He put a log on the fire and turned to Beau, who'd jumped off the couch to follow close on his heels. "And this one, too." He bent to rub the dog's long ears, making the basset moan in pure pleasure.

*He even likes my dog. And my dog adores him. How much more irresistible can the man get?*

Struggling to get off that train of thought, she indicated the coffeepot.

"Another coffee...by the fire?"

"Thanks, but I'd better head back to my place. I just had an idea for a new song. I need to get a handle on it before it slips away."

"I understand. It's the same with my stories. Sometimes a scene bursts over me, and I have to capture it before it can escape."

"Good, you understand. Thanks for a great meal…and the company." He headed for the door but stopped abruptly, his hand on the knob. When he turned back to her his expression snatched her breath.

Long strides brought him back. He pulled her into his arms. The next moment she was reliving all the ecstasy of that kiss in the moonlight on an Alberta ranch…and more. This time there was something else, something deeper. This time she was kissing a man she knew and liked, not a fantasy. His arms around her, his mouth over hers, his tongue caressing her lips, seeking gentle admission. His body against hers, strong and hard, sent waves of eroticism engulfing her from head to toe.

As suddenly as it had begun, it was over. Releasing her to rub his hands down his thighs, he backed away.

"Well"—he paused—"I should be going. Better get back to my place before the rain gets worse…or I lose the inspiration for that song. Good night and thanks again for a great supper…dinner."

He opened the door on the darkness of a night alive with wind and rain. And paused. "Etta?"

"Yes?"

In two strides he was with her again, taking her into his arms and kissing her with a passion that swept her out of reality.

"Etta, I'd like to stay the night." He breathed the words against her hair.

"Travis…"

"Your decision, darlin'. If it's not what you want, if…"

She didn't reply. Instead she gazed up at him for a

moment. Then she took his hand and led him into her bedroom.

\*\*\*\*

Etta rinsed conditioner from her hair and found she was humming, actually humming, one of Travis's hits. She smiled into the water cascading down over her and marveled. The wonderful reality of the night kept her floating on a cloud of utter happiness.

She'd just spent the night with the man of her dreams, corny as that sounded. And Travis Masters had proven all she'd imagined in her wildest fantasies. The best lover she'd ever dreamed up to be the hero of one of her books. Only now that lover had become reality. He was actually in the kitchen, singing and frying up their breakfast.

*Let Emma top this!*

She turned off the water and stepped out of the shower. Still humming she grabbed a large bath towel and began to rub herself dry. Sunshine flooded in through the window. It was going to be a glorious day. As she dressed, she recalled the intimate conversation that had followed their passionate lovemaking, that had kept them awake until dawn.

He'd told her of his parents' work helping people in remote regions of Africa, teaching farmers how to raise and tend livestock. He explained about their deaths during a tribal war, how Shelby had hidden them both until their father's brother, Jack Masters, had arrived to rescue them and bring them back to his farm, the Ebony M. Jack and his wife Jane had become their parents.

Jane had died the year Shelby entered university, but Jack had insisted she continue her studies to fulfill her dream of becoming a vet. The year Shelby graduated, Jack had been killed in an accident. Shelby had had to take over running the farm and raising a fifteen-year-old boy, while establishing her veterinary practice.

He told how Jake had come to the family farm for riding lessons, how he and Shelby had fallen in love, how Jake had wanted to quit the band to be with her, and how Annie Wyse had allowed Travis to take over from him.

After some hesitation, he went on to explain how all the band members had been in trouble with the law until Jordan had taken them into his group, how they'd been discovered by Annie Wyse while she was on vacation to PEI, and how first Jordan and then himself with Lili and Joe Farrah's help had taken on the responsibility of seeing they got into no further trouble. He told her about Paulie and his drug problems and how what had happened in New York had been the main reason for the band taking a hiatus until things were sorted out.

She'd had no idea his early life had been anything other than a peaceful, bucolic one. As he talked, she'd laced his fingers into his and leaned her head against his chest. Her life story, the one she shared with him later, sounded tame and idyllic by comparison. Raised by loving parents in Ottawa, one of three children—her brother Andrew, known as Drew, being the third— she'd gone to school and studied journalism at college before going to work on a national magazine. Later she'd resigned to write romance fiction, and the rest he knew.

"So no deep, dark secrets?" She'd felt his hand

tighten around hers.

"Not a single one. Sorry."

"Etta…"

Fearing he was about to ask more questions about the incident at the Calgary airport, she silenced him with a kiss.

**\*\*\*\***

They were enjoying a second cup of coffee on Etta's veranda when the sound of an approaching vehicle made them turn toward the trail. A black Jeep appeared out of the tree-lined lane and came to a stop behind Travis's truck.

"Ah, damn!" Hot annoyance surging through him, Travis watched Lanie Lanson get out.

*The woman has one rotten sense of timing.*

"So here you are." She swaggered toward him in her skin-tight jeans and cowboy boots, a denim jacket over her red tank top. "And you have company. My, my, do my eyes deceive me, or isn't that the little fugitive from the Calgary airport, the one with a double police escort? Travis, sweetie, what have you gotten yourself into?"

"How did you find me?" Anger tightened a knot in his gut.

"Well, as you might recall I told you, baby, my daddy was a woodsman—hunter, trapper, fisherman. He taught me a few tricks about how to track down prey. All you have to do is watch and wait, he used to say. I managed to follow you to Carleton. It wasn't all that hard. Plane reservations and the like. I went out to your family's farm, but that sister of yours is one stubborn gal. She wasn't about to give you away. In fact, she told me you'd gone off somewhere to relax. So

I hung around town for a few days. I had a gut feeling you were in the vicinity and that you'd have to surface for supplies. And guess what. You did. The rest is obvious."

"So what is it you want?"

"I want to know when you'll be getting your game on again. I want to know when I can start planning for Europe. I want a hard and fast contract for a duo with you on your next album."

"First of all, I have no idea when I'll get my game on again." He rubbed the heel of his hand over his forehead. "Right now, that European tour is next to never happening. As for us singing a duo on the next album—no way. You and I have voices that blend about as well as a crow and a rooster trying to harmonize."

"You backwoods bastard! You're the one that kept Annie from agreeing to represent me. You're the one who…"

"Lanie, Annie Wyse handpicks her clients, no influence accepted. You're an okay vocalist, but you're no show stopper, and you for sure don't fit in with our band. We're down-home country. You're sex on the hoof."

"So you're saying I'm too hot?" Instantly her outrage turned into purring cat. She swaggered up the steps to stand inches in front of him and reached out a long-nailed finger to run it along his jaw.

"Put a stopper in it, Lanie." He jerked away. "I'm not interested."

"Oh, and just why not? Have you turned into some kind of hermit? Don't tell me"—she put her hands on her hips, feet planted shoulder-width apart—"it's her"—she narrowed her eyes to give Etta a nasty stare—"Miss Dowdy, wearing a baggy jogging suit, for God's sake!"

"Not every woman feels the need to flaunt her wares, Lanie." *My blood pressure has to be topping out.*

"You used to like it when I did, sweetie." She glanced over at Etta with narrowed eyes.

"What are you talking about?" Only his sister's painstaking tutoring on being a gentleman kept him from yelling for her to get the hell out of here. That kind of language wouldn't do in front of Etta.

"Wonderful! Deny those hot nights in Calgary! I'll be leaving!" She swung away. "But first I need to use your facility. Is it indoors, or will I have to head around back?"

"It's indoors…over there." He jerked his head to indicate his cabin. As Lanie Lanson swaggered away, he glanced at Etta. She gave him a look he interpreted as a mix of hurt and disappointment, stood, and went inside. Beau got to his paws, stretched, gave Travis a disdainful glance, and waddled after her. The basset paused at the screen door that had swung shut and howled for admittance.

*Great! Now even her dog hates me!*

Chapter Eleven

"I'm going." As she flounced past him, Lanie Lanson gave him a parting shot. "Bastard! I'll make you pay for this!"

"I don't doubt you'll give it your best shot." He watched as she headed for her vehicle. "But if you're half as clever as you think you are, you won't. Don't go burning too many bridges, lady. You never know when I might get my game on again and you can make use of me."

"Argh!" She swung into her vehicle and peeled off down the trail.

*Now, damage control…if I can manage it.*

He turned to the door and wondered if he'd be admitted. Maybe if he howled like Beau she'd take pity on him.

*Man, I am desperate!*

"Nice lady, right?" Travis stood looking through the screen. The sound of Lanie Lanson's vehicle gunning down the trail was fading.

"You apparently thought so in Calgary." She made no move to invite him in. "When did you romance her? Before or after we went riding at the Turner ranch?"

"Aw, come on, Etta, you can't seriously think that her and me…"

"Are or were Country Couple of the Year? I read the magazine article. She all but announced your engagement...at the very least, a steaming hot romance."

"I can't believe you read trash like that!"

"I do when someone I like...liked is on the cover."

"You can't seriously be jealous of Lanie Lanson." *Bugger all! I knew that trashy story would come back to bite me big time.* "Does she strike you as my type?"

"I didn't think so...until now." She crossed the room and shut the inside door.

\*\*\*\*

"Etta!" Her name was a bellow as she slid the bolt into place, then leaned her forehead against it. She couldn't compete with a confident, sexy creature like Lanie Lanson, and she wasn't about to try. If that was the type of woman Travis enjoyed, then let him have her. Etta Prescott didn't belong in the world of country music.

"Go away, Travis. Just go away!"

Silence. Then the sound of his booted footsteps leaving.

Something in her chest pained. Too much fried breakfast? Or heartbreak?

She dropped to her knees to take Beau into her arms.

"She called me dowdy, Beau," she said. "You heard her. She was right. I'm plain and dowdy. How a man like Travis Masters ever gave me a second look, I'll never know. Well"—she pushed herself to her feet and drew a deep breath—"there's only one cure."

She went to her computer and began to type.

\*\*\*\*

Back in his cabin, Travis slammed the door shut. Damn Lanie Lanson! Just when he and Etta had had that great night together. His thoughts ran back to those hours. The sex had been great, hot and fulfilling, but there had been more, so much more.

In those hours of darkness just before dawn, after their passions had been satiated, she'd lain with her head on his shoulder, their fingers intertwined as they'd shared their thoughts, the stories of their pasts. Well, sort of. Etta hadn't confided an explanation about those armed guards escorting her onto a plane. Sinking into a chair by the hearth, he groaned.

Probably he'd been a fool to let last night happen. But damn, he'd wanted it to, wanted Etta Prescott like he'd never wanted any other woman. Last night, after the loving, after those moments of amazing passion, in the soft darkness just before dawn, he'd felt a closeness, a bond that was warm and comfortable, that made it easy to share thoughts and memories.

Still she hadn't gone so far as to explain the airport incident.

As more thoughts invaded his mind, he rubbed his forehead with the heel of his hand. Maybe Lanie's intervention had been a sign that he shouldn't get further involved with Etta Prescott. Eventually he'd have to go back to his band, back out on the road, and that would be the end of any future plans he had involving her.

*Snap out of it, man. Remember, she's made it clear she's not about to tell you the truth about having an armed escort in Calgary. So let it go. We had one hot, one really hot night, and that's it.*

He snapped on a lamp. Another rainstorm was moving in. He headed for the fireplace and hunkered down to build a fire. As he readied paper, kindling, and split logs, the coldness of the room sent a shiver wafting over him. After he'd thrown a match into the mix, he stood, hands on his hips, and watched the flames leap up into the chill air.

*Damned empty and lonely. Maybe I should get a dog. Maybe... Forget it, man. Get on with nailing down that song that's running around in your head.*

He crossed the room and took up his guitar from where it had been resting against a far wall. Sitting down in a chair by the fire, he strummed it, at first randomly, then with purpose as a tune and words entered his mind.

It didn't take long for him to realize the song was for and about only one woman. Etta Prescott had become what Shelby would have called his muse.

*Damn it!*

\*\*\*\*

With a grunt, he pulled himself out of bed. Daylight was peering in at the window, and he hadn't slept more than three or four hours. He'd worked on that song until well after midnight. Afterwards, in bed, he'd been troubled beyond sleep by memories of Etta Prescott in the cabin only yards away, and the previous night of passion they'd shared.

With a guffaw, he headed into the bathroom and a hot shower. As the water cascaded down over him, he found he was humming the song he'd composed the previous night: "When you give me one of those lovin' looks, I know happily ever after isn't only in your books."

As he finished the final verse, he decided the ballad was the best thing he'd ever written. Not that he did a lot of composing. He left most of that to Paulie. Only occasionally did he try his hand. And only when, like last night, he felt an overwhelming desire to capture his feelings in song.

*That woman is getting to me big time! I never wrote a song for one before. Scratch that. There was Jenny Miller in Grade Ten. And it was a pretty lame effort. No wonder she never dated me.*

He stepped out of the shower and grabbed a towel. As he rubbed himself dry with a vigor that threatened to chafe him raw, he came to a decision. It was no use. He couldn't put the woman out of his head. There was only one thing he could do. He had to find out the truth about her, discover whatever secret she and her sister were hiding. But how?

He needed someone with whom he could talk. His sister wouldn't do. Maybe Jake could help. He was one smart guy, and he could trust him to keep quiet.

Another thought hit him. When the Ebony M's stallion Midnight Black had been stolen, Jake had hired a detective agency. He'd get the name from his brother-in-law, contact them, and let their agents find out the truth about Etta.

Twenty minutes later, he climbed into the old farm truck and hoped the engine would start halfway quietly. He needed to get away from Loon Lake without another encounter with Etta.

The aged vehicle had other ideas. It roared to life with the vigor of a steamroller.

"Damn!"

Glancing apprehensively toward Etta's cabin, he was relieved to see no sign of life. He shifted into gear and drove away.

****

He had to pass through Carleton to get to the Ebony M. As he did, he realized it was probably too early to pay a social call at the farm. The residents would be busy with morning chores. The town's favorite coffee shop caught his eye. He could use a cup, strong and black, before he sought Jake's advice.

Inside, he purchased a large and took a seat in the sunshine near the front window. He'd barely sat down when a woman he recalled with no fond memories appeared outside. Spotting him, she waved and bustled into the shop.

"Travis Masters, as I live and breathe!" Mildred Carter, whom he remembered as his math teacher years ago in high school, confronted him, ample bust thrust forward in a jacket that threatened to burst its buttons, thick glasses perched on her snub nose. "I haven't seen you in years."

"Nice to see you, Miss Carter." Travis, mindful of his manners, stood.

"My, my, you haven't changed much." She peered at him critically. "Maybe filled out a bit, but still the same boy I recall having all kinds of difficulty with Grade Twelve math. We have a lot of catching up to do. I'll get a coffee and join you."

As she scuttled off toward the counter, Travis stifled a groan and sank back into his seat. The woman hadn't lost her ability to order him around or make him ill at ease.

A few minutes later, she was sitting down opposite him. "You've become quite the celebrity, I understand. Traveling the world with your little group. Of course, I don't listen to country music—I prefer classical—but apparently there are a lot of people who do. I expect you never were exposed to Mozart or his likes, what with being brought up by your sister out on that farm. She did her best, I suppose, but she had her hands full with starting her animal doctoring business and being without any mature person to guide the pair of you. I've always said it was no wonder you made such a poor showing in mathematics and that you ended up in a career such as yours with no college degree or anything to recommend you for a secure position."

"Shelby did a great job of bringing me up after our aunt and uncle died." Even though the woman had lost little of her ability to cow him, he couldn't sit by and let her demean Shelby. "It wasn't easy for her, setting up her veterinary practice, running a farm, and raising a teenage boy on her own."

"Oh, I'm not saying that it was. But then she ended up marrying that singer…Jordan Brooks or whatever his stage name was. Not the best choice, in my opinion. People like him have gypsy blood. I'm expecting to hear any day that he's left her to go back on the road playing music."

"I doubt it, Miss Carter. Shelby and Jake have been together for over six years now. They have a daughter."

"Time will tell." She sipped her coffee before continuing, "We've had a few unorthodox marriages around here of late. There's the guidance counselor at our school, for instance, claiming she married that fellow with whom she was living up at Loon Lake last year. Supposed to be an assistant professor of biology at the provincial university. I've checked with the university. No one was willing to confirm or deny that he works for the institution.

"And no one, mind you, no one from our staff was

invited to the wedding. They wanted it to be quiet, Emma said, but really! Why? Now he's gone, disappeared like a puff of smoke. It makes one wonder if there ever was a legal marriage." She pursed thin lips, shaking her head in a display of sad acceptance.

Travis had been about to excuse himself and get away from the woman's nasty tirade, but the mention of Etta's sister and her absentee husband changed his mind. This gossipy woman offered an opportunity to find out more about Etta, or her family at least.

"You know Emma well?"

"I know her and her kind all too well." The woman sniffed and settled back in her seat. "Let me tell you, she's not the angel most of the staff and students think she is. Rumor has it she and her so-called husband were instrumental in getting our physical education teacher, Mr. Brock, arrested for trafficking drugs, never mind that she broke poor Mr. Worth's heart."

"Mr. Worth, the English teacher?"

"You remember him. A dear, quiet man who loves the Lake poets. He used to read poems to Emma every time she sat down to lunch in the cafeteria. Then she up and married this so-called associate professor. I can tell you, Mr. Worth was shattered by her duplicity."

"Did Emma give him reason to think there was something between them?"

"What else was the poor man to assume, with her hanging on his every word as he read, putting his heart into every line."

"Maybe Mr. Worth misinterpreted kindness for interest on Emma's part." Travis had to suppress a grin as he imagined the balding, bespectacled little man reading poetry while Emma listened, quite probably to avoid hurting his feelings. "That doesn't seem to be much of a black mark against her."

"Possibly not to a man who has lived the life you have, with hordes of women running after you and leaving a string of broken hearts in your wake, but for a sensitive person like Brandon Worth, such a rejection was shattering."

"I hardly see Emma being to blame." He finished his coffee and started to stand.

*Leaving a string of broken hearts in my wake? Where does this woman come up with her ideas?*

"You haven't heard the worst. She and that sister of hers, her so-called twin, although there's barely a family resemblance, have been involved with male dancers…exotic male dancers."

"Yeah?" She regained his interest. He dropped back into his seat.

"Oh, yes. Last fall Emma had what is called these days a bachelorette party, up at one of the cabins at Loon Lake, for another teacher, and she hired a…dancer…from the local male dance hall."

"I think that's par for the course with such shindigs, Miss Carter. I don't see what this has to do with her twin."

"I'm getting there." She shoved her glasses up her nose and peered over at Travis. "This spring, before Emma supposedly got married, her sister held another such party up at the infamous place. She hired the same exotic dancer…Roc Hard. I learned his name from some of the female teachers who attended."

"Roc Hard?" Travis couldn't prevent his lips from curling at the corners.

"Yes. He's apparently become friends with both

sisters. I've seen them having lunch with him right here in this coffee shop. I don't know why Thomas Pentland tolerates such goings on."

"Thomas Pentland? Mr. Pentland? He's still principal at Carleton High?"

"Yes, he is, and mostly doing a fine job...except when it comes to his ability to put up with behaviors such as Emma Prescott's...and her sister. Do you know this Etta person writes romance novels? Probably the kind young girls keep hidden under their pillows and read with a flashlight late at night unbeknownst to their parents."

"I've read a couple, Miss Carter, and, believe me, there would be no need for anyone to feel guilty about reading them. Now, I have to go. Thanks for the update. Say hello to Mr. Pentland and Mr. Worth for me."

"I feel I must warn you further." The woman drew herself up indignantly at his abrupt departure. "Beware of that nasty little dog of Emma's. It's the most flatulent creature I've ever encountered. Every time I go near him, he breaks wind in the most embarrassing and unpleasant manner."

"I'll keep it in mind." Travis rubbed a hand over his mouth and strode out of the restaurant before a chuckle overwhelmed him.

****

Travis drove into the yard of Ebony M Farm and stopped. Jake was sitting on the veranda, strumming his guitar. After the storm of the previous night, it was a beautiful autumn morning, everything fresh, newly washed by the rain.

*Looks as if Jake is alone. Great.*

"'Morning, Jake." He went to join him and

dropped into a wicker chair that sat next to his brother-in-law's. "Not often I find you all by your lonesome."

"No, not often. Shelby and Katie Rose are off to some kind of kiddie thing at the playground in Carleton, Grady is working with a new mare that got delivered last evening, and I'm having a Saturday morning to myself. Coffee? I think there's still some in the pot."

"No, thanks. What I need is some information."

"Oh, yes?" Jake laid his guitar aside. "Since you're well past the age for the birds-and-bees talk, I haven't a clue what you can possibly want from me…except maybe something to do with the band. Are the boys all okay?" The last sentence came out sharp with concern.

"Yeah, sure."

"Well, then, what?"

"It's about Etta." He leaned forward to stare down at his hands as he rubbed them together between his spread knees.

"Go on."

"It's like this, Jake." He straightened up to face his brother-in-law and dove into telling him about the incident in the Calgary airport, about Etta's reticence to explain.

"Now you're finding yourself getting serious about this woman of mystery and don't know how to proceed," Jake finished his story.

"Yeah, well…yeah." He squinted over at his companion in the morning sunlight flooding the veranda. " 'Getting' is past, after the other night. More like 'am.' "

"O…kay." Jake settled back to be an attentive listener.

"Yeah."

"So?"

"Later we talked about our lives, growing up, all that kind of stuff."

"Definitely more than a one-night stand."

"Definitely. Even before that, Etta and I had been getting to know each other, to like each other. Jake, I'm not into casual sex—recreational sex, some of the guys call it. Maybe for a while, back five or six years, when I was caught up in the craziness of concerts and the like, I might have been…a bit. But that kind of stuff is pretty empty, right?"

"Right. Sorry, I'm not catching the problem. You like her, I'm assuming she likes you. What's wrong? Sounds as if you're either falling in love with Etta Prescott or you're already there. Good for you!" He reached across to slap Travis on the back.

"It's not that simple. This morning Lanie Lanson showed up."

"What did she want?"

"Promises of a contract for the European tour and a record deal, neither of which she's likely to get if Annie Wyse has anything to say about it."

"I assume you told her as much and sent her on her way."

"Not so simple as that. She got really steamed and started talking about the hot times we had in Calgary…in front of Etta. None of which was true."

"What happened?"

"Pretty much what you'd guess. Etta has locked herself in her cabin and refuses to speak to me. And it gets worse. This morning, I found out a few things about Etta and her twin that threw another curve into the relationship. I was talking to Miss Carter…Mildred

Carter. You probably know her from working at Carleton High."

"Oohhhh, yes." Jake dragged out the words. "Otherwise known as Nasty Gossip Central. What has the oh-so-righteous Mildred been telling you?"

Travis told him.

"Damn it, Travis, if you're going to let Mildred Carter's innuendoes turn you off, you're not ready for a serious relationship with Etta. You don't deserve to have one."

"Don't go getting your tail in a knot. The stuff about the bachelorette parties was crazy. I imagine most brides-to-be would be disappointed if their friends didn't throw one for them. It's the airport thing that's driving me nuts."

"Why should that concern you so much?" Jake stood and went to perch a hip on the veranda railing. He looked squarely at his brother-in-law. "Etta's told you neither she nor Emma have done anything criminal. Loving someone means you have to have faith in them, trust them."

"You're saying I have to get over myself, right?"

"That's step number one. Then you have to get her to listen to you, to get her to understand there's nothing going on between you and this Lanie woman, never was…was there?" He raised an eyebrow as he looked over at Travis.

"No. Hell, no."

"Well, then you need a reliable witness to substantiate the fact. Not one of the band members. Etta would think they were sticking up for you. What about Lili? No one could doubt that woman."

"I'll think about it."

"As for any nasty innuendoes about Emma, I can tell you, from firsthand knowledge, she and Associate Professor Frasier MacKenzie did an excellent job busting Brock for trafficking drugs to students in our high school. As a result, I'd be inclined to think those officers were escorting Emma for protection. Drug connections reach right across this country, you know. The RCMP may have gotten a tip that she was in danger."

"Could be, but a bit far out, don't you think.? I've been around deceptive women too long to be able to shove suspicions aside without proof." He hesitated before continuing more slowly, cautiously, "That's why I've come to you. Remember when we lost Midnight Black and you hired a detective agency…?"

"Aw, come on, Travis. You can't seriously be thinking of having Etta investigated!"

"Jake, I'm getting in pretty deep with her. I have to know. Now, will you give me the name of that detective agency, or do I have to start looking though yellow pages for some guys I know nothing about? Most are probably creeps who are ex-cops fired from the force for behavior 'unbecoming an officer of the law.' "

"The Transcontinental Detective Agency." With a resigned shrug, Jake gave out the information. "They're highly reputable but also damned expensive. You're sure about this, are you, brother? Because if she ever finds out…"

"I'm sure. Thanks, Jake."

"Listen, Travis, for the record, I think this is a bad idea, a real deal breaker." Jake stared down the road to the highway. "Furthermore, I see no good reason for it. I know her twin sister. We work together with troubled teens at the high school." He swung back on Travis. "I can't believe anyone in Emma's family could be anything but upright and decent."

"Emma's supposed to be married, right? To this Frasier MacKenzie?" Travis wasn't about to let it go easily.

"Yes. What do you mean 'supposed' to be married?"

"Well, not many people in Carleton have seen this guy. None, actually, as far as I can find out, since Emma and he hooked up. He's vanished without a trace."

"Not vanished." Jake went back to his chair. "He's a professor of biology with the provincial university. According to Emma, he was sent off to investigate the effect of global warming on wildlife in Canada's far north."

"And this newly married guy hasn't been home in nearly a year? Come on, Jake. If I was married to someone like Emma Prescott, MacKenzie, or whatever her name is, I'd be getting back here as regular as clockwork."

"Apparently it's not easy for him to leave the place where he's working."

"Yeah, well, Mildred Carter tells a different story. She said a lot of people think there's something fishy about the way Professor MacKenzie vanished. They're saying he never really married her, that he made a promise just to get her in the sack and then took off."

"All rumor and gossip, but if you feel hiring a detective to check Etta out will quell your worries, go for it. Only don't say I didn't warn you if this backfires and you end up losing one fantastic lady."

\*\*\*\*

"Etta?" The voice of her editor, as always, gave her a mental start. Although she'd been doing well with her stories, she lived in latent dread of her next one not hitting the mark with critical Alesha Coin.

"Hi, Alesha. Did you get the three chapters and summary I e-mailed to you yesterday?"

"Definitely. And, Etta?"

"Yes?" *Relax, Etta, relax.*

"I must say, this has the makings of being the best thing you've done so far. Your hero is so flesh and blood, I'd know him anywhere."

"Really?" Butterflies of delight fluttered. "He's a new creation. I wasn't sure if you'd go for the idea."

"What woman wouldn't. Etta?" Alesha's voice became soft, inquisitive. "Is he based on someone you've met? He seems all too human to be a mere product of your imagination."

"As a matter of fact…"

"Never mind. You don't have to confess anything to me. Just keep this guy going for seventy thousand words or more, holding in mind I see him as a character in a series."

"Wonderful. Thanks, Alesha."

"And, Etta, if this man is real, if he's in your life, take my advice and don't let him get away. Contact me when you have the finished product."

"Of course. Thanks, Alesha. Bye for now."

Etta dropped the phone on her desk, leaned back, and closed her eyes. What a relief! She'd most definitely been venturing into untried territory with this new hero, this shy country boy with gorgeous blue eyes, a killer grin, and the manners of a gentleman. She was thankful Alesha had liked him. Etta didn't know if she could have abandoned him, at this point, to write about any more devil-may-care cowboys.

The sound of Travis's old truck coming up the road brought her back to the moment and trepidations. She didn't want to see him…but she did…no, she definitely didn't want anything more to do with this man who didn't trust her, who lived among women like Lanie Lanson. Agitated by indecision, she stood and began to pace. Beau, stretched out on the rug in front of the hearth, raised his head to cast his hound eyes on her.

"I know, I know, I'm driving you crazy, but I'm in a turmoil."

The truck stopped in front of the cabin next door. A few seconds later, the vehicle's door slammed shut. She heard his booted footsteps pounding up to the veranda and then another door shutting as he apparently went inside.

She plunked down in a chair by the fire and put her face in her hands. He hadn't tried to see her, hadn't tried to further explain.

Reasonably, why would he? He'd given it his best shot after that woman had left. Besides, he didn't need someone like Etta Prescott playing hard-to-get when he had any number of beautiful women ready and willing to have him no matter what. He was moving on, and she had no one to blame but herself.

Well, that wasn't entirely true. There was Frasier MacKenzie.

She heard another vehicle coming up the trail. Going to the window, she saw not one but two cars bearing the RCMP logos drive up in front of the cabins and stop. Two uniformed officers got out of the second vehicle. Another stepped out of the driver's side of the first.

She caught her breath as an officer held open the back door and a fourth man emerged. Dressed in rumpled clothes, tangled dark hair curling below his ears, and a stubble disguising his face, he paused to look around the area and out over the lake.

*Frasier MacKenzie! Good God, what is he doing here?*

"Okay, let's get on with it." One of the uniformed officers jerked his head for Frasier to move toward the cabins. "We didn't bring you along just for the ride."

*Oh, God! It can't be! Not some kind of undercover sting. Not with Travis…and Frasier involved.*

****

A half hour later, with Beau by her side, she watched from her veranda as Travis, handcuffed, was brought out of his cabin. Behind him, one of the uniformed officers carried his guitar case.

*Oh, my God! What's happening?*

Travis glanced over at her, his look so dark, it struck a knife through Etta's heart.

*Surely he can't be blaming me! Surely he can't be equating this with what he saw at the Calgary airport…*

"Move along." One of the officers urged him toward the rear door of one of the cars. "We haven't got all day. Miss?" He turned to her. "I think you'd be wise to move away from here. This man had enough drugs in his guitar case to supply a rock band for a major concert."

"No, that can't be right! I know him. He wouldn't…" Her words were jumbling.

"Take my word for it. The man's a dealer." He

returned his attention to his prisoner. "Come on, get in."

Travis gave her one more dark look before following the man's urging.

"Travis, you've got to believe me!" She ran to the window of police car. "I don't know what's going on! I have no idea…"

"Save it," he snapped. He focused on the grille in front of him.

The officer climbed back into the driver's seat. Frasier hesitated before getting into the other police car. She thought she saw something like regret in those blue eyes her sister found so irresistible—as many women did—when he glanced over at her.

"Go on, get in," an officer snapped. "You've served your purpose, but we're not about to let you go gallivanting off into the trees."

Frasier was responsible! He'd somehow managed to get it to appear Travis was involved with drugs. Was this some kind of revenge for her being Emma's accomplice in Calgary? No, that would be just too crazy. But why?

As the vehicle turned and headed down the trail, Beau threw back his head and howled.

Anger suffused pain as she watched the vehicles disappear into the trees. How she'd kept from screaming at Frasier MacKenzie, how she'd kept from "blowing his cover," as her sister had termed it, she didn't know. Her loyalty to her twin and her twin's spouse had to be ridiculously overwhelming.

\*\*\*\*

"Emma!" Etta pounded on the door of her sister's Carleton apartment. "Emma!"

"I'm coming, I'm coming," her sister's voice

responded. "Don't break it down!"

"Emma, it's awful, unbelievable." The moment the door opened, Etta burst inside, Beau waddling behind her.

"What's awful?" Emma caught her by an arm and drew her to the living room couch. "Calm down and tell me."

"Your husband and a bunch of his RCMP buddies came up to the cabin this morning and arrested Travis!" she blurted. "They said they found drugs in his guitar case. They suggested he might be trafficking…"

"Etta, try to slow down. Take deep breaths. Now tell me in the most coherent way you can."

\*\*\*\*

"And that's the whole story." A half hour later, Etta, clutching a mug, leaned back on the couch and closed her eyes. Emma had paused her part way through her narrative to provide cups of strong, black coffee for them both.

"Etta, I'm so sorry." Emma's words were soft and comforting. "Good God, what could Frasier be thinking? What…?"

"Emma, don't go blaming your husband." She opened her eyes. "As I'm calming down, I realize he was only doing his duty. He doesn't know Travis personally. I'm guessing that traveling music groups often fall suspect when it comes to drugs. Frasier must have gotten a tip from someone…" Her voice trailed off, an idea forming.

"Etta, what are you thinking? I know that look. You've either hit on a great scene for one of your books or you've had a giant epiphany. Tell me."

"Lanie Lanson. She came up to the cabin to try to

convince Travis to promise to take her to Europe with his band, to force him to sign a contract with him for their next album. When he refused, she flew into a rage."

"But if you both witnessed her tirade, both were with her all the time…"

"That's just it, Emma! We weren't. She said she needed to use the facility, as she called it, and went into Travis's cabin alone. She would have had time to plant those drugs."

"Etta, you can't really believe the woman would be that nasty, that vindictive."

"Yes, oh, yes, I can." Etta stood and began to pace, clutching the mug. "You didn't see her, hear the things she threatened." She rounded on her sister. "She even called me dowdy."

"Dowdy! The nerve! But she must be crazy, to try to get Travis arrested for trafficking."

"As I've said, musicians, especially the itinerant ones, often fall suspect for the activity."

"Hard rock and the like." Emma stood and began to pace the room, coffee cup clutched in her hands. "Not country groups…at least, not ones like Travis's."

"Emma, all the members of Travis's band have criminal records. When they were teens, Jake, who was a teacher at their school, got them released into his custody to form the band. Travis told me their songwriter Paulie has a history of drug abuse."

"But they're reformed…all of them. Frasier can't go chasing after them for a past they've put behind them." Bruiser, on the floor beside Beau, howled in response to his mistress's raised tones. Beau uttered a muffled grunt.

"It's his job." Being with her sister, hearing her twin raving about the injustice of what had happened, calmed Etta. Emma was, as always, on her side.

"Never mind all that." Emma plunked herself down into a chair. "Right now we have to concentrate on getting your man out of jail."

"Oh, God, Emma, don't make this sound like a country ballad. It's deadly serious. And he's not my man. As for getting him out of jail, I'm sure he's got his manager and agent Annie Wyse working on it already. He told me she was a practicing lawyer before she got into the music business."

"Wait until I change." Emma stood. "Then we'll head out to the RCMP detachment in town...that's where the jail is. We shouldn't have any trouble getting information when we tell them we're family."

"Emma, we're not family." Etta made an attempt to protest as her sister disappeared into the bedroom. Drawers and doors banged.

"You will be soon, if you play your cards right." Her twin, in sexy panties and bra, glanced briefly out at her. "Now..." She vanished into the room again. "What to wear. Do I want Frasier...on the off chance he's at the detachment...to see me as desperately sad or wildly sexy? Hmmm!"

*This visit to the police department has the earmarks of a bad movie, but there's no stopping Emma when she's in full rescue mode. I can only keep my fingers crossed we don't end up incarcerated as well.*

"Beau, you stay here with Bruiser." She looked down at her dog sitting beside Bruiser in front of the electric fireplace. "If my sister and I get arrested, I'll make sure some kind people from the SPCA rescue you both and send you to Ottawa to live with our parents."

Beau's head dropped to his chest, his ears trailing on the carpet. Bruiser's curly tail straightened.

Chapter Twelve

Emma came out of the bedroom, dressed in a navy pantsuit, hair pulled back into a bun at the back of her neck.

"What's with the getup? You look as if you're ready to do battle in a courtroom."

"I've decided this isn't a time for eye candy. We're heading into a legal battle. Here"—she pulled off her diamond engagement ring—"hold out your left hand."

"What…?" Etta tried to pull back as Emma determinedly shoved it on her third finger.

"Keep it there. We may need it." She grabbed the briefcase she used for school files. "And this will give me an official look."

\*\*\*\*

"We demand to see Travis Masters!" Emma stood outside the bulletproof glass at the Carleton RCMP detachment and barked the words at the desk officer.

"Good morning, miss." The man looked up at her, his countenance undisturbed by the outburst.

*Training, training. Probably Emma is one of the less threatening people the man has to deal with in the course of his shift.*

"Yes, yes, good morning." Emma rushed through the pleasantries. "We want to see Travis Masters."

"I'm afraid we can't give out information about individuals." Again the placid calm.

"I understand not to just anyone, but this is his fiancée." She grasped Etta's left hand to display the diamond ring.

"Engaged?" The man stood and leaned toward the glass to get a better look.

"Yes, engaged. They're going to be married in a couple of days. So you see, it's imperative you release him. The man has a lot to do."

"Sorry, miss. There's no way…"

"What in hell is going on here?" Annie Wyse, looking even more official than Emma in a gray pantsuit and her signature six-inch heels, swept into the detachment office, briefcase in hand.

"And you would be?" As unruffled as he had been by Emma's demands, the desk officer queried.

"I'm Ann Wyse, Travis Masters' attorney." She ignored the two women. "He called me."

"Ah, yes." He looked down at the paperwork in front of him. "I'll let the officer in charge of the case know you're here." He picked up a phone.

"Miss Wyse?" Stepping forward, Emma took advantage of the moment. "I'm Emma Prescott-MacKenzie and this is my sister Etta. She and Travis have a relationship…"

"Oh, my God!" The agent's words came out in a breathed expletive as sunlight glinting in the window fell on the ring on Etta's hand and set it sparkling. "He didn't! The fool!"

"Fool!" Emma snapped back. "Don't you dare brand my future brother-in-law a fool! He and Etta are in love! They're planning to get married…soon."

"Emma, please!" Etta hissed.

"Are they, now?" Annie Wyse turned to face the

woman, eyes narrowing. "Well, then I hope they've based their plans on his having a lot less income. His fans won't tolerate a married man. He'll be finished."

"Miss Wyse?" The officer interrupted her tirade as he put down the phone. "You'll have to wait. Mr. Masters is being interrogated at the moment."

"He has a right to have his attorney present."

"Not in this case, I'm afraid. A judge has issued an order making an exception." He waved a paper.

"Let me see that!"

"Sorry, miss, it's confidential."

"I just bet it is. No judge has the power to issue such an order."

"I'm afraid one just did. Now if you'll take a seat…"

"Argh!" The woman strode across the waiting room and plunked down onto one of the hard plastic chairs. "What a merry mess this is. And you two are to blame!"

**\*\*\*\***

"Travis Masters?" In a small, windowless room at the rear of the detachment, the scruffy-looking man who'd been with the officers at the cabin stood from where he'd been sitting on one of two plastic chairs, the only furnishings. In the light of a single bulb high in the ceiling, he looked even more disreputable than he had out at Loon Lake.

"Yeah." Travis stood with his back to the door and heard a lock click behind him.

"Frasier MacKenzie." He held out his right hand.

"What…?"

"Sergeant Frasier MacKenzie. Emma's husband. Have a seat." His introduction ignored, the man swung his arm to indicate a chair that faced the one he'd vacated.

Travis remained where he was. *What in hell is going on here?*

"I know this must come as a shock to you." The man who'd introduced himself as Emma's husband resumed his seat. "If you'll sit down, I'll explain. Yes, damn it." His tone changed to one of angry annoyance. "Sit down. I've put myself in jeopardy to do this, and by God, you'll listen."

Moving as if hypnotized, Travis did as the man ordered.

*Is this some kind of crazy dream? Have I really been arrested, handcuffed, and now thrown into a room with a guy who looks like a back alley bum but declares himself Emma Prescott's husband?*

"You're really married to Emma?" Travis found his power of speech returning as he faced the man's grim expression.

"God help me, I am." He heaved a sigh before continuing. "Now to business. We don't have long. You have to swear you'll never reveal that fact or any of what I'm about to tell you. I'm putting my life on the line here."

"Yeah, well…"

"Swear?"

Travis met the man's clear, blue-eyed gaze and hesitated. Finally he drew a deep breath and muttered, "Swear."

"Good, because you can't even imagine the viciousness of the people I work among. There are no holds barred when it comes to doing violence to anyone who endangers them. They also have a nasty way of wreaking vengeance on family and friends of anyone they perceive as standing in their way. Remembering those facts should serve to keep your mouth shut."

"That's one big, nasty threat."

"Not a threat, a statement of fact."

"Fine. My mouth is zipped. But you referred to yourself as Sergeant." Travis was still struggling to come to grips with the situation. "I was told you were a professor of biology, off somewhere in the far north…"

"Now you know that's not true. You're being let in on highly confidential information, and I'm trusting you'll keep this strictly to yourself. Here's the major fact: I'm an undercover cop, working on drug trafficking."

"What! No shit?"

"Definitely no shit."

"But how…?"

"Long story short, when I was in university, I became a member of a rock band that later was known as The Sound."

"Yeah?" Mesmerized by all that had happened and now this man, Travis sat and stared at his companion. "I remember them. Hard rock, tough guys."

"Not as tough as we should have been. Our lead singer got into drugs, big time. One night I found him dead in a pool of vomit in our hotel room."

"Jesus." Thoughts of Paulie rushed to mind.

"My father, an RCMP inspector, got the news and hauled me out of the band. I was damned bitter about Larry's death, so he found it easy to recruit me into the force as an undercover drug squad officer. I was on assignment, posing as a biology professor up at Loon Lake, when I met Emma. We discovered a drug stash.

As a result, we both were very nearly killed by traffickers. Now you can understand why I'm so dead set on not involving her in any further operations."

"Man, you're walking one narrow tightrope." Impressed, Travis stared over at Frasier MacKenzie.

"Emma came close to blowing my cover when she tracked me to Calgary this past summer. I had a couple of members of the force escort her and Etta to the plane to make certain she wouldn't further insert herself into my life at that point. My wife is something of a handful, as you probably know. I've been told you witnessed this bit of damage control and that it caused major trouble between you and Etta."

"But why are you telling me all this now?" Travis, still suffering from a sense of unreality, could barely form coherent questions.

"Because my wife has threatened to track me down wherever I go, possibly blowing my cover, which would also endanger her life, if I didn't confide in you, if I didn't let you know the truth about Etta and that incident at the airport." He rubbed his forehead, his shoulders lifting in a deep intake of breath. "I know she's perfectly capable of doing it. But she didn't stop there. She called my mother." He looked up at Travis, a sheepish grin on his face.

"Your mother?"

"Sounds crazy, doesn't it? But my mother can be one determined lady…and my father's only known Achilles heel. Emma's aware of the fact. Add to this that she and Emma are thick as thieves, to use a hackneyed expression, and you'll understand why my wife chose this first line of attack. When Emma told her about you and Etta, about how my work was ruining your relationship, she...my mother...turned on Dad. Ordered him, in fact, to let you in on the truth. Of course, he refused. It caused a major rift in the family, I can tell you."

"Sorry."

"Don't be. This isn't the first storm my parents have weathered, and it won't be the last." A small smile curled a corner of his mouth. "If all turns out well, I'm thinking they'll be off on another of their makeup honeymoons."

"So how did all this happen?" Travis waved a hand to indicate the austere room.

"I don't know how well you know my wife, but she can be one charming, convincing creature when she wants something, especially from men. When she believed my mother's efforts had failed, she turned on my father. He told her there was nothing he could do. Unbeknownst to her or my mother, however, he had you investigated from the day you were born. Deciding you were squeaky clean, he arranged this complicated arrangement for us to meet."

"Hell and damnation!"

"Yes, hell and damnation." He stood. "Now I have to get back to work...that is, get a judge to release me on a suspended sentence. Don't make me have taken this risk in vain, Masters. Get down on one knee as soon as possible and ask that woman to marry you."

"But what about you? Are you ever going to get out of this line of work? Seems like you and Emma aren't having much of a marriage."

"I promised my father another year. Then someone else can take over, sleeping in filthy hotel rooms, never being able to relax. Emma wants us to build a house down the shore road on the waterfront between your farm and the old Turner place. And…"

"And?"

"She wants to have a family. There's no way that can happen while I'm doing this job. It's hard enough worrying about Emma and even her Pug, never mind a baby. Now, remember—keep all this to yourself, or there may not be a someday for Emma and me."

"Swear on the Bible."

"Good man."

"Just one question. All that shit about finding drugs in the lining of my guitar case…was it planted as an excuse to bring me in here?"

"Lanie Lanson, as she calls herself, is one of us. She put the stuff in your cabin. Travelling around with your band gave her a perfect cover to watch for drug dealers. She's not much of a singer, but she is one hell of an agent."

"So that's why she's been trying so hard to stay with my guys, so anxious not to be dropped."

"Another secret for you to shove out of your mind." Sergeant Frasier MacKenzie went to the door and rapped three times. It swung open and a uniformed officer reached inside to grab Frasier MacKenzie by an arm to hustle him out into the corridor.

"Come on." He snapped handcuffs on the man's wrists. "The judge is waiting."

"Take it easy, buddy." Back in character, Sergeant MacKenzie smirked over his shoulder at Travis. "Good luck on getting away from these bastards."

"Get going." The officer nudged him, and Frasier MacKenzie moved away.

\*\*\*\*

"Of all the stupid stunts!" Annie Wyse's anger burst as the three women left the RCMP detachment with Travis an hour later. "Getting yourself caught with drugs! I still don't know how they came to drop the charges. I thought they had you dead bang, that Paulie had hid the stuff in your guitar case. Travis, do you have any idea how much damage control I would've had to do to fix this mess? Thank God no reporters got wind of it, that there wasn't a crowd of paparazzi ready to confront us!"

"In Carleton?" Travis smirked. "You've got to be kidding. The town has one weekly newspaper. Jim Waters, who owns it, is reporter, editor, and publisher. He wouldn't have time to come out to snap a picture of a local boy charged with possession of a bit of marijuana."

"But it wasn't marijuana, was it?" She grabbed his arm to halt him. "It was hard stuff. I'm heading down to Nova Scotia to give Paulie one hell of a calling down. He's got to smarten up or you'll have to dump him, Travis."

"Dump the guy responsible for most of our hits? Come on, Annie."

"Well, anyhow, I'm off. Try to keep your nose clean, will you, sweetie?" True to her mercurial personality, Annie raised on tiptoe to kiss his cheek before turning and striding off toward her rented vehicle.

"I won't be needing this any longer." Etta removed Emma's ring from her finger and passed it to her sister.

"No, you won't." Travis caught Etta by a hand. "On to the next order of business. Too bad it has to be fast. I have to get to Nova Scotia and protect Paulie from the dragon lady."

"But can't that couple who travel with you do that…Lili and Joe?"

"Not like I can. I sign the contracts and the checks. Emma"—he turned to her sister—"will you let me have a few minutes alone with Etta?"

"Oh, sure, of course." Emma winked at her twin. "I'll be in the coffee shop."

"Travis, Emma is my ride…" She glanced at her rapidly retreating sister.

"Just give me a minute, will you?"

"Okay, a minute."

"Etta, I know this is the wrong place." Travis glanced around the RCMP parking lot. "But it won't wait until I get back." He dropped on one knee, still holding her hand. "Etta Prescott, will you marry me?"

"What…Travis…" She stared down at him.

"I love you, Etta, and I'm hoping you feel the same about me. So what about it?"

"Travis, get up." She glanced at a pair of officers exiting the building behind them. They grinned at the couple as they proceeded to their vehicles. "People are staring."

"Let them. Come on, Etta, give me an answer."

She paused. For a moment he thought she was about to refuse. Could he really blame her, with all those suspicions he'd let muddy their relationship?

"Yes, Travis Masters, I'll marry you."

He shot to his feet and pulled her into a passionate kiss.

*Hot damn! Etta is going to marry me.*

The officers, driving past, honked their horns.

"Travis." Their good-natured approval broke the

spell. She pulled back to look up into his face. "Are you sure about this?"

"The possibility of a long incarceration made me realize any of the stuff that had come between us was a drop in the bucket." He had to come up with a reason that didn't include his meeting with Sergeant Frasier MacKenzie. "The idea of being separated from you for God only knew how long made me realize that if I got out of the mess I was in, I had to make my move as soon as ever I got to see you again. Come on. No time to waste. Annie ignores the speed limit when she's on a mission."

"Where are we going?" She had to trot to keep up with his long strides as he started down the town's main street, gripping her hand.

"You'll see."

\*\*\*\*

A half hour later, Etta Prescott stood in the parking lot of a rent-a-car facility, staring down at the diamond glittering in the ring on her finger while Travis went inside the office to sign up for a vehicle. She still couldn't accept the reality of being pulled down Carleton's main street and into the town's jewelry store, where Travis had asked to see their finest diamond rings. Ten minutes later she was wearing one of them.

*I'm engaged to Travis Masters! This has to be a dream, some kind of crazy dream.*

But when he came toward her, the pleased grin he wore told her she was wide awake and the tingling happiness coursing through her was justified.

"I've got to go." He led her over to a gleaming four-by-four truck. "But when I get back, I'll be in full courting mode. And I do plan to court you, Miss Etta

Prescott, just like one of those guys in your books."

"Travis…" She looked up at him.

"Kiss me again, woman, and wish me safe journey." He took her into his arms.

"But what about clothes and things? You haven't got anything…"

"There are stores in Nova Scotia." He kissed the tip of her nose. "I'll shop. I'll be back just as soon as I can. Now, take care."

He climbed into the truck, closed the door, and put the window down.

"Aren't you going to give me a real kiss before you leave?" Etta looked up at him.

"Hey, I'm one tough guy, but not that tough. One more of your hot kisses, and I won't be able to go. Take care, darlin'. I'll be back soon."

Etta waved and watched as he drove away. When he had disappeared from view, she turned and ran toward the coffee shop, heart pounding. She had to find Emma, to share this intense happiness that had overtaken her in the space of less than an hour.

As she paused at an intersection to let a truck pass, she noticed a gray car moving slowly along the street behind her. Where had she seen it before? Yesterday? The day before? Was it following her?

*Ridiculous.* Carleton was a small town. It was highly probable to encounter the same car more than once within its boundaries. Eager to share her news with her sister, she brushed the thought aside.

\*\*\*\*

"Etta, this is wonderful!" Back in her apartment, Emma cranked at the cork of a bottle of white wine. "Definitely something to celebrate. And to think I engineered it all!"

"What do you mean 'engineered it all'?" Etta caught up her sister's remark.

"Oh…you know…the trip to Calgary…invitation to that ranch party, et cetera." She kept her back to her sister as she replied.

"Not to mention nearly ruining it due to your escapade with Frasier that resulted in that police escort to the airport."

"Oh, well, that." She poured wine into two glasses and swung back to her sister, one in each hand. "A minor glitch in the road to romance. Here. I've been saving this for a special occasion."

"Then shouldn't you keep it for Frasier's release from his present duties?" Etta accepted a glass as Emma sank down beside her on the couch.

"At some time in the unforeseeable future? Etta, I'm so weary of keeping secrets, of being married to a ghost. When I informed Frasier I'd told you about his work, he had a major snit. But I've never been able to keep anything from you. Twins are like that. He should know." She sipped her wine.

"But he's promised in a year or so…"

"Yes, yes, in a year…or so."

The discouragement in her normally exuberant sister's voice tore at Etta's heart. Being married to her hero wasn't turning out to be all Emma Prescott-MacKenzie had thought it would be. And now that she'd had time to reflect, Etta wondered about her own future with the number one country music star. He'd said he was on a break. What would happen when he went back on the road with women like Lanie Lanson? Had she been too hasty in accepting his proposal?

\*\*\*\*

"Hi, darlin'." Travis's voice over her cell sent a thrill of joy coursing through her.

"Travis, hi. Where are you?"

"At Joe and Lil's. Paulie has moved out to their guest house, and I'm staying there with him for a bit. He's having a tough time, what with not being able to take pain meds because of his addiction. Add to this the fact that Annie showed up almost the same time I did. Her pressuring him to straighten up and get back to writing hit songs didn't help."

"Travis, I'm so sorry."

"She and I had a major blowout...I'm glad Shelby couldn't hear it. I wasn't much of a gentleman, I can tell you. Bottom line, Annie stormed off with a bee in her blonde head. In spite of all this, I'm not so sure she won't be back to torture Paulie, or that she won't tackle the other guys in the band. They've rented a cottage here in Yarmouth."

"That woman is unbelievable." Etta caught a pause in his narrative to give a response.

"So you can see Paulie, not to mention the other guys, need support. I can't expect Lil and Joe to do it all. I owe Paulie big time for all those great songs, never mind that he's my friend. So it looks like I might not be getting home for a while. I'll have to play it by ear. Sorry, darlin'."

"Don't be. I understand. There's been a threat of snow these last few days, so your sister has insisted I leave the cabin and move into the guest room at the farm. I've packed up all our stuff, both yours and mine, and now I'm here at the Ebony M."

"Hey, that's great. I was getting worried about the

weather up there. Now listen, Etta, will you do something for me?"

"Certainly, if I can. What is it?"

"Will you start furnishing the log house? I'd like it ready for folks to enjoy at Christmas. Shelby has my Visa number. Charge everything you need to it, right down to bedding, dishes, and towels. Pick what you want, what will make you comfortable and happy. Remember, it'll be our home…soon."

That final word brought questions and concerns gushing into her mind.

"Soon?"

"We'll talk about that later, darlin'. Right now, my major concern is Paulie. If you're willing to get the house set up for Christmas, that will be a big issue off my mind. Are you willing to do it? I know Shelby will help you."

"Of course." *Stop crossing bridges before you come to them, Etta Prescott. The man said "soon." Let that satisfy you for now.* "Do you have preferences or ideas about furniture or other things?"

"Just keep it simple country."

"Got it. That suits both the house and me right down to the ground."

"Gotta go, darlin'. Paulie is having a bad turn. Love you. Talk soon."

\*\*\*\*

"Etta?" Etta recognized the agent's voice on her cell and something inside her shuddered. She didn't want to talk to Annie Wyse.

"Yes."

"Etta, I'm glad I managed to get in touch with you. I've been wanting to meet with you ever since I discovered you're Vanessa Dean. I've read a few of your books, and I think we can do business."

"Business?" Warning bells began to ring in Etta's thoughts. Travis had told her about the woman's no-holds-barred business tactics, had told her how she'd sought to manipulate Shelby and Jake.

"You've got some good stories, but the company you're currently with isn't promoting to the extent necessary to put them on a bestseller list. I can get you a deal with a major publisher who will recognize your talent and get your work moving, really moving."

*I give Annie Wyse full marks for method. If ever anyone knew how to hold the carrot of success under a nose, it's she.*

"I thought you dealt with musicians."

"I do, but I'm not opposed to taking on a rising literary talent. I definitely see you as one, Etta a.k.a. Vanessa."

"Why now? My books have been out there for a few years."

"No one introduced them to me until Travis bought a couple and I had an opportunity to read them. You're good, Etta, too good to be puddling around with a small-cheese publisher. I'm in Montreal at the moment, but once you say the word, I'll have you a lush contract in no time at all. In fact, I've already booked a flight to New York."

"Then you'd better cancel it." Although she saw a golden professional opportunity slipping away, Etta forced herself to reject it. "My current publisher has been very good to me, took me on when I was struggling to get my first manuscript published. I couldn't possibly leave the company."

A moment of silence, then: "You realize I can make your books bestsellers. You've seen what I've done for Travis Masters and, before him, Jordan Brooks. You'll be letting the chance of a lifetime slip away."

"Quite possibly, but I've heard of some of your methods, and I don't want to be a part of any of them."

"Are you still thinking you and Travis will get married and live happily ever after? Don't delude yourself, sweetie. Travis is not about to give up fame and fortune to settle down and marry some little mid-list writer. Furthermore, I don't think you really know the man. You're not the first he's charmed into bed, and you won't be the last. I'm telling you that, in spite of his innocent hometown boy appearance, Travis Masters is a musician in the big time and as much a tomcat as the worst of them. In fact, he and I had a few magic moments when he first replaced Jordan."

"Thank you for that unsolicited information." Etta's hand had begun to tremble. She wasn't a tough business woman; she wasn't a tough anything. Keeping pace with this underhanded negotiator was turning her into a heap of shivering nerves. And the mere idea of her and Travis…

"Think about it, sweetie. Your books on bestseller lists, publishers vying to contract your next effort… Here's my private cell number. Feel free to contact me at anytime."

"Etta, come on, we're going to town!" Shelby burst into her room as Annie Wyse ended her call. "We've got big plans for you!"

*Doesn't everyone!*

\*\*\*\*

"This is so premature!" Etta sat in the passenger seat of Shelby's four-by-four king cab as the vet pulled into the mall parking lot and stopped. "Buying a wedding dress when we haven't set a date, when Travis and I haven't even discussed plans…"

"It's best to be prepared, isn't it, Emma?" Shelby shut off the engine and swung toward Etta's twin in the rear seat. "I know my brother. He's not likely to give you much warning once he feels able to leave Paulie." She turned back to Etta. "I'm not about to let him whisk you off into some quickie, unplanned little ceremony. You've spent most of your time these past weeks furnishing his house from stem to stern. Now it's time you got yourself fixed up."

"Agreed." Emma's tone sounded wistful. Etta remembered that her sister and Frasier had been married quickly and quietly in Ottawa with only their immediate families present. She knew Emma had longed for a true RCMP wedding with her groom in his red serge, leaving the church to ride away on a pair of white horses. Fairytale stuff, but still Etta hoped that someday she, Etta, would be able to bring off a second wedding for her sister, the wedding of her dreams with her hero Frasier MacKenzie. In the meantime, she recognized that Emma was trying to do the same for her. She couldn't refuse to go along with her twin's well-wishing plans, no matter how premature.

"Okay, okay." Etta snapped off her seat belt and opened the door. "Let's get on with it."

"I can't believe we got away from Katie Rose," Emma said as they walked though the first light snowfall of the season toward the mall doors. "She definitely sensed something is up."

"Her dad offering to take her on a trail ride and then to McDonald's for lunch had a lot to do with it." Shelby chuckled. "It would have been a disaster to bring her along. She's adorable, if I do say so, but she can't keep a secret. She's been so gung-ho to get you and Travis married, Etta, she'd be blurting out the story of our looking at wedding dresses to anyone who would listen, my brother included."

"We plan to keep him in the dark about all of this until the last minute," Emma said. "Therefore, even if he does decide he wants to get married sooner than soon, surprise, surprise, we'll be ready."

She pulled open the shopping center door and made a mock bow. "After the bride."

\*\*\*\*

"Oh, Etta, it's positively perfect...perfect for a winter wedding!" Emma's critical gaze taking in every inch, she walked around her sister, who stood in a shimmering gown that draped softly to the floor, its satin overlaid with a cloud of glittering snowflake designs in lace that sparkled with rhinestones as she turned to view herself in the mirror.

"It is...*nice*." She felt her breath catch in her throat. Etta Prescott, wearing the fairytale-worthy dress, a matching veil cascading about her shoulders, could barely contain the thrill bubbling through her. No character from any of her stories had been more beautifully arrayed on her fictional wedding day.

"Nice! Etta Prescott, you're gorgeous!" Emma's face glowed with pleasure. "You'll positively floor the man when he sees you."

"I agree." Shelby stepped forward to adjust the delicate material at one side. "If my brother isn't already totally besotted, he will be after he sees you in this."

"It is lovely." Etta brought herself back to reality. She glanced over the dress for a price tag. "But it must cost a fortune."

"Must you always be so practical!" Emma continued to circle her sister. "It's my gift. I never got to pick out a wedding dress. Let me do this, Etta." She paused and touched her sister on the arm, her expression wistful.

"Emma…"

"Don't go feeling sorry for me." Emma brightened. "One day soon I'll glide up an aisle toward my handsome husband arrayed in full dress uniform, and we'll get married 'right and proper' as one of the characters in your books would say. Now, get yourself out of that thing and let the saleslady who's been more than patient pack it up. The next item on our agenda today is a visit to a nice restaurant for a fancy lunch."

"Fancy lunch?" Etta felt her sister's fingers beginning to release the back fastenings. "Don't you think you've spent enough already?"

"Carleton doesn't have a wide variety of eateries, and we can't risk McDonald's." Shelby removed the veil from Etta's head. "Can you imagine the uproar if we ran into Katie Rose and her father and she sensed we'd done something without her?"

"You're right, Shelby," Emma said. "There's a perfectly lovely place a few miles out of town. Frasier took me there last year for lunch. Very romantic." She sighed, her eyes taking on a soft expression of remembrance before she snapped back to the moment. "Let's go. At this time of year, seafood won't be their specialty, but beef bourguignon definitely is. Since you're worried about my spending too much, it will be your treat, sister dear."

Chapter Thirteen

"Emma, do you see that gray car behind us?" Etta looked into the truck's side mirror as they drove toward the restaurant.

"Yes." Her sister twisted to see it. "Why?"

"Nothing...that is, I may be imagining things, but I'm certain I've seen it before...several times, in fact...almost as if..."

"As if it was following you...or me. Oh, my God, Frasier wouldn't dare! Shelby, put on your emergency lights and pull over. We're going to get to the bottom of this right now."

\*\*\*\*

Emma jumped out into the swirling snowflakes and rounded the rear of the truck to step into the road, waving her hands at the following vehicle. The driver had no choice, short of running her over, but to stop. She pulled off to the shoulder behind the truck.

"What's the matter?" A tall thirty-something woman stepped out. She wore jeans, boots, and a gray quilted jacket.

"May I see your badge, officer?" Emma planted herself in the front of her, hands on her hips.

"Badge? What are you talking about?"

"I know you're an RCMP officer. You've been following me. Now I want it to stop."

"I'm not police. Is something wrong with your

vehicle? How can I help?"

"Fine. You won't admit to anything." Emma pulled out her cell. "I'm calling the local RCMP detachment and having you arrested for harassment."

"Stop." The woman put a gloved hand on Emma's arm. "Okay, I'll admit it. My cover's obviously been blown. I've been following Etta Prescott. I'm with the Transcontinental Detective Agency. We have offices across North America." She pulled out a wallet and offered her ID.

Emma examined it. She gave a rueful sigh.

"Okay, it all looks according to Hoyle. But why?"

"We were hired by a man named Travis Masters. He wanted information on Ms. Prescott."

"Travis?" His name came out in an incredulous gasp. Etta's hand flew to cover her mouth.

"Travis Masters is my brother." Shelby stepped forward, eyes bright with indignation. "He's engaged to marry Etta. He'd never do anything so despicable!"

The woman pulled out a cell phone and began to scroll down. When she found what she was looking for, she handed it to Shelby. "Here's his authorization for the surveillance."

A sinking sensation started in Etta's chest as she watched the vet's expression first become a frown, then deepen to outrage.

"What on earth could Travis have been thinking?" She thrust the phone back to its owner. "Getting a detective agency to investigate the woman he loves!"

"Let me see that." Emma grabbed the phone and examined the text. "Maybe it was before…"

"Never mind when he did this!" Doctor Masters didn't try to hide her fury. "It makes my blood boil that he'd do something so underhanded."

"It's okay, Shelby." Throughout the arguments, Etta had remained silent. "I understand his concerns. Did your agency send him a report?" She faced the detective.

"Not yet." The woman retrieved her phone and stuffed it into her jacket pocket. "So far there's been nothing to report. Apparently you, Etta Prescott, are just exactly what you appear…a nice girl."

"You'll be sending your findings on to Travis?" She faced the detective squarely.

"May as well. Now that my cover has been blown, I'll be throwing up the case. Good luck to you all." She went back to her vehicle and got into the driver's seat.

As she drove past them, she waved to the three women, a look that could be interpreted as amusement on her face.

"Damn it!" Shelby kicked a tire of her truck. "I'm that furious with my brother! Wait until I get my hands on him!"

"Shelby, it's okay." Etta touched her arm. "Maybe this was meant to be." She stopped and looked off across snowy fields.

"Meant to be? Etta Prescott, what do you mean?" Emma was quick to follow up.

"Lately I've been thinking that maybe we were a bit hasty in getting engaged, that Travis's lifestyle and mine won't merge. After Paulie is well, Travis will most likely go back on the road. His loyalty to that man and the other members of his band is blatantly obvious. He's not about to leave them on their own. Emma, I've seen how lonely you are and how desperate you are to be with your husband. I'd feel the same if I were married to Travis, but chasing him around the country, maybe even across Europe, isn't my style."

"Etta, what are you saying?" Shelby stared at her.

"I'm saying maybe we moved way too fast after he was accused of drug possession and then released, that maybe having great chemistry, and even love, isn't enough." She turned back to the truck. "I'm going to our parents' house in Ottawa. Writing in that basement apartment of theirs isn't all that bad."

****

"Etta, what is going on?" Travis's voice over her cell made her flinch. She'd been expecting this call and dreading it but knew, in fairness, she had to talk to him. "I've been going crazy, girl. You haven't been answering my calls and texts, and Shelby won't help me out. She keeps saying you've gone off somewhere to write. Finally, I got Emma to act as a go-between, to get you to take my call."

"She did what you asked. I am taking your call."

"Etta, I need a chance to explain. Don't hang up on me. Shelby tore a strip off one side of me and down the other for hiring that detective agency. I deserved that and much more."

"Travis, you don't have to explain."

"Yeah, I do. I hired those people when things first started really heating up between us, when it was getting beyond a hot physical attraction, when I saw our relationship as heading into something real serious. After my arrest, I realized I'd been a fool not to trust you, that I knew all I had to know about you. Then the trouble with Paulie started up again, and I forgot all about that damned detective agency. Etta, you gotta believe me!"

"I do, Travis. You're not the lying kind. But aside from your hiring the detective agency, I have other concerns now that I've had time to think rationally, away from you and what you've termed 'a hot physical attraction.' Your first loyalty is to your band. Your lifestyle and mine will never mesh. You're a celebrity who'll be on the road with your band for weeks, probably months at a time. I need peace and quiet to work. I'm definitely not the kind of woman who can live out of a suitcase and bounce from one hotel to another. I don't want to end up like Emma, desperately lonely for her husband. She has to manufacture elaborate schemes just to see him."

"Etta, this won't be forever. Once I'm sure the guys can find someone to replace me…"

"And when might that be, Travis? Annie Wyse was blessed with good luck when she found you to take over from your brother-in-law. That kind of thing doesn't happen over and over again."

"Etta…"

"I'm sorry, Travis, truly I'm sorry. I love you and probably always will, but I won't marry you. It won't work…for either of us."

She ended the call. She couldn't talk any longer. A lump blocked her throat.

When the phone rang seconds later, she hit mute and dropped it beside her computer. She yanked a tissue from a box beside it, blew her nose, and tried to go back to her story about a romance writer who fell in love with a country music idol. Her fingers shook.

**\*\*\*\***

"Damn it, Shelby, tell me where she is!" Travis confronted his sister in the farmhouse kitchen. "I paid the pilot of a private plane a big lump of change to get me up here as fast as possible. Now I want to see Etta."

"She made me promise not to tell." Shelby pushed past him to put a pot roast into the oven. "And I'll thank you not to swear. Katie Rose is in the living room watching videos. She doesn't need any new words added to her vocabulary."

"I love the woman, Shel." Travis caught her arm as she started to return to the counter by the sink. "I can't imagine life with her. You gotta understand. You have to. You feel that way about Jake, don't you?"

"Of course I understand. Of course I feel the same about Jake, but I can't violate a promise." She put a hand up to touch his stubbled jaw. "Trust me, Travis. If circumstances change, if she decides she can manage your lifestyle, I'll be the first to send you racing off to her."

"Okay, okay." He heaved a deep breath. "I'll join Katie Rose watching videos until supper is ready."

"Okay." His sister's eyes narrowed. "Just don't try to pump Etta's whereabouts out of your loquacious niece."

"Wouldn't think of it." Travis went to join the child on the couch in front of the television where Bugs Bunny was once again doing a number on Elmer Fudd.

"He's one smart-ass rabbit, isn't he, Uncle Travis?" She snuggled up to him, and he thought how great it would be if he and Etta had a kid like her some day.

"He sure is, but watch the language, cowgirl." He leaned down to speak softly into her ear. "Your mom has super powers when it comes to hearing."

"Right, right." She replied in the same tone.

"Have you heard from Aunt Etta lately?" Again the

below-normal tone. He glanced toward the kitchen door to make sure Shelby wasn't nearby.

"Last night." She snuggled closer against the side of his chest. "She and Mommy talk all the time."

"And you talk to her, too?"

"Sure," she replied, her attention returning to the screen. "Wow! Did you see that? Elmer near blew the tail off Bugs!"

"Katie Rose, did Aunt Etta say where she is, where she was calling from?" This time he was all-out whispering, a shaky eagerness in his voice.

"Nooo." She shook golden curls vigorously. "I asked her, Uncle Travis." She looked up at him, blue eyes round. "I figured you'd come looking for her and I'd be able to tell you, but she wouldn't say. I guess she's like Mommy and doesn't think I can keep a secret."

"Yeah, well, maybe they've got that right." Travis eased away from the child and stood. "Think I'll go for a little ride before supper. I've been missing Midnight Brandy."

"Can I come?" The mention of riding immediately took the little girl's attention from the video, and she was on her feet beside him.

"Not this time, cowgirl. It'll be dark in an hour or so, and we both know your pony is afraid to go out at night."

"He is." She heaved a sigh as she climbed back onto the couch. "But tomorrow, a trail ride…you and me, right?" She made a thumbs up at him.

"Tomorrow." He returned the gesture.

\*\*\*\*

"I'm going to take Brandy for a canter out to the

log house, Shel," he informed his sister as he crossed the kitchen. "I'll be back in lots of time for supper."

"Travis, I don't think that's a good idea." She paused in setting the table. "That gelding hasn't been ridden in weeks. He's inclined to be a handful under the best of conditions."

"He's my horse, I know him backwards and forwards." He paused to kiss her on the temple. "Remember, I'm the guy who rode a bronc in the Calgary Stampede last summer and managed to stay in the saddle."

**\*\*\*\***

"That critter ain't been rode for a good spell." Grady, retired movie horse trainer, now wrangler and jack of all trades around the Ebony M, leaned on a pitchfork and shook his head as Travis went into Midnight Brandy's stall. "He's got a torpedo's worth of energy stored up."

"Grady, this guy knows me." Travis led the gelding out into the corridor. "He won't try any of his stunts when I'm in charge."

"Well, take care, lad. He ain't winter shod yet, and there's still snow on the ground from that little fall last week." He squinted up at the ominous whiteness of the clouds. "Looks like more is on the way."

"Sure, sure."

As he fastened the big gelding in the crossties and began to saddle him, Travis ignored the horse's prancing and head shaking. When he led Midnight Brandy out into the yard and swung into the saddle, the animal half-reared.

"Easy, boy, easy. We're not out to run the Kentucky Derby."

The animal responded with a snort and an equine dance. Travis turned him down the trail to the log house and let him break into a gallop.

*Damn, but if feels good to be back home, back in the saddle with a handful of horse.*

Even at the speed Midnight Brandy was moving, Travis recognized that the road had been leveled, that it could now accommodate trucks and SUVs. Low-hung sports cars wouldn't be able to handle it. That was exactly how he wanted it and how he would endeavor to have it kept, in the same condition. With any luck, it would keep away women with penchants for such vehicles. (Annie Wyse, Michelle Layton, and Lanie Lanson sprang to mind.)

\*\*\*\*

He allowed Midnight Brandy to canter twice around the house before reining him in and dismounting at the front steps leading to the veranda. As he tied the horse to the railing, he looked the place over. It appeared exactly as his construction foreman had said, finished, with only a bit of landscaping to be done in the spring. And it would be only a bit. He wanted the natural ambience of the place to remain intact.

Long shadows stretched out from the trees as he mounted the steps to the dark-windowed house. He inserted the key into the lock, opened the door, and stepped inside. The cold of an unoccupied building in late November engulfed him.

"Welcome home, man." The words tinged with sarcasm spilled out. The place he'd planned for so long, had envisioned for years, held nothing but a near-icy chill without the woman he loved. "Damn it, Etta, where are you?"

He ran his hand along the wall until he found a light switch and flicked it.

"What the…!" He stared around.

The room had been fully furnished. Couches and chairs bearing horse motifs, pillows in their corners, with oak end and coffee tables in place near them, surrounded the fireplace, where logs and kindling were laid ready for a match. The kitchen and dining room area held a large pine table and matching chairs. Places had already been set with dishes and napkins bearing country motifs. It couldn't have been more exactly what he wanted if he'd chosen each item himself.

*Etta. She did this. She understands me right down to the ground. Damn it, I need that woman. I'll get her back even if I have to hire that detective agency again. I don't care how pissed she gets about it. Once I find her, I'll fix everything.*

Still gazing around, drinking in the perfection of it, he crossed the big, open room and went upstairs. Each of the four bedrooms had been fully furnished, right down to bedding and bathroom linen. But it was in the master suite, as he snapped on a light, that he caught his breath as he gazed around at Etta's handiwork.

A king-size pine sleigh bed, inviting with an array of pillows, had a bedcover with a print of a horse that looked amazingly like Midnight Brandy. Dressers and tables matching the bed were scattered around the room. In front of the fireplace, two overstuffed easy chairs faced the hearth. His agitated breath came out in a mist in the cold room. This was the room she'd decorated with them in mind.

Determination flooded over him.

This was the room he and Etta would be sharing.

Damn it, he'd find her. He had to.

He took the half-log pine steps two at a time as he returned to the ground floor. Outside, he locked the door and leaped over the veranda railing to gather up Midnight Brandy's reins. Come hell or high water, he'd convince his sister to reveal Etta's hideout.

The startled horse snorted and reared back as Travis sprang into the saddle. He barely noticed that it had begun to snow, that it was coming down thick and fast, as he headed for the main trail at a full gallop. He had one thought, one mission burning in his brain. He had to find Etta. He had to get her back.

As he swung his gelding sharply to the right to head back to the farmhouse, the animal's hooves slid in the snow. Shrieking, hooves flaying, Midnight Brandy went down, his rider discharged from his back.

Travis's head struck a tree. As his horse galloped off toward the barn, he lay unmoving in the deepening snow.

****

"Travis?" He returned to consciousness and to the sound of his sister's voice.

Forcing his eyes open, he tried to turn his head in its direction. A sharp pain stopped him, made him grunt.

"Take it easy, brother." Jake's voice. He and Shelby were both with him…where?

He squinted, trying to focus. He was in a bed, but not anywhere he recognized. A shadowy white room with a humming sound.

"Shel?" He succeeded in turning his head enough to see his sister's worried expression. Her husband stood behind the chair where she sat close to the bed.

"What…happened? Where am I?"

"You took a spill off Brandy." As he became aware he was hooked up to an IV, she put a cool hand on his arm. "You've got a concussion. Aside from that, you're mostly bruised and scraped."

"How…?"

"It appears, from the hoof prints at the scene of the accident, that you were going flat out when you rounded the turn from your house onto the main trail," Jake explained. "It was snowing hard, and Brandy hasn't been shod for winter. He slipped and went down, tossing you against a big ol' pine." He quirked a corner of his mouth. "So I'm not the only one that black devil has tossed on his backside. Appears he can even throw a bronc rider."

"I was distracted." He was coming back into his own, getting a handle on reality, but when he tried to move, he grimaced and stopped.

"Rest." Relief was moving over his sister's expression as she stood. "We'll leave you alone for a while, but we won't be far if you need us."

"Etta? Where's Etta?"

"Rest."

****

Travis wasn't sure how long he drifted in and out of consciousness, only vaguely aware of doctors and nurses moving him, shifting him from one position to another, their ministrations making him bite his lip to contain sounds of his discomfort.

Suddenly, he opened his eyes to a miracle.

Etta Prescott sat beside his bed.

"Etta." He breathed her name over dry lips. "You're here? For sure? I'm"—he choked—"not havin' another crazy dream?"

"No." She smiled, and his whole world brightened. "I'm here. It's not every day a man who's successfully ridden a bronc in Calgary Stampede gets tossed by his own horse. I thought it such an anomaly that I had to come."

*Teasing. She's teasing me. And looking at me with those beautiful emerald eyes.*

"And you're gonna stay?" He made an effort to draw himself further up on his pillows and flinched.

"Don't go rushing ahead, cowboy." She stood and assisted him.

"Etta, you have to. I saw what you've done with the house. It's exactly what I want, what *we* want." He caught at her arm with a bruised hand.

"Rest. We'll talk later." She bent forward to brush a kiss on his forehead below the bandages.

"Sure, sure." He closed his eyes, her presence soothing him more than any treatment or drug he'd been given since the accident. And she'd kissed him.

*Damned meds! I'm drifting off again...just when I need to talk to her.*

\*\*\*\*

"Where's Etta?" Travis, propped up on pillows, his head mainly cleared, asked his sister when she entered later in the day. He'd been moved from ICU to a private room for less critical patients. Although he still ached in what seemed like every bit of his body, he knew that meant he was on the mend.

"That's a nice greeting." Shelby bent to kiss his forehead. "No 'hi, sis'?"

"Sorry. Hi, sis. Good to see you. Now, where's Etta?"

"Travis, you have to understand…" Shelby stepped back from the bed.

"Understand? Understand what?"

"Etta only came to be with you when you were in serious condition. Now that you're out of danger…"

"Don't tell me she's gone again!"

"She had to get back to her work. She has a manuscript due…"

"Manuscript be damned!" He hoisted himself further up on his pillows and grunted. "Doesn't she know…"

"Travis, she only knows nothing has really changed in your situation." Shelby put a placating hand on his arm above the IV. "She understands your loyalty, your obligation to the band, and accepts it. She also accepts that she can't become a gypsy or spend days and weeks waiting for you to come home. She's seen too much of that kind of life through her sister."

"Yeah, well, I'll show her." His face contorted as he tried to move again. "Just as soon as I'm out of here…"

"There's also that little matter of your hiring that detective agency to spy on her."

"Aw, shit! One huge mistake. I realize it now. But you have to understand, Shel. I've been living with deceptive women for so long…Lanie, Annie, Michelle…"

"I get all that, but Etta doesn't. I think you've got a bit of explaining to do before you can entertain any expectation of winning her back."

"And I will…on bended knee."

"Okay, okay. But you'll have to wait until you're out of here. On to more immediate matters. The doctor has told us we can bring Katie Rose to visit. She's in the waiting room with Jake. I'll bring her in, if you promise to watch your language." Shelly paused before continuing more slowly, "Travis, we've cautioned her that you look different. We didn't want her to be…startled."

"Different? What do you mean?" He put a hand to the left side of his face and grimaced. "What's wrong with the way I look? Shel…"

"Calm down. Aside from a bandage around your head, you've got some bruising. We wanted her to be prepared, that's all."

"I need a mirror." His face contorting, he struggled to move higher on his pillows. "Shel, I need a mirror. You must have one in your purse, in that compact thing."

"Travis, I've never known you to be vain…"

"Now, Shel! I need to see what Etta was looking at!"

"Okay, okay, calm down." She dug in her purse. "Here."

He took the opened compact she handed to him and squinted into its small mirror.

"Ah, shit! I look like something out of a horror movie." Gingerly he turned his head to better view his entire countenance. "No wonder she left."

"Language, please. If you think Etta Prescott is going to be turned off by mere physical appearance, you don't know her at all." Shelby snatched back her property and returned it to her purse. "If you perceive her as being that shallow, then she definitely shouldn't marry you."

"Yeah, well, you just watch me." He leaned back

on his pillows. "I'm going to get that woman back if it's the last thing I do."

"Travis, Etta's leaving again had nothing to do with your appearance, and you know it." She hesitated.

"Okay, Shel, let's have the rest of it. I know you too well not to recognize when you're hiding something."

"If you must know, that high powered agent of yours called her. She tried to do what in essence was bribe her away from you. She promised her a contract with a major publisher and huge promotions for her books if she agreed never to see you again."

"Ah, hell!" Travis slumped against his pillows. "The woman is a witch, and no doubt about it. She never stops stirring her cauldron of tricks."

"Cauldron?" Shelby cast him a skeptical look. "Sounds like something from Shakespeare...from one of the plays I tried to interest you in to make your way through high school. Good to see some of it sank in."

"Etta didn't take her up on it, did she? No, of course she didn't. Etta is a whole lot smarter than I am. She knows not to get involved with that woman."

****

Travis leaned back in the recliner in the farmhouse living room and heaved a sigh. It was great to be back home, away from hospital smells and regimentation and rules...back in actual clothes. The only downside was that there was still no Etta. He thought about how perfectly she'd furnished the log house, how her face lighted up when she smiled, her delight in the horses he also loved, her pleasure in a quiet rural life. The perfect woman for him, if only he didn't have obligations... obligations he'd promised to fulfill when he'd taken over the band from Jake.

He heard a vehicle coming up the lane to the house. Patients or clients for Shelby or the farm. He shifted in the chair and tried to focus on the hockey game he was absently watching. Suddenly a cacophony of voices erupted from the kitchen.

His sister, a wide smile on her face, entered the room.

"What?" He looked up at her.

"You have visitors…in fact, a whole bunch of visitors. I think you'll be glad to see them…and hear what they have to say."

Lili and Joe Farrah, followed by Jessie, Matt, Paulie, and James, came into the room.

"Ah, hot damn!" Delight burst over him. "Man, it's good to see you guys."

"And lady." Lili stepped forward to plant a kiss on his forehead below the bandages.

"And lady." His hand fumbled for hers, and she took hold of it.

"How are you doing, man?" Matt shoved his hands into the pockets of his jeans and shifted his feet. The rest of the group, aside from Lili, looked equally uncomfortable.

*Nervous. Not used to visiting a dinged-up buddy.*

"Good, good. You guys?"

"Pretty good. We miss you, Trav." Paulie stepped forward. Aside from a scar on his left cheek, he showed no lingering effects of his accident. He'd put on weight and appeared a lot less strung out.

"Travis, we've been speaking with Shelby these last few days." Lili looked down at him, her face softening into lines of deep compassion. "As a result, we have a proposition to put to you."

"Yeah?" Apprehension welled up. "Best way to do that is to get right to it."

"Jessie, maybe you should start." Lili released Travis's hand and stepped back.

"Well, it's like this." Jessie drew a deep breath and began. "Matt and I have been itching to stay in Nova Scotia. Last spring, when we spent time with Lili and Joe down there, we spotted a car dealership we'd like to take over. It's got a service bay with an auto body repair shop attached. Right now, the owner is looking to retire. It's the perfect opportunity to get into a business that will be there when we get too old to wiggle around a stage, when we're too old to turn the ladies on." A wry grin creased his face.

"I've heard you talking about that place, but I didn't realize you were all-out serious." Travis could barely believe what he was hearing. *These two former outlaws wanting to go into a legitimate business?* "Good show. We all should be getting into something substantial. But what about you, James?" He turned to the big drummer.

"You remember when we started out, when Jordan first took us all on, my mother was recovering from a bad car accident?" The two-hundred-pound drummer wet his lips and looked shyly around at the group. "Well, thanks to the money I've made with the band, you know she's had a successful rehab. Now she's looking to open a bed-and-breakfast back home. Tourism is the meat and potatoes of Prince Edward Island, what with it being the land of Anne of Green Gables. Mom would like to open her place near Cavendish, with a tea room and gift shop attached. I've been saving, and I got more than enough to set her up in style."

He paused, looking around at his friends before continuing, "I bought an old farm. Mom and I are going to set up her business in the house, restoring it as a heritage site, as well." He paused again. "There's a cottage on the shoreline of the property." Grinning sheepishly, he continued, "I plan to live there with Amy…as soon as we're married."

"Amy?" Matt looked over at him sharply. "Who is Amy?"

"Someone I've been seeing every time I went to visit Mom. Someone I've been calling and texting while we're on the road for nearly a year now."

"Hey, that's great, man!" Jessie's pleasure was sincere as he looked over at his friend. "Congrats."

"Good for you, James." Travis's acknowledgement was equally hearty. "Lili and Joe, what about you?"

"Joe and I haven't had many opportunities to enjoy our Yarmouth place since we were married and I went on the road with you vagabonds. We'll be happy to settle down. There's a guest house on the property that will accommodate Paulie and give him the peace and privacy he needs to get back to writing those wonderful songs. Actually"—she smiled across the table at her husband—"we're glad to be off the road."

"Paulie, you okay with that?" Travis, acutely aware of his friend's sensitive nature, looked up at him, concerned.

"I'm fine with it, Trav." His tone and expression told Travis he meant it. "Being on the road didn't help my…problem. Over the years, as you know, I've received a few offers from Nashville artists to write for them, no performing involved. I'm going to sift through them and see if there's anything I can handle. Whoever I decide to sign with will have to agree to my terms. I don't plan to leave Nova Scotia."

"Then it's settled." A wave of relief and happiness gushed over Travis. "We're officially breaking up our band, heading out into real life. Shel..." He spoke to his sister, who'd quietly followed the group into the room. "Call Etta. Tell her she doesn't have to worry about becoming a gypsy." He turned to the group surrounding him. "You'll be staying in the log house. Etta has it fixed up real fine. But don't mess it up. With any luck, she and I will be moving in real soon."

## Chapter Fourteen

"Etta?" The sound of Travis's voice flushed familiar internal butterflies into motion. "It's Travis."

As if he had to identify himself.

"Yes."

"Etta, Shelby told you about the band's breaking up, about our future plans?"

"Yes."

"Okay, okay. I'm goin' out on a limb here, darlin'. Since you seem to be stuck on one-word answers, here goes. Now will you marry me? We can live in the log house, you can write, I can work with the horses. No more traveling."

"Travis, I…"

"Aw, damn, woman, if you could see me, I'm trying to get down on one knee. I'm still stiff as a board from that stupid spill I took, but…"

"Travis, don't!" More softly, "Please don't. I'm coming to New Brunswick, to Carleton."

"To marry me, right?"

"We'll talk when I get there." A sudden imp leaped out from among the wild mix of ecstatic emotions whirling through body and soul. "See you tomorrow."

"Etta…!" But she punched End and threw her arms around herself in an elated hug.

****

"Damn it, Shel, why of all days did a blizzard have

to snow in the Ottawa airport? Why of all days can't Etta get here?" Travis strode back and forth in the farmhouse kitchen. He paused to look out a window toward the highway. "Ah, hell, it's even starting to snow here."

"Travis, relax." At the table, Jake looked up from term papers he'd been marking and removed his reading glasses. "The woman loves you, and you love her. That's the important stuff. After that, it's just formalities…like getting you two married."

"That's one hell of a formality." Travis eased into a chair opposite his brother-in-law. "I want us to be together forever, and that's the best way I know of to make it happen."

"You're right, little brother." Shelby shut the dishwasher door, touched Start, and went to put an arm about his shoulders. "Emma and I can't wait to start putting the finishing touches on your wedding."

"So get on with it, Trav." Jake rubbed the bridge of his nose. "Life will be so much better for me once those two women are assured their quest for what Ross Turner would call 'a wingding of a wedding' will be rewarded." He put his glasses back in place and returned his attention to the pages in front of him. "Right now, what would make me happy are students who didn't place their faith in spell checkers and made an effort to figure out on their own which 'two,' 'too,' or 'to' to use."

Looking over at him, Travis suddenly chuckled.

"What's so funny?" Jake glanced up at him.

"Jordan Brooks in spectacles, grading papers and complaining about grammar. Six years ago, when I was your biggest fan, I never could have imagined such a sight. Also, as I recall, a whole lot of your songs included words like 'ain't' and 'gonna.' "

"Yes, well, I'm not exactly twenty-six anymore. With these teacher cutbacks, every licensed body in the school has been harnessed to instruct at least one academic subject. The music teacher has a couple of hours of math to teach each day, the Phys Ed specialist is presiding over Level 2 Science three afternoons a week, and the guidance counselors…that would be Emma and me…have been roped in to take over several Language Arts sessions four mornings out of five."

"Once Etta and I get hitched, maybe we could volunteer at the school once in a while…you know, Etta to talk about writing, me to talk about farming and horses…"

"Thanks, but I see a couple of major pitfalls in that plan." Jake was scanning the page in front of him.

"Such as?"

"Well, first…" He looked up. "You have to get Etta to marry you. Then I doubt any kids would want to hear you talk about farming or even horses. You'll have to wait until your fame dies down…which, if history repeats, shouldn't take long. Otherwise, all they'll want to hear from you is how you got to be such a big star and about life on the road with sexy women."

"You're a giant pain, Jake, you know?" Travis ignored the teasing and returned to a window to look out into the fast-falling darkness. "Shit!" He swung back to face the couple. "How long will it take for this cursed storm to blow itself out over the Atlantic?"

"Speaking of Language Arts, watch it, little brother." Shelby sat down across the table from her husband. "The good news is, it's moving west to east. If it's arriving here, it probably has moved out of the Ottawa area. I'm thinking Etta will be boarding the plane first thing tomorrow morning."

"You're right." The words raised Travis's hopes. "Sure, by now, this storm is probably clearing out of Ontario and snow removal is underway in Ottawa. Yeah, that's it. I've always known I had a smart sister."

****

"Emma, hi." Shelby answered her cell an hour later while she, Travis, and Jake were watching a weather broadcast on the living room television. Katie Rose, curled up against her uncle, clutched the huge stuffed rabbit Ross Turner had given her for her birthday the previous year, and dozed.

Instantly alert, Travis moved to face his sister so quickly Katie Rose awoke, blinking.

"She left by train? It got through in spite of the storm? She arrived in Carleton around six this evening?"

Travis was beside his sister on the couch. "For God's sake, Shel, let me talk to her!"

"It's not Etta, it's Emma." Shelby punched out and turned to him. "Etta arrived by train in Carleton about an hour ago. She called Emma and told her she was grabbing a hamburger before she rented a car and headed down here. Emma wanted to know if she arrived."

"Ah, hell!" Travis bolted to his feet and grimaced. "Just look at how fast snow is moving in across the bay. And listen to that wind! The shore road will be blocked by drifts in a dozen or more places. She'll never make it."

His cell vibrated and he answered.

"Travis…"

"Etta! Where in hell are you?"

"My…car went off the road about a mile from…the farm. Travis…"

"Etta…Etta!" He was yelling even as he realized the connection had been broken.

He Iistened for a few seconds longer before throwing the phone on the couch. "Shit!"

"Travis, please." Shelby jerked her head toward the child.

"Sorry, sorry." The words came back as he strode out of the room and into the kitchen. When Shelby, Jake, and Katie Rose caught up with him, he was pulling on his boots.

"Travis, where are you going?" His sister grabbed his arm. "You won't be able to get through either. Think! It's entirely probable Etta never got out onto the shore road. Generally, as you know, during storms, the RCMP block it off. She's likely in Carleton, headed for Emma's apartment and a safe haven for the night."

"No, she isn't." He thrust his arms into a jacket. "She's stuck in her car a mile down the road. I'm going after her." He pulled on a toque and grabbed truck keys from a hook by the door.

"Travis, you'll never get a vehicle out of the yard, much less up to the highway." Jake yelled out the door after him as he waded down the steps. "I'll call Andy next door. He has a snowmobile."

"Can't wait." He paused to look around at the swirling snow. "Maybe one of our trucks won't get through, but I know a horse that will."

"Travis, don't be foolish!" Shelby was beside her husband in the open doorway. "Andy can be here in a few minutes! He'll take you to her."

"Sorry, sis." His words blew off in the gale as he headed down the lane to the barn.

\*\*\*\*

Inside the stable, he didn't hesitate. He knew exactly the animal for the task ahead. Going into Silver's stall, he caught the albino's halter.

"Come on, mister. You're the strongest, sanest guy we've got. We're heading out to find a lady."

Ten minutes later he had the big gelding saddled up. Leading the horse out of the barn, Travis ducked his head against blizzard conditions.

"Okay, Silver, here's where we find out just how tough we both are."

He swung into the saddle and headed up the lane, past the farmhouse. In the window he saw his sister's worried face. Beside her, her husband held his cell phone to his ear. Calling Andy Crowell, no doubt. They didn't believe he could get through on horseback. Well, he would. He had to.

The footing was good for the distance between house and barn, having been swept clean by gusting winds, but as he headed onto the road toward Carleton, drifts blocked his way. Between them was snow packed hard to an icy consistency, which made footing treacherous. At times he had to dismount and lead the horse. Chafing at the pace but with memories of his accident with Midnight Brandy still fresh, Travis forced himself to the modified progress. If he allowed the horse to flounder into a ditch, he doubted he could get him out without help.

In the eerie half light the blizzard produced, he squinted to keep to the road. Snow sleeted into his eyes, at times momentarily blinding him.

Then he saw it. Lights slanting into a ditch ahead.

"Etta!" He leaped from the horse and floundered toward the car almost entirely submerged off to the side of the road. "Etta!"

He yanked at the driver's door, a thick drift fouling his efforts. Desperate, he began to shovel with his hands. "Etta, push!" He jerked at the door again. This time it gave, and she tumbled out into his arms.

"Travis, you came." Her words were a gasp.

"Yeah, yeah, I came." He held her tight, too tight, he knew but, hell, she was alive. "Come on, we have to get you to the farm." He released her and pulled the hood of her jacket up over her head before reaching into the car to turn off the motor and shove the keys into his pocket. Grabbing her gloved hand, he started to where Silver stood ground tied, head bent against the driving wind.

"A white horse." He turned to look into her pale face and saw the beginnings of a smile.

"Yeah, just like in one of your books, right? Put your foot into the stirrup. I'll give you a leg up."

\*\*\*\*

"What? Hey, no way! Not in a million years!" Travis sat at the kitchen table the following morning, nursing his second cup of coffee as he stared across it at his sister. "I nearly lost Etta permanently last night. I'm not about to let you separate us for the next two weeks!"

"You've been separated from her for longer periods." Shelby calmly began to remove breakfast dishes and load them into the dishwasher. "Emma and I are determined to make this a storybook wedding, and

Etta has agreed. She's a romantic. So as soon as the roads are cleared, Jake is taking Etta to stay with Emma in Carleton. We're not about to let you convince her to run off for some quickie ceremony. You'll see the bride on your wedding day, Christmas Eve. It will be picture perfect.

"Furthermore"—a devilish twinkle lighted her eyes—"it will give Emma and me time to arrange for one huge bachelorette party. You guys are to take Katie Rose and stay at Emma's apartment in town for that night; we've arranged to hold it here. It wasn't easy to set a date…Roc Hard is so popular."

"Roc Hard? The male stripper?" Jake stared at her.

"Yeah, sis. I never imagined you'd go in for anything like that." Travis added his surprise.

"A bachelorette party is part of the festivities. I missed out on the fun because at the time I didn't have any party-type girlfriends to throw one for me. I plan to make up for it with Etta's."

She paused, the mischievous twinkle in her eyes increasing.

"Why do I get the feeling there's more?" Jake sounded apprehensive.

"Because there is." His wife broke into an all-out grin. "Emma will be inviting a bunch of female teachers from Carleton High. She wants to make certain there will be enough of them to carry lots of tales back to Mildred Carter."

"Ah, now you two are playing with fire." Jake leaned back in his chair. "You know I have to work with the woman every day. I'm not sure I'd be comfortable with that old gossip soaking up stories about how my wife entertains strippers in our home, embellishing them and spreading them around. Thomas Pentland might not take them in stride."

"Loosen up, my love." Shelby went to put an arm around his shoulders and slip onto his lap. "You know the principal doesn't take a word that woman says seriously. Furthermore, his wife will be attending. All that's left for you to do is arrange a stag party for Travis."

She gave him a quick kiss, stood, and swaggered back to the counter, casting a sly glance back over her shoulder.

"I don't need…" Travis began.

"You may as well give in, Travis." Jake stood and went to replenish his mug. "I've learned that one of the first rules of a successful relationship is to knuckle under as often as possible. I'll get things moving for a stag the night before the wedding." Jake slapped him on a shoulder. "Just don't get drunk like you did on your twenty-first birthday. Man, you had a major hangover."

"And what am I supposed to do in the meantime?"

"There's always lots of work down at the barn. Grady could do with some help." Shelby turned back to him. "The horses are in need of training, and there are students for riding lessons most afternoons, scheduled in the arena. With Jake having to take on more responsibilities at school, we're super busy. Furthermore"—she headed for the coffee pot—"it will be good for you to get back to the work you'll be doing as soon as the honeymoon is over. It will give me an opportunity to evaluate your efforts. You have been away from it for a while."

"Aw, Shel." He caught her teasing. "Okay, okay, I'll give in to this romantic wedding thing if that's what

Etta wants. But after we're married, no interference, agreed?"

"After you're married, I'll be absolutely content. Having you and Jake settled here on the farm and happy is all I want. Actually, I'm thinking of taking on an assistant to help me in the clinic. What with having to take time off next summer"—she lowered her voice and jerked her head in the direction of the living room, where Katie Rose was watching cartoons—"when the baby arrives."

"Baby?" Travis choked on the mouthful of coffee he'd just taken.

"Shhhh." Shelby held a finger to her lips. "We haven't told Katie Rose yet. We're waiting until we're sure all is going well."

"Well, damn it!" Travis was on his feet and gathering his sister into a bear hug. "Great! Wonderful! Etta and I will be pleased as punch to help out." He released her and swung on Jake to shake his hand. "Congratulations, man."

"Thanks. We are pleased."

"But this wedding"—Travis turned to his sister— "it won't be too much for you? I'm thinking you should be taking it easy."

"Travis, love, never fear. I'm strong as the proverbial horse."

"Well, then, good. But take care. Mustn't disappoint Katie Rose. This news should make her stop asking when Etta and I are going to have kids. Now I think I'll head into town. Roads should be plowed by now. I want to pick out a wedding ring. Should have done it when I bought the engagement one, but I was in a rush."

"Travis, a heads up." Shelby stopped him as he was reaching for his jacket. "Michelle Layton has been seen in Carleton. Apparently she's on vacation at her father's summer place a few miles below here. I remember your saying she was after Paulie, so watch your step."

"Damn! Will that woman ever stop being a major pain in the behind? Thanks, Shel, I'll be on my guard."

\*\*\*\*

"Well, well, look who's perusing fine gems."

As he stood looking over the tray of rings the jeweler had placed in front of him, the sound of her voice made Travis all but cringe.

"Morning, Michelle." He forced himself to be civil. "At your dad's place downshore for a vacation, I hear?"

"Daddy had some strange desire to have a country Christmas." She sauntered over to stand beside him encased in black leather, her hair done up in some kind of odd style he imagined only fitted into a rock video. "So here I am. I'm assuming the night life around here is still as dead as ever?"

"Wouldn't know. I haven't been in Carleton much lately." He focused his attention on the rings, hoping she'd take the hint and leave him alone.

"What can I do for you, Miss Layton?" the jeweler asked. "I'm sure Mr. Masters won't mind if I leave him to make his decision while I wait on you."

"You know a good customer when you see one, don't you, Mr. Aube?" Out of the corner of his eye, Travis caught her arrogant smirk. "Today I'm looking for something for a gentleman. A gold chain with lots and lots of carats."

"You can't buy Paulie with that kind of junk!" Travis could hold back no longer.

"Who said anything about your precious Paulie? It's for a record producer in Toronto. If Nashville can't recognize my talent, I'll go elsewhere. As for that drugged-out songwriter you work so hard to protect, consider your worries at an end. He made a state-of-the-art fool of himself in New York and showed me just how reliable he isn't. I have no time to babysit a creep like him."

"That's not what you said a while back, when you demanded to know where he was while you hung onto my horse's bridle."

"And you let that black monster run me down!"

"Run you down? You got in his way big time…all in an effort to find out Paulie's whereabouts."

"I've had time to think since then." She tossed her waist-length black hair back from her shoulders. "I don't need an addict I have to babysit, who can't keep himself clean."

"He was clean until you got your hooks into him."

"It didn't take all that much persuading for him to jump off the wagon." She took a ring from the tray, held it up to the light, and frowned. "Really, Travis, you should have made your purchase in New York City, or even Toronto."

"Yeah, well, Etta isn't into what stuff costs." He snatched it back and returned it to its place in the tray. "By the way, aside from getting Paulie back on that junk, I've been told you didn't stick around after that cab hit him, that you hightailed it away as fast as those fancy boots could carry you."

"What do you think it would do to my reputation to be caught with someone so high he thought he could fly? I did call 911."

"I didn't see you at the hospital…not once."

"What could I do?" She shrugged. "I'm not a doctor."

"You're a real piece of work, you know?"

"Miss Layton, I've found some chains I think might suit you." From across the store, the jeweler called for her attention.

"Be right there." She paused to favor Travis with a seductive look and a wink. "Remember, sweetie, if you get bored with little Miss Sugar and Spice, I'll be only two farms away, next summer vacation."

"Don't hold your breath on that one, Michelle."

"I can't believe you're really getting married." She peered again at the rings on the tray. "Will the little wifey be going on the road with you, or will you stay a free man for appearance's sake? I don't think that arrogant agent of yours will want to advertise the fact that her heart-throb client has a ball and chain."

"Etta and I will be staying at the farm."

"What! You're quitting? What about your band?"

"Forget it, Michelle. The band is retiring, too."

"Ah, well"—she turned away from him—"they weren't that great anyway. Mr. Aube, about those gold chains…"

A wave of relief washed over him as she sashayed away.

*That's two troublesome women out of the way. That leaves only Annie, but what she'll be up to next, I have no idea.*

**\*\*\*\***

"Jessi, you should be up at the house with the guests." Etta stood in the tack room that had been cleaned for the occasion as Jessi Turner fussed over the gown she, Shelby, and Emma had chosen weeks previous. "I still can't believe you came all the way from Alberta, you and Ross and both your families, for the wedding…especially now." She gestured toward Jessi's belly.

"We wouldn't miss it." She adjusted Etta's veil and gave the skirt a fluff. "Ross and I have been given the all-important task of getting the bride ready and delivered on time. As for her…" She ran her hand over the front of her dress. "She's not due until April."

"She? You've had an ultrasound? You know it's a girl?"

"No, but Ross is determined it will be, that it will be the ultimate way of besting his brother with his mom. His mother, as you know, has always lived in a house full of men. To add to this male population, his brother Chase's child is a boy—you met him when you were in Calgary. So Ross is dead set on giving his mom a little girl. Now come on." Jessi stood to one side of the doorway that led into the barn's corridor. "We can't have the bride late for her wedding."

As she stepped out of the room, astonishment stopped Etta short. Ross Turner stood grinning at her, by his side the little palomino mare she'd ridden in Alberta—saddled with the strangest bit of equipment she'd ever seen.

"Come along, my lady." He held out an inviting hand. "Let me get you aboard this pretty little girl."

"Ross…Jessie." She turned from the man in the rancher's sheepskin-lined jacket, black Stetson on his head, to the woman following her and attempting to keep her gown from dragging on the barn floor. "What…?"

"Sidesaddle." Ross indicated the contraption on the mare's back. "Had a hell…heck of a time finding one, but the ladies insisted that while they wanted you to arrive at your wedding on horseback they didn't want that outfit you're wearing crushed in any way. Here, let me give you a leg up. Get your right leg over that hook," he instructed, "and your left in the stirrup. At least, I think that's how it goes."

"Wait, wait!" Jessi scuttled into the tack room and returned with a long white satin cape lined with a soft faux fur. "It's cold out there." She swung it around Etta's shoulders and adjusted her veil out over it.

"Okay?" Ross looked at his wife.

"Okay."

Taking her in strong hands, Ross hefted Etta onto the horse. He stood back as Jessi adjusted the gown into position.

Ross's cell rang. He pulled it out. "Yeah, we're ready. Okay, we're headin' out."

Ending the call, he turned to the women. "They're waiting for us up at the house. Let's go."

With Jessi by his side, Ross led the quiet mare out of the barn and into the crisp, starlighted night. Beyond the house, over the frozen bay, a full moon brightened their way.

*Can this really be happening?* Etta drew a deep breath of the frosty air, heart pounding at her ribs. *On this perfect Christmas Eve, with a wedding that is like a beautiful fantasy, I'm going to marry—corny as it sounds—the man of my dreams.*

"Oh, by the way." Ross looked up at her. "This little palomino gal is yours, Travis's wedding present. He had her shipped here all the way from Alberta. Cost him a fair amount of cash, I can tell you. If that isn't love, I don't know what is."

At the veranda steps in the front of the house, Ross stopped the mare. Jake's voice singing "O Holy Night" wafted out into the quiet night. Etta saw her father standing by the door, his white hair making him all the more distinguished in his dark suit.

"Look here." A photographer appeared and held a camera toward her.

"Hope you don't mind," Ross said. "We all felt this wingding should be captured. Then, when you and Travis get old and gray, you can flip open an album and recall the day."

"Of course." Etta smiled in the direction of the camera. "I want to remember this time always."

"Got it?" Ross turned to the photographer.

"Got it," she replied.

"Okay." Ross reached up to lift Etta down from her mount, and there was another flash. The mare shook her head but stood still. Etta was grateful to the woman holding the bridle.

*Jessi has trained her well.*

"Come along, daughter." Her father joined them as Ross placed her on the ground. "We're to make an entrance as soon as Jake finishes singing. We don't want to cause a glitch in this moment Shelby and Emma have worked so hard to make perfect…never mind your mother. We have to make an exactly-on-cue entrance. By the way"—he smiled down at her—"you are beautiful."

She swallowed hard. It was too perfect. Apprehension suddenly invaded her feelings. Her father tightened his grip on her arm, and she looked up at him.

He was smiling gently. "Come on, daughter. Let's get you married."

Together they started up the veranda steps.

Inside the house, Katie Rose, Shelby, and Emma, dressed in matching blue floor-length gowns, waited to lead the way up the path between the rows of chairs filled with family and friends.

"You're a knockout, Aunt Etta," Katie Rose managed to whisper before her mother hushed her and set her in place to lead the way for the bridal procession.

As Jake finished his song, Shelby nudged her daughter into motion. In perfect time to the wedding march, the child, smiling proudly, started off, strewing rose petals ahead of them. Shelby and Emma fell into step behind her.

Etta, on her father's arm, followed the trio, her heart fluttering with joy…until she caught sight of the woman sitting in the back row. Wearing a flame-red dress, she stood with the rest of the gathering as the bridal party advanced.

*Annie Wyse!*

The agent's presence sent a wave of apprehension washing over her. What was she doing here? What trick was she about to pull? She missed a step and her father, glancing down at her, frowned quizzically. Quickly she remedied her pace.

As she proceeded across the living room, she had her first sight of Travis. Her view had been obscured by the two women ahead of her. When she did get a look at her future husband, standing by the fireplace with his best man, her breath caught. He was so incredibly handsome in his dark suit, white shirt, and string tie.

Beside him stood her brother-in-law, Frasier MacKenzie, in full RCMP dress uniform of red serge, jodhpurs, and gleaming, knee-high leather boots. A final scene from one of her books couldn't have been more perfect.

The expression on Travis's face when she arrived beside him, when her father lifted her veil, kissed her, and handed her to him, swept her heart into a whirl. He was gazing at her as if she were the most wonderful creation on earth.

"You're beautiful." His lips formed the words as the minister took his place in front of them and opened the Bible.

Enchanted, Etta missed her cue to give her vows. Emma's nudge alerted her to the moment.

"Travis, I am a writer, but describing my love for you eludes me. This time last year I could never have imagined in my wildest dreams marrying you. Now I cannot imagine my life without you. The poet Elizabeth Barrett Browning may have attempted to count the ways one person can love another. I cannot. I only know that, as she wrote, I love you to the depth and breadth and height my soul can reach...and I always will."

He swallowed hard and wet his lips.

"Henrietta, I sometimes write songs, love songs mostly." His voice was deep and hoarse. "But I can't speak the right words to tell you how I feel. So I'll have to do it in a song. For now, know I love you and will do my best to keep you safe and happy all the days of my life."

He paused and looked at the minister, eyes bright with something Etta thought might be tears.

"Sorry, Reverend. That's the best I can do. You'll have to take it from here."

A soft chuckle went up from their guests. A similar response crinkling his face and voice, Reverend Mason lowered his eyes to the Bible in his hands and proceeded.

"If anyone present has any reason why these two may not be joined together as husband and wife, let him speak now or forever hold his peace." After such perfect moments, the clergyman's statement doused her joy and sparked fear in Etta's heart.

*Oh, God, please, please don't let Annie Wyse say something! Please don't let her have come up with some wild reason to ruin everything!*

Silence.

Reverend Mason cleared his throat and continued with the remainder of the ceremony.

"I now pronounce you husband and wife." The minister closed his book and beamed at the pair. "You may kiss the bride."

As Travis gathered her into his arms, the assemblage broke into clapping, with whistles and yells from Ross Turner and the members of Travis's band.

"Yehaw!" Ross Turner yelled as the couple started down the path between the chairs, a rain of rice falling over them. "Now it's out to Travis and Etta's house for one winging of a good time!"

"Yeah, a whale of a winging!" Katie Rose raced to the big cowboy, and he caught her up in his arms. "Give me a ride out to the truck, Uncle Ross. Mommy will have a fit if I get my boots wet!" She pulled up her dress to reveal blue cowboy boots. "She paid a fair chunk of change for them."

\*\*\*\*

Food and drink were plentiful at the log house, where tables had been set up around the common area. There were many toasts to the bride and groom. Finally, when the meal was finished, Ross in his role as master of ceremonies called for attention.

"Now, folks, if you'll lend a hand, we'll clear back these tables for some dancing."

Within a few minutes, the center of the floor had been cleared. Travis's band, with equipment previously arranged, readied themselves.

Then, to Etta's utter amazement, her husband kissed her on the cheek and stood.

"If you'll bear with me for a few minutes, folks, I'd like to give Etta my wedding gift, one I made for her way back when we were at the cabins at Loon Lake and I was falling head over heels in love with the woman."

He moved to stand in front of his band and took the guitar Matt handed to him. He strummed it a few times, and then, with his gaze focused on Etta, began to sing. The ballad was so beautiful, so heartfelt, Etta felt lightheaded with happiness.

When he finished, everyone burst out in applause and calls of approval. And when he passed the guitar back to Matt and returned to Etta, she had to fight to keep tears at bay.

"Travis, that was absolutely beautiful." She caught his hand when he returned to her and bent to kiss her cheek before resuming his seat. "I thought Maisy was the ultimate gift, but you just topped it."

"Glad you liked it, darlin'."

"Now, folks…" Ross Turner raised his voice to regain control of the gathering. "We have another treat for you. Jake and his daughter Katie Rose are going to give us a toe-tappin', maybe even foot-stompin' tune. Jake and Miss Katie Rose, take it away."

He stepped back as father and daughter took Travis's place in front of the band.

"Hold it! Hold it just a minute!" Ross intervened. He strode forward to hoist the child onto a table beside her father. "Now you folks can get a good view of this young lady's talent."

Jake looked at his daughter. She nodded to him, signaled to the band, and the performance began. Shortly she and her father had the entire room clapping in time as she sang in tune with Jake and the band and danced on the table.

When their performance ended to thunderous applause, Jake handed his guitar back to the band and swept his daughter off the table into his arms. He planted a kiss on her cheek before he set her on the floor.

"Now the bride and groom will lead us off in the first dance." Ross, grinning widely, held out a hand to indicate Travis and Etta. "Come on, folks, let's give them a big hand to get them started."

Travis stood and held out his hand to Etta. "Come along, Mrs. Masters...or whatever you decide to call yourself."

"Mrs. Masters will do just fine, thank you." She accepted his offer as she got to her feet.

****

During a pause in the dancing, Emma, glowing with happiness, drew Frasier over to join Etta and Travis.

"Wonderful news, Etta!" She grasped her twin by

the hand. "Frasier is no longer doing undercover work!"

"I guessed as much when I saw him standing in front of the fireplace with Travis in full dress uniform."

"And that's not all!" Her sister's enthusiasm bubbled over. "He's bought the old Turner place from Ross. We're going to renovate it and live there! We'll be neighbors!"

"Terrific!" Travis was the first to react. "It'll take work, but it's got a great beachfront and a topnotch view of the bay. Best of all, it's no more than a mile or so along the shore from our place. We'll be able to ride over often. Do you two ride?"

"Not enough to call myself an equestrian," Frasier replied.

"Not at all," his wife said.

"Then we'll be signing you up for riding lessons." Travis was enthusiastic. "It'll give you a reason to visit regularly."

"I'm in." Emma looked up at her husband, green eyes bright.

"Why doesn't that surprise me?" Frasier put an arm about her. "Okay, me too. Actually, it will be good for my professional image. A mountie should be able to ride."

"There you are." Annie Wyse maneuvered her way through the crowd, drink in hand. "Travis, I need your help."

"Yeah?" His tone reflected suspicion.

"I want you to convince your sister and brother-in-law that he and his child can be a show-stopper of an act at any country music venue. Those golden curls and sweet, mischievous grin will wow any crowd, never mind that Jake as Jordan Brooks is far from forgotten."

"No way." Travis's tone couldn't have been more decided. "Her father and I lived that life. There's no way I'd want my niece involved in it."

"I can make sure she'll get rich quick, build up a college fund second to none."

"I think her family will be able to afford to see her educated." Travis held his ground.

"Okay…for now." The agent sipped her drink before continuing. "But you know me well enough to understand I don't give up easily." She turned away. "Now, where is that handsome neighbor of yours…Crowell I think is his name. Andy Crowell. I do fancy country boys."

"Don't worry." Travis caught Etta's concerned expression as the agent moved away. "Both Jake and I know how to handle her. And don't concern yourself about Andy. He's no country bumpkin when it comes to women. Now…" He leaned to speak softly into her ear. "It's time for us to get out of here and on with the honeymoon. Go up to our bedroom and change into something warm. We're headin' out, lady."

"But, Travis, we can't sneak away from our guests." She looked up at him, startled by his proposal.

"Does it look as if they'll miss us?" He jerked his head to indicate the crowd dancing to the music of his band or clustered in groups, laughing, eating, and drinking.

"Well…"

"Go on. I'll meet you up there directly. If they see us heading upstairs together, they'll get suspicious."

"Okay." She paused to plant a kiss on his cheek before heading for the stairs.

Chapter Fifteen

In the bedroom that was to be theirs, she got yet another surprise on a day of surprises. Laid out on the bed were winter outdoor clothes from long underwear to a windproof, water-resistant jacket, pants, and boots.

She sat down on the bed abruptly, ignoring the crushing of her gown. What did all this mean?

\*\*\*\*

"Etta." Her name was a hiss.

"Travis?" Involved in struggling to get out of her back-laced wedding dress alone, she turned toward the patio doors to the balcony. He was dressed in winter gear right up to a peaked woolen cap with earflaps.

"Let me in." He tapped lightly on the glass.

"Travis, what are you doing? How did you get up here?" She opened them to face her bridegroom. Without answering, he swept her into his arms in the kind of kiss she'd been longing for. When he finally released her, he was grinning again, not the shy grin that had driven girls and women to fall in love with him or the men to want to emulate him, but with his mouth curled in a special way Etta had come to know was meant only for her.

"What are you wearing?" She touched the hat on his head, a chuckle brimming in her throat. In it, he didn't look much like the Stetson-wearing superstar he was on stage.

"A cap. Honey, it's cold out there. What's so funny?"

"Katie Rose would absolutely love it. It looks like something one of those characters in a Bugs Bunny cartoon would wear."

"Elmer Fudd."

"That's the one. Only Elmer never had such a handsome face."

"Don't try to dig yourself out of a hole with flattery, Mrs. Masters. Now get a move on. We're leaving, taking off on our own before any of the mob below can stop us or douse us with more rice."

"Oh, Travis, I don't know. Wouldn't that be rude? They're our guests."

"Not in my books at this time." Travis held her out at arm's length. "We've done our bit by having this big wingding of a wedding to satisfy family and friends. Now it's our turn. Get yourself out of that bunch of rhinestones and lace and into some good, warm winter clothes. I have a surprise for you. Hey, what's this?" He turned to the dresser where a flattened red rose and small card lay side by side. He picked up the piece of white cardboard and read, " 'To Cinderella, all my best, Travis.' You kept this? And one of the roses?"

He turned to her, astonishment in his expression.

"As you can see."

"So even away back then you had a soft spot for me?" He dropped the card and returned to her.

"A souvenir, nothing more." She tossed her head, pretending disdain. "After all, you are something of a country music star."

"Was, darlin', the verb is 'was.' " He came up behind her to gather her into his arms. "Man, Shelby would be proud of me, remembering that part of speech. Now enough talking. Let's get this show on the road."

He began to unlace the length of fastenings down the back of her dress.

\*\*\*\*

"Travis, this is crazy!" Etta grasped his hand as he indicated the ladder he'd put up to the balcony.

"Shhh!" he cautioned. "Be careful. Don't slip. We'll be out of here in no time."

Catching the spirit of the adventure, Etta chuckled.

"What?" Travis paused in helping her over the balcony railing to the ladder.

"This is so like something Emma would do."

"Maybe. But let's get a move on. We'll have to walk to the farmhouse. I left my truck there earlier so no one would hear it starting up." He kissed her again, then looked at her, blue eyes bright in the moonlight. "This is only the beginning of the adventure, darlin'."

"What about clothes?"

"All taken care of. I had to bring Emma in on the plan. She packed your bag. It's ready and waiting."

Shortly, they were scuttling away from the brightly lighted log house and up the well-packed road to the farm. Once there, Travis hustled her into his truck, and they were off, with him driving at the top of the speed limit in spite of the snowy roads.

"Travis, you've got to tell me! Where are we going?"

"Somewhere romantic. Somewhere that would fit right into one of your books." Etta watched his mouth curl into a sly grin in the shadowy dashboard lights. A tingle washed over her. Here she was, Etta Prescott—

now Masters—the shy introvert, speeding off through a beautiful winter's night with a man a year ago she'd only ever seen on an album cover. And his wife, no less! Fairytales do sometimes come true, no doubt about it. With a little help from an audacious twin sister.

They passed through Carleton and headed up the highway to turn off on a familiar secondary road. Travis's plan began to clarify in her mind.

She suppressed a gasp as they approached the trail to Loon Lake. A double-seated sleigh hitched to a pair of dappled gray horses stood waiting at the entrance.

When Travis stopped the truck, she was still further amazed to see Grady holding the reins in the driver's seat. Beside him sat Beau, wrapped in a red blanket and wearing a Santa hat.

"Oh, Travis, this is…this is…" She couldn't find words.

"I must have done it right…knocked the words right out of a writer." He pulled the keys from the ignition, got out, and strode around to her side. He opened the door and drew her into his arms to kiss her.

"Travis, Grady is—" she managed breathlessly when he released her.

"Grady was a wrangler on movie sets for years before he came to work at the Ebony M. He's seen a lot worse. Now, come on. Can't keep him and the critters waiting. There's a cabin at the lake with a fire that probably is burning low by now. We may have to heat the place all by ourselves."

He handed her into the rear seat of the sleigh.

"You even thought to bring Beau."

"Yeah, well, I figured it wouldn't be much of a

honeymoon with you worrying about him. Anyhow, he was kind of a cupid for us."

"Cupid?"

"Yeah, you remember. He ran off so I could come to your aid in finding him, in getting him to the vet, playing the hero…"

"You're thinking all of that was intentional? I know Beau is a perceptive guy, but even he has limits. Anyhow, he barely knew you back then."

"Dogs have great instincts. They know a good thing when they get a whiff of it. You'll remember he did enjoy the way my truck smelled the day I arrived at Loon Lake. Now enough stallin' around." He turned his attention to Grady. "We're all set, driver. Let's move out."

"You got it, sir." Grady clucked to the team, and they started at a sedate walk down the trail that had been plowed for the event.

"Travis, that song you wrote for me is wonderful." She snuggled up against him. "It is a beautiful gift. And Maisy! What a surprise. I'm afraid I have nothing so amazing to give you. All I did was write a book about you."

"A book! Now that's something." He pulled her out from him to look down into her face, his own bright with pleasure. "What character am I? A half-assed country singer who isn't a real cowboy, an idiot who tries riding a bronc in a major rodeo without any experience…" He was grinning down at her, teasing.

"Actually you're kind of the hero." She cast him a sly, sideways glance. "A hero who is absolutely adorable when he's wearing an Elmer Fudd hat."

"Look." He pointed overhead. "Just look at that."

Above them, the night sky had come alive with a brilliant array of northern lights. Green and white, they rose up and up before doubling back on themselves. They made the heavens dance.

"Quite a display." His mouth curled at the corners as he looked down at her. "Can you believe I arranged it especially for you?"

"After all the magical moments you've already provided this evening, I almost can." She stretched to plant a light kiss on his cold cheek. It wasn't enough for her husband, she quickly discovered, as his mouth covered hers.

On the front seat, Beau threw back his head and issued a full-blown howl up into the magic of the night.

## A word about the author...

An award-winning author, Gail says, "This is my 38th traditionally published book. I'm delighted to be an author with The Wild Rose Press, where writers are encouraged, tutored and mentored in the best of ways."

Contact her at:

macgail@nbnet.nb.ca
Twitter: tollerbeagle44
Facebook: Gail MacMillan

~*~

This is the third book in the *Cowboy Country Connections* series. The first book is *Counterfeit Cowboy,* followed by *Cowboy Confessions.* Readers can also enjoy the antics of Emma, Frasier, and Bruiser in *Holding Off for a Hero.*